THE GHOST OF BETHEL CHURCH

OTHER BOOKS IN
*THE HAUNTING MYSTERIES OF
MAGGIE STYLES* SERIES:

THE DARK LEDGER

THE GHOST OF BETHEL CHURCH

Wil Hodge

ISBN: 978-0-9894848-3-1 – Paperback
eISBN: 978-0-9894848-4-8 – eBook

Contact: wil@wilhodge.com

Printed in the United States of America

∞This paper meets the requirements of ANSI/NISO Z39.48-1992 (Permanence of Paper)

0 2 1 5 2 3

This book is dedicated to the memory of my parents,
JIMMY AND RUTH HODGE.

The brilliant and the beautiful.

"A writer writes. Always."
Billy Crystal
Throw Momma from the Train

FOREWORD

When a writer creates characters he becomes close to, he's never alone. They live within his abilities to shape their loves, lives and legacies.

The characters in the Maggie Styles series are that for me, as they have made me laugh, hurt and feel things within the pages I normally would have not had the good fortune of experiencing. I hope they find a place in your reading that brings you joy and fueled imagination. It's there where fantasy lives and good triumphs.

Nothing more can be asked of a reader.

Chapter 1

THE CHURCH FIRE

The year was 1802. The midnight sky in Randall, Arizona was illuminated in an eerie orange glow that could be seen for miles as flames summoned the townspeople out of their homes to the church at the edge of town. Screams could be heard coming from inside the burning structure as a lone man, Pastor Jeremiah Bolt, stood sentinel as the chain that bound the doors glowed a hot white with flames exploding around it. Jonathan Carriage, the town Sheriff, was the first to arrive on the scene.

"Goddamn preacher, what did you do?" Carriage yelled, holding his hand up to shield his face from the inferno that had engulfed the church.

"It had to be done!" the preacher cried. "It had to be done. The Devil is in there burning with them. Listen to him scream. Listen at it. The Sword of God won out tonight!"

Carriage demanded, "Who's in there, you fool?"

Bolt declared, "All four of them, the whole lot. Witches. Devil's work. No more!"

"Witches? Are you crazy? Who's in there?" Sheriff Carriage grabbed the preacher's coat and yelled to his face, "Who's in there? Tell me or I'll shoot you right here and now."

With the look of a madman, Pastor Jeremiah Bolt feigned a smile and answered, "Your daughter and her coven of devil worshipers are in there. She's going to hell with the rest of them."

The preacher then pulled away, held up his bible and shouted, "The Sword of God has won tonight! The Sword of God has won against the evil that consumed these women. The Sword of..."

It was then a thunderous gunshot shook the town as the pastor's words were cut short. Bolt glared at the flaming church as he dropped to his knees, still clutching his now bloodstained bible. The silhouette of Sheriff Carriage pointing his revolver could be seen against the smoke-filled night sky as the pastor fell face-first into the baron churchyard.

It took two days for the fire to cool so the remains of the four women inside the church could be exhumed from the ashes. A funeral was held in the cemetery behind the church as people came from all over the county, mostly out of curiosity, to pay their respects. The newspaper printed headlines big and bold that heralded the actions of Sheriff Carriage for shooting down the crazed pastor who took the lives of the seemingly innocent girls, all in the flower of their youth.

Pastor Jeremiah Bolt was buried in an unmarked desert grave. A sandstorm later in the week erased all markings that would show where he was laid to rest. Relatives of the four killed were said to have gone in search of Bolt's grave to condemn the man who burned the women in what was to them an act of delusion, but the grave was never found.

The church was rebuilt and maintained, withstanding the test of time for two hundred years through war, threats of demolition and an onslaught of weather. Only soot-stained mortar blocks in the basement would be the only indication of the fire that shook the small Arizona town. Stains no one living knew were there.

As the town grew, so did the cemetery behind the church. Family mausoleums were built for the wealthy, shadowing the meager stones of the desolate in this barren garden of the dead. The town was built around it as Randall became a stop for miners headed to California from as far away as the eastern coastal states. "It was a long way to go to dig a hole," was a local saying directed at the men and women passing through.

Randall was founded by miners who themselves had decided to give up dreams of gold and riches for a simpler life of selling cattle and dry goods. Oddly, two sizable gold nuggets were found while digging out a foundation for the town's Courthouse. It sparked a flurry of "Gold Fever" in the town, which prompted settlers and prospectors to mine there, but no additional gold was ever reported.

The two gold nuggets were on display at the Courthouse and survived numerous attempts to steal them. A century later when a new courthouse was built, the nuggets were moved to the first Randall, Arizona Museum. The museum was mostly dedicated to the town's mining history and local legends, including Sheriff Jonathan Carriage. His revolver, along with Bolt's bible, were there with a summary of the church fire.

Chapter 2

VERA CHASE: TOUR GUIDE

Now abandoned and marked as a historical site, Vera Chase knew Bethel Church well as she worked as a part-time tour guide for the town. Not a normal tour guide in the historical sense, but a paranormal tour guide taking people on a walk of haunted places of legend, where the dead were said to mimic the living and haunt the town. The church, over time, had found its way onto its roster of 'must see' places where the spirits of the four dead women could sometimes be heard screaming for their lives as Pastor Jeremiah Bolt watched outside the church.

Another highlight were the stories of attempted christenings that somehow went awry. One such incident in the 1920's told of a couple who wanted their daughter christened in the church. As the ceremony began, a cold chill came over the congregants as the temperature plummeted in the tiny structure. When the minister reached out to put his hand into the holy water, he found the water frozen solid. The people left the church and walked out into a clear August day. It was said to be "Summer hot" outside.

Vera had always known she was different. She never played with dolls as a child or did other girly things, having always identified herself with boys into her early teens and had been perfectly fine with it. One day she happened to walk into the living room of her house where her mother was watching a talk show. One of the guests on the show was a woman who had gone through a sex change and Vera was fascinated. The woman told of how she had always felt there was a man living inside her and she realized that she had to become a total man or go crazy. Now 'he' was happy with himself. He had a wife who was pregnant with an implanted child, he owned his own successful business and would make the same decision over again if given the chance. From that moment on Vera's destiny was laid out for her as she decided right then and there to someday, somehow, recreate herself as a man. Even if it was for a short while, she wanted the experience to let the man out.

Now twenty-five years old she had come to terms with the promise she made to herself all those years ago and was pondering her transformation. Her partner of four years, Cat Tucker, adored Vera and would stand by her through anything. They met in college and had an immediate connection. Cat's real name was Cathy. Vera commented on her "cat-like" eyes one night and started calling Cathy her "Cat". The name stuck and now everyone called her that. For some reason, Cat liked it.

One of their friends had passed away recently and while at the funeral, the minister said she had been, "Reborn. Transformed to another part of life that we all make at some point." While looking at the body in the coffin, Vera was amazed at how good her friend actually looked. Her hair was fixed just right; her clothes were perfect and dainty, and her makeup was model-like and flawless.

Cat looked down and remarked, "Some send off, huh? I hope I look that good when I'm dead."

When the minister said the word "transformed," it resonated in Vera. She had been using the word a lot recently and it touched a nerve deep inside her. She looked down at her friend in the coffin and it all became clear. Without hesitation Vera turned to Cat and declared, "I have to die."

Cat stepped back and replied, "What? What do mean?"

"I have to die, Cat. I want to be reborn as a man. The

woman I am now has to die to become that man, so I have to arrange my funeral."

Cat was bewildered. "Are you crazy? Vera, this is a joke, right?"

"No joke. I need a coffin and a place." She then remembered the old church on the outside of town she knew so well. "I have the place, Bethel Church, now I need a coffin. Any ideas?"

Cat stood there looking at Vera and realized she was serious. Suddenly it all came into view for her. Transformation. Vera had to let go and say goodbye to her feminine self to recreate herself as a man. Vera Chase had to die.

"I'll make some calls," Cat said looking back at Vera, who was literally shaking. "Vera Chase has to die, but I have to tell you I don't think you can rent a coffin. People that buy them usually don't bring them back in a day or two. This place here won't rent you one. That guy is an asshole and these things are worth a fortune." Cat looked over at the high browed mortician standing in the parlor and observed, "Only dead people can stand him."

"Good point," Vera agreed. "How about a prop rental place? Surely somewhere there must be a coffin for rent for a Halloween show or something."

Cat was cautious. "Is this like a permanent thing or are you just going to drive this man you become around the block for a while? I like girls, Vee. I love you, but damn, this could get weird."

Vera grinned. "I just want to feel it. Even if it's for a week or two, I want to let the man inside me out for a stroll. That's all. Besides, my tits are too big and they aren't going anywhere."

"Can I get that in writing?" Cat asked as she admired Vera's figure.

Chapter 3

BETHEL CHURCH

The last stop on the Randall Ghost Tour was the old church. A small group of three people had followed Vera throughout the town as she recreated gunfights and pictures of a past long gone. The tour started at the supposedly haunted Courthouse then continued by hotels and saloons where spirits were said to have been seen by patrons on a regular basis. As they walked onto the church property Vera noticed the mayor, Vernon Collier, driving by and offered him a wave. He smiled, nodded at Vera and drove on by.

"It helps to have friends in high places," Vera said to the group. "That's the mayor."

"I'd rather see a ghost," the man snapped.

Giving the man a dirty look, Vera announced:

"And this is the last stop on the tour, and my personal favorite, Bethel Church. In 1802 Pastor Jeremiah Bolt chained four women in here and burned them alive saying they were witches who consorted with the Devil. Bolt was shot dead in the yard with a single bullet through the heart by Sheriff Jonathan Carriage. Bolt is buried in an unmarked grave out in the desert... somewhere. The grave was covered by a sandstorm and never found to this day. His blood-stained bible, along with Sheriff Carriage's revolver are on display at the Randall Museum."

Vera walked to the old church double doors, unlocked and opened them wide for the tourists to enter. As the doors opened, Vera glanced up to the front of the church to see a hooded woman with searing dark eyes staring back at her. Vera was shaken and dropped her keys. When she looked up, the woman was gone.

One of the teenage girls laughed, "What's wrong, see a ghost?"

Vera stood silent as she tried to grasp what she'd seen, having never come across anything in her three years as a tour guide to indicate there was any truth to the legends of hauntings that pulsed through the town. Old wife's tales to enhance the tourist trade was all she thought the legends were, until now.

"No, I wish," Vera nervously sighed as she regrouped.

"Have you ever seen a ghost anywhere in town?" the girl then asked.

"No, not to my knowledge. I did see a man I thought was a ghost walking down the street one night swaying from side to side. When he finally turned around, I could see him holding a bottle of Jack Daniels. He was stone drunk," Vera answered with a forced chuckle.

Vera then heard the question, "Why did the Pastor burn them? Have you sought the answer?"

Vera turned around and answered, "No, I haven't. When you think about it, someone really should, I guess. After all it was a mass murder."

"You haven't what?" one of the girls asked as she curiously studied Vera.

"I haven't looked into it," Vera replied.

The girl pressed, "Looked into what?"

"The deaths of the…" Vera stopped there and realized the voice she heard was not one of the teenage girls on the tour. "Never mind. I'm just thinking out loud. Any other questions about the fire at Bethel Church?"

Vera felt herself slipping into a panic. What was happening? She reached into her pocket and tightly grasped her key chain, feeling the metal begin to cut into her hand as the man walked to the front of the church with his boots making a big booming sound across the aged wood.

"This place has a basement," he stated. "It sounds hollow under here. I didn't think buildings this old had basements in them."

Vera realized it actually did sound hollow under them, never noticing it before. Vera was curious. "Why would you ask about a basement of an old church?"

The man replied, "Because that's where the ghosts are. They either live in a creepy old basement or in the attic. I don't see an attic happening here, but a basement might be of interest."

One of the girls got excited. "Oh, you are right! I seem to recall basements being a dastardly place for single women to go."

The man moved to the front of the church, walked to the wall and found a crack in the paneling. He ran his finger up and down the seam, pushed in, then pulled forward as a two-foot-wide doorway appeared out of nowhere. It was just an outline on the wall until now, when it made an eerie creaky sound as the opening was revealed.

"Wo! Creaky door and everything. How cool is this?" one girl said as she moved to look down into a seemingly black abyss. "There are steps leading down there. Can we go? Come on, let's see what's in the basement."

Vera was stunned. No one had ever hinted at a basement and now here she was out of her element about to go into a part of the church she never knew existed. She had already begun to feel panicked and this was very much out of her comfort zone, but she had to admit, she too was curious as to what was down there. Taking a deep breath, she gave in. "Okay, but I have to go first."

"Yes ma'am," the man said stepping back.

Vera took out her trusty flashlight, walked to the opening and shined the light down the stone steps revealing a dirt floor at the bottom, as a musty smell rose up to greet her. Turning sideways, she put one foot on the first step and cautiously squeezed through. The two girls followed while the man stayed upstairs.

"Aren't you coming? This was your idea," one of the girls said to the man.

"Those small steps don't look like they were made for me. Tell me what you find. It's better I stay up here in case you fall into trouble down there," he replied.

As Vera landed on the soft basement floor, she shined the light around the room. In front of her she could see the mortar brick walls still scorched from the fire long ago. Her light panned the space as she made way for the other girls to join her. With everyone at the foot of the stairs, she shined the light behind them and found a large box resting on mortar blocks. In the shadows, it looked like a chest of some sort. She walked towards it, then suddenly stopped and stared at the object in front of her.

"Holy shit!" the girl behind her exclaimed. "Is that a…"

"Casket," her friend replied.

Vera curiously answered, "I can see it's a casket. The question is, whose casket?"

One of the girls then commented, "More than whose casket is it, how did it get down here? The door is far too small for that thing to fit through. This is only a partial basement that must have been used to store or hide stuff back in the day."

"People kept a lot of stuff for emergencies down in old cellars," Vera acknowledged. "I never heard of anyone storing a…"

Then Vera heard the sounds of the girls going back up the dirty stone steps as one said, "I'm not wanting to find out who, or what is in that thing. I'm outta here!"

Standing there frozen, Vera looked up at the wooden ceiling. It was like a scene from a cheesy teen movie where someone happens upon a vampire's lair, then opens the casket to reveal a vampire inside with fangs and all the glory of an old immortal. Vera decided right then she needed an answer. She urged herself forward, one small step at a time, until she was standing by the box. Upon studying it, she could tell it was very old with elaborate carvings on the side that appeared to be some sort of ancient text. She had no idea what it said but marveled at the detail of the letters.

Vera put her flashlight in her mouth, and with one hand under the lid, pushed upward. The hinges were silent as the casket opened, void of any vampires or decaying corpses. There was a certain beauty to its emptiness. She took the flashlight out of her mouth and shined it all around the inside of the aged box and stood in awe as she let her hand rub up and down the carefully manipulated wood. It was like finding a fine piece of furniture stored long ago and then forgotten.

"Whoever you were made for sure must miss you. You're mine now," Vera said aloud as she closed the lid. Her funeral was at hand and now fate had offered her the crown jewel in her scheme to be reborn… an old wooden casket. But whose was it? She had to find out.

Vera ascended the steps that led up to the Church, pushed the door open and walked out into the sanctuary remembering the vision of the old woman she had seen earlier, wondering if it was indeed real or not. She scanned the room and saw nothing but emptiness but kept telling herself she had seen a woman looking back at her when she entered the church. There was no sign of the tourists who vacated the premises upon the discovery of the casket, almost making her laugh at their need to flee. Vera closed the small door and saw it all but vanish inside the lines of the paneled wood on the wall.

"Crazy," she thought to herself.

It was now ten-thirty at night. Vera pulled into the driveway where she lived with Cat in a large house owned by the college where Vera taught math. The house was a six-bedroom Victorian for guests, visiting faculty and foreign exchange students who were coming in to either give a lecture or view the college. Vera and Cat moved in when Vera first got her professorship with the college. They agreed to let her manage the property in return for a place to stay as she would be living in Randall the year round. It was now Summer and there were no classes. With she and Cat the only ones there it was a great setup.

Vera walked to the front door, took a breath and walked in. Cat was sitting on the sofa watching television and devouring a bag of instant popcorn as Vera sat down across from her. Looking up from her popcorn, Cat asked, "Hey doll. Where've you been?"

Vera sat up, leaned forward and whispered, "You won't believe what happened to me tonight."

"Go on," Cat coaxed, now pausing the T.V. and realizing something was up.

"I took a tour down to Bethel Church. When I opened the door, I swear, I saw something. It looked like a woman staring back at me with dark eyes. I dropped my keys and when I looked back up, she was gone."

Cat was excited. "No lie? You finally saw a ghost? Are you kidding me? We have been here for years and finally one of us sees something in a town that's supposed to be haunted as shit. I'm relieved. Now at last we have a ghost story to tell the relatives."

Vera wasn't smiling. "I'm serious here, Cat. I really think I saw something, and there's more. My search for a casket is complete. I found one, or it found me."

"A casket? Are you serious? Where did you find one? I've been all over the place looking for one." Cat felt like she had been beaten in a treasure hunt.

"At Bethel Church, down in the basement," Vera revealed.

"What?" Cat said sitting up. "You found a casket at Bethel? Is there a funeral or something going on there now? In the basement? I didn't know there was a basement."

Vera explained, "That is the freaky part. We went down there because a girl said she wanted to see it because stuff happens in old basements. This guy walked to the wall and found a small door, then I, with the two girls, squeezed through it and went down there. I didn't realize there even was a door. It was so small, I missed it and as far as I know, everybody missed it. When we got down the stairs, I swear there was a casket."

"No lie?" Cat questioned. "You really found a casket in the basement? Darlin' this doesn't sound good."

"I'm telling you, it's there. The crazy thing is, I don't know how it got there. It's too big for the door. Someone had to have had it built there or it was there when the church was built. I can't figure it out, but Cat, it's beautiful. Smooth aged wood with cool carvings on the outside and perfect for me to die in. We need to have the ceremony in the basement at Bethel Church."

Cat studied Vera for a moment and then said, "Show me," and got up to put on her jacket.

"What? Now?" Vera said, as she watched Cat getting dressed.

"Yeah, now. You said you found a casket in the basement of a church; you want to die in the thing and get re-born with people there to celebrate the man living inside you. What am I supposed to say? You are my best friend, my lover and my confidant. In other words, my everything. I can't go forward another minute without understanding what you just told me. If you found a casket in the basement of Bethel Church then we are going back there now to see it. I'm serious, now let's go."

All Vera could do was smile. Cat was her everything as well.

On the way there, Vera was like a little schoolgirl planning a birthday party. "I know where I can get some old rugs for the floor, we can put flowers all around and even hang some fake windows on the walls. We can bring in folding chairs I can borrow from the college and I want to get a huge candelabra like they have in the old movies. It'll be so cool. I'll lie in the casket all prettied up and people can walk past me. Beth can give me a sedative to knock me out so I'll look dead. It'll be perfect!"

Cat was concerned. "You'll look dead? Listen to yourself. You are taking this thing way too far," she advised as they turned into the parking lot of the old church. "Beth is on probation with her hospital. Did you forget that? She's not just going to hand out some drug to knock you out. Now show me this casket."

It was late at night and all was quiet along the street as Cat and Vera got out of the car and walked to the front door of the church. As Vera took out her key she hesitated. "Wait, this is when I saw the woman staring at me. Look to the back of the church when I open the door and see if you see anything."

Vera put the key in the lock and slowly turned it. Hearing the release, she slowly opened the doors as the glow from the streetlight behind them flooded the room. They stood in the doorway studying the back of the church to find nothing there, only the empty space behind the pulpit.

"No ghost," Cat said. "Are you sure you…"

"Yes, I'm sure. I know what I… think… I saw," Vera said with some reluctance.

"So, where is this casket?" Cat asked as she began moving about the church.

"It's over here." Vera shined her light to the back as they slowly made their way through the empty pews. Finding the entrance, Vera proclaimed, "See? Here is the doorway. No knob." She reached her fingers in the crack of the door and slowly pried it open, then shined her light down the steps. "It's down here."

Cat cautiously said, "Shit, it's creepy as all get out down there. Why did you go down there?"

"Some guy made me," Vera replied as she began squeezing through the small opening and onto the stairs that led down below.

Cat laughed. "This is why we are gay. Men are freakin' stupid."

As the two women reached the bottom of the steps Vera turned to shine her light on the casket.

"See? A casket," Vera announced.

"Unbelievable," Cat admitted as she eyed the large, out of place box. "And you have no idea who or where this thing came from?"

Vera approached it. "Nope." Reaching down under the lid she again raised the top and shined her light down to reveal the smooth wooden inside. "See? It's beautiful, huh? I could lie dead in here."

"Will you quit saying that? This is nuts, Vee. How did it get down here and why is it down here?" Cat asked eyeing the box.

Vera shook her head. "I have no clue, but I know it's perfect. Look, we can put chairs over there, hang some wall art and I gotta have that candelabra."

Cat looked around and tried to get into what Vera was offering but she was still reeling from being shown a hidden casket in a church that was supposed to be haunted. After finally settling down, she asked, "Are you sure you want to go through with this?"

"I have never been more serious about anything. I want this. Don't you see it's perfect? I'll be reborn as a man and for a while we'll be like a normal couple."

Cat snapped, "Vera Chase, we are a normal couple. I can't believe you said that."

"You know what I mean. I want to promote my masculinity, even if it's just for us. There is a man living down inside me. I know that. I've always known that, as have you. Why can't I have a ceremony to become that man? I'll still be Vera Chase to the people at work and all, but to us, our closest friends and a few of the professors at school, I want to be..." and she stopped.

"Be who?" Cat said. "You are going to change your name as well? I hope not because I'm not calling out a man's name during sex, even if it is you."

Vera was suddenly silent. She started to sway a little and had to catch herself on the side of the casket as Cat reached out and grabbed her.

"Are you alright? Vee? You Okay?" Cat asked, looking into her face with the light.

"Did you hear that?" Vera questioned. "Did you hear it? Tell me you heard it."

Cat looked around the room. "Heard what? I saw you almost fall but I didn't hear anything. What are you talking about?"

Vera steadied herself on the casket. "When you asked me if I was going to change my name, I heard a voice as I was talking to you. You didn't hear it?"

"Vera Chase you are scaring the shit out of me. What voice? I think we need to go now. There is so much mold and dust down here it's probably got us both hearing things. Let's go and talk about the funeral later. What did the voice say?"

Vera looked around the room and pointed to one of the walls.

"It came from over there. When I said what I was going to change my name to a voice said 'Bevan.' I heard it plain as day."

"Bevan? Who the hell is that?" Cat asked, now looking where Vera motioned. "I've never known anyone named Bevan. Are you sure?"

"Yes. It said 'Bevan'," Vera said coldly. "Like 'Kevin' but with a 'B.'

"Okay, Bevan. Let's go. I don't like this," Cat insisted, now moving toward the stairs.

"I'm beginning to feel the same way," Vera admitted as she followed.

As they got to the top of the stairs and turned to look back down into the dark, Cat said, "Man, if I didn't love you like I do I'd never set foot back down there. There are some creepy ass vibes around that place."

Vera agreed. "I hear you, but in the daylight, I bet it's a different thing. Let's come back tomorrow and see."

"Daylight? What daylight? There is no daylight down there. Dark is dark, Vee. It's weird as all hell down there any time, day or night."

The two women exited the front door of the church. As Vera turned to close the door behind her, she glanced back and saw the woman she had seen earlier rapidly coming up the aisle towards her. Vera watched as the woman reached up and placed a hand on the side of Vera's face. Vera sensed a coldness and immediately felt faint, hearing the same voice she'd heard earlier saying, "Find me!"

Gasping, Vera fell backwards. Cat turned to see her lying there and ran up the steps. "Vera! What on earth? Did you trip?"

Vera looked up at Cat and whispered, "It was her again. I saw her. She touched my face. Here…"

Vera took Cat's hand and placed it on the side of her face where the woman had touched her.

"My God!" Cat pulled her hand back. "It's ice cold! Really ice cold. Are you all right? Does it hurt?"

Standing up from the floor Vera pulled herself together and looked back into the empty church. "I'm fine," she assured Cat as she dusted herself off and reached up to feel her face returning to its proper temperature. Handing the keys to Cat she said, "Here, you lock up."

Cat was tightly clutching the steering wheel as she drove through the empty streets.

"Vera, I don't know about this. We've got a front row seat to one heck of a creep show here. Now you have ghosts touching you freezing your face. Doesn't that scare you at all? I'm shaking. This is way off the page here."

"She told me to find her," Vera said as she stared straight ahead.

Cat was freaking out. "Find her? Find who? The ghost that touched you? I'd say you pretty much already did there, darlin',"

"No. She said for me to look into why Bolt burned the four women in the church. Nobody has ever really found out why he did it, only that he was crazy and there was talk of them being witches. The voice of the woman told me to dig. I have to find out why Jeremiah Bolt killed those women."

Cat assessed the situation as she found her way home.

"I'd say you need to find out where that damn casket came from. That's crazy. A ghost woman touching your face? A casket? You have your work cut out for you; I'll say that."

The next day, Vera went to the college library and set up shop in a lone corner. She was determined to find all she could about the deaths of the four women that occurred over two hundred years ago. After hours of research online as well as through old town biographies, she found nothing other than what she already knew. There was some history about the event but not anything about the women themselves. More luck needed to come her way. Remembering the voice the night before, "Find me!" she knew she had to broaden her search.

Vera reached up and let her hand brush across the part of her face the woman touched the night before. She could vividly remember the cold sensation she felt while lying there on the front steps of the church recovering from…something. The memory wouldn't leave her.

Chapter 4

MRS. JENKINS

Vera decided to try the Courthouse as she was familiar with most of the building having taken ghost tours through it every Halloween. Every supposedly haunted site in Randall opened its doors to the public on Halloween night and the Courthouse was on the 'most haunted' list.

It was quiet on that particular day. The Courthouse was usually a busy place, but today Vera was surprised to find few staff members on hand. She met an elderly woman who'd worked there for fifty-three years. Mrs. Jenkins was the stereotypical old school librarian type, complete with a round bun hairdo with a long pin through it.

"Hello, Mrs. Jenkins," Vera began with an adoring tone.

Looking up to see who spoke, she recognized Vera and said, "Well, hello sweet girl. Here you are again. It's not Halloween yet. Or is it?"

Laughing, Vera reassured her it wasn't Halloween, and then a thought hit her; if anyone would know about the Bethel Church fire it would be her.

"Mrs. Jenkins, I'm doing a little research on the old Bethel Church. I need information for my ghost tours because people want to know more about the four women who died when Jeremiah Bolt chained them in the church. Do you know where I might find anything on them? Who they were, where they lived, any relatives still living?"

"That was a terrible thing," Mrs. Jenkins began. "My grandfather used to tell us bedtime stories about it to scare us to death. It worked, too. My sister and I would cower under the covers at the thought of old Pastor Bolt yelling at the top of his lungs how The Sword of God had won out over evil.”

“So, you know the story?” Vera questioned.

“I was a little girl here. A friend of mine was a descendent of one of the women burned in the church. Rebecca Middlebrook was her name. She lived near me and we walked to school together.” Mrs. Jenkins then took a long gaze out the window. “It was so very long ago.”

“Mrs. Jenkins, where is Rebecca Middlebrook now? Is she still here? Is she still in Arizona?”

“Rebecca passed on when she was seventeen years old from being in a sledding accident. The horse pulling the sled somehow got spooked and bolted. The sled left the road, hitting a boulder when the horse broke free. Rebecca was thrown and broke her neck. We were all so close back then. Small town, you know. She was really a nice girl. She’s at rest out in the cemetery. I’ll pay her a visit soon and take her some wildflowers. That will be nice.”

“Mrs. Jenkins, I’m sorry about your friend, but I need to know anything at all about the four women. Rebecca Middlebrook was your friend’s name?” Vera took out her notebook and scribbled the name down. “Would there be a record of the church burning? Any old newspapers from back then in a vault somewhere?”

Mrs. Jenkins seemed still lost in the remembrance of her friend. She stood silent a moment then, “In the basement. I believe what you need is in the basement now.”

“Can you show me the room or just tell me which one? I’ll look around on my own, just tell me where. I’ve never been down there.” Vera was becoming anxious at the prospect of finding any leads on the women and it showed in her hurried disposition.

Mrs. Jenkins took Vera to the top of the stairwell and began her slow descent. Vera followed her trying not to rush. On the way down, Vera took a chance and asked Mrs. Jenkins if she knew anything about an old casket at Bethel Church.

"A casket you say? At the church? No, I can't say I know anything about a casket in the basement of the church, Vera."

As the two women reached the bottom of the stairs, Vera realized she hadn't said anything about the casket being in the basement or mentioning there was a basement. Just as Vera was about to question her about it, Mrs. Jenkins walked two doors down and said, "Here we are." She slowly turned the antique doorknob then gently pushed open the door. As light from the hallway flooded the storeroom, Vera realized she had her work cut out for her. There were boxes on top of boxes, old file cabinets and pieces of scenery from long forgotten happenings on the square. Basically, the forgotten records of a small town.

Vera walked in and said, "Thank you so much. However, I think I'm going to be a while."

She couldn't believe the task before her as she walked into the room and scanned for a place to start. There was no light switch on the wall and no light fixture to be found in the storeroom. She reached in her shoulder bag and took out her ever-present flashlight, turned it on, then shined it around the room. "If I need anything, I'll..."

Vera turned around to find Mrs. Jenkins had left her alone with the task at hand. She walked to the door, scouted around and then heard another door close down the hall. "Must be a bathroom down there," Vera said aloud. "Good to know." She rolled up her sleeves and began the task of trying to find a needle in a stack of needles.

Sometime later, after going through boxes, file cabinets and parade artifacts, Vera at last found a file drawer containing old newspapers from the time of the church fire. "Yes!" she heralded as the papers went by one by one. She looked at dates and knew she was getting close, and then, there it was; the front page of the newspaper with the date and headline;

May 29th, 1802: Special Edition
CHURCH FIRE KILLS FOUR
SHERIFF SHOOTS PASTOR

Vera froze as she studied the writing that seemed to ooze from the old newspaper and absorbed every word. She sat on the floor of the storeroom as she read the newsman's recollection of the fire. It was all there. From the four young women down to the hot glowing chains that held the church doors closed.

Vera read aloud, "The hero, Sheriff Jonathan Carriage, stood in the glow of the flames with his revolver in hand as crazed Pastor Jeremiah Bolt lay dead in the churchyard from a single bullet through the heart." It was poetry. It was almost word for word like the speeches she had given on her ghost tours.

She continued reading aloud; "Sara Carriage, Rebecca Middlebrook and two unknown girls were the victims in the Pastor's deluge of insanity.

"Rebecca Middlebrook? That was the name of Mrs. Jenkins' friend. It can't be the same one. Mrs. Jenkins would be over two hundred years old," Vera said aloud. "And two unknown girls? I gotta find out who the two unknowns were now as well? This is getting deep."

Most of the paper's news was dedicated to the fire. It was a small-town paper of only six pages, being three front and back. Vera turned them carefully so not to do any harm to the fragile pages when a name caught her eye; "Bevan." It was a small article about a man who bought the land Bethel Church and the cemetery sit on.

Vera carefully folded the newspaper back the way she found it and then once more before sliding it into her purse. She figured no one would miss a two-hundred-year-old paper. Besides, it was all she had on the fire. She left the room and the door closed behind her. As she began her climb up the stairs, she held her arm down firmly on her shoulder bag. She harbored a shade of guilt, like she was stealing an artifact, but that quickly faded as she rationalized she was doing a favor for the town by clearing up some missing historical accuracies. "It's a gift to Randall," she thought. "Screw it."

Cat was busy planning a funeral. She'd contacted several

of their friends who'd agreed to come, and she'd gotten excited over the prospect of it all coming to fruition. Hearing the door open, she turned to see Vera coming in.

"Vee! I got your funeral covered. I can see it. You lie in the casket all girly-like and we have a few of the guests get up and talk about you and say how they are sad to see you go and talk about girl stuff you did. Then, we all go upstairs for lunch. While we are gone, you do the change-a-roo, we go back down, open the casket and you get out resurrected as a man. Just don't say, 'ta-daaaa!' It will spoil the effect. So, what do you think? Cool, huh?"

Vera was taken by surprise. She had thought about the funeral, but not in that much detail. She knew she wanted Cat's blessing and had wondered how that would happen. Now she knew. By letting her plan the festivities it would make her feel as though she were a part of it. Vera then blurted out, "Perfect!"

"Perfect?" Cat questioned. "You wanna do this funeral thing, I plan it and all you can say is 'perfect?' No input on the staging or anything? This isn't like you. What's up?"

Now trying to focus on the moment, Vera came back to her senses realizing how much thought Cat had put into all this. She was doing it all for her.

"I'm sorry. I've just spent hours over at the Courthouse going through old newspapers looking for whatever I could find about the fire at Bethel Church. I found a paper with an article about the whole thing."

Cat sat up at the good news. "You did? What did it say? Anything about the women themselves?"

"No obituaries on the girls," Vera sighed, "But I found an article with the name 'Bevan' in it. I guess he was rich. He bought the land the church and cemetery sit on. I guess that was news back in 1802. He seems harmless enough."

"Vee, this is crazy. Why are you so dead set and determined to find out who died in a fire back in the 1800's? Now you're defending a guy that seemingly spoke to you through a freaking wall in a basement you didn't even know was there until yesterday? Are you hearing this?"

Vera decided right then and there to take a leap. She knew it was crazy, but she had to say it.

"Because I think I was involved. I think somehow, some way, I lived back then and ended up at Bethel Church the night Jeremiah Bolt chained the women in the church. I feel it, Cat. I know it sounds nuts, but I know it and now I have to find out why. I don't know if I was one of the four women or what, but when I researched all this and read the article, it wasn't like I wasn't learning it, but remembering it."

Cat was dumbfounded. "Holy crap, you're serious. You actually think you're one of the women?"

"No, I didn't say that. I believe I was there in some capacity. Maybe just a bystander or something. I really do believe I was involved," Vera said with her ever confident tone. "I really, really do. How am I supposed to find out why I feel this way?"

Cat looked at Vera standing in the aftermath of what could very well be the strangest thing she'd ever heard her say. She was amazed to see a tear running down Vera's face; something she'd only seen one time before in their relationship. She knew Vera was a strong-minded woman, but an emotional woman? No. She was rock hard when it came to showing that side of herself. Then a thought hit her. Maybe she did have a way for Vera to clear up some of this bizarre circumstance.

"I have an idea. It's a long shot, but it is something. What about your aunt that lives in Colorado? Remember you said you used to be close before she moved down to Florida and you lost touch? You said she's back in the mountains with her husband. Aunt Audrey? Was that it?"

Vera thought for a second and said, "Oh, everyone calls her 'Lovey' now."

"There you go," Cat confirmed.

"Past life regressions?" Vera sighed. "That's her thing. Really, Cat, I don't see it. I don't believe in that stuff. Never have and you know that. I'm a math geek. Two plus two equals four. I can prove that, but hypnosis and such? That's not me. Why would we want her involved?"

"Look, I researched her when you first mentioned her. She seems like the real deal, babe. She has a reputation for helping people like us who need answers they can't explain any other way. She's helped a lot of people get some serious shit out of their head. I think she can do some good here. What do you think? We can get in touch with her and she can at least give us something. It's all I got. Let me call her. What do you say? We need help here, Vee, and she could be the answer. And what are the odds you'd be in this place and have a clairvoyant aunt? It's a no-brainer."

Vera sat holding her Kleenex and trying to imagine what a past life regression would be like. At the moment it was all bullshit hocus-pocus to get vulnerable peoples' money. Still, there was a sincerity in Cat's voice that was speaking to her. She needed answers. Vera was seeing ghosts now and finding caskets. This was off the map for them both. Vera took a deep breath and said, "Screw it. Let's get in touch with her, but I gotta tell you, I can't call her because she and her husband use carrier pigeons. They don't use phones. Her husband is afraid the government is listening."

Cat laughed and fell back into the sofa cushions. "They don't use phones, they use pigeons?"

"Yeah, her husband is a little odd," Vera sighed. "He's like stuck in 1975. You think they can help me figure out why I'm seeing ghosts?"

Cat ran her hand across Vera's face.

"We need to get her out here. I really feel like she can help. We are supposed to work this thing out together."

Vera let out a deep sigh. "I know a guy I have to call who sends his carrier birds to Colorado. He'll get in touch with Wood and Lovey and we'll go from there. If anyone can really do this regression thing, it's her. That's a fact."

"Wood?" Vera questioned. "Why does she need wood?"

Vera laughed. "'Wood' is her husband's name. It's short

for 'Woodstock.' Long story, don't ask. I'll send a bird tomorrow. She will probably think I've lost my mind, which at this point is not out of the question."

"So, why exactly do you think you were involved?" Cat asked as she was obviously becoming more aware of Vera's sincerity.

Vera took a deep sigh and walked over to the window.

"When I research this thing, it's like I can hear the crowds, I can see Bolt standing there, waving his bible and that thunderous gunshot seems to pulsate with me. It's like I can hear it. Cat, I can almost…remember it."

"You really think you were there? Vee, this is off the chain even for you. You've never mentioned anything like this before. I know little to nothing about ghosts or past lives," Cat admitted. "Maybe your aunt is the ticket here. If she can help, I'm all in."

"Why now?" Vera asked. "I've been in that church a hundred times and never seen or heard a thing out of the ordinary. Then, all of a sudden, I'm engulfed in something crazy. Why now? That's what I can't seem to figure out."

Chapter 5

THE BIRD ARRIVES

Wood was in the backyard of his mountain house. Maggie, Wood's daughter, bought another place down the mountain with her boyfriend Jack Reynolds and moved out, leaving Wood's old house for sale. Wood and Lovey had decided to leave Florida and move back to Colorado when marijuana was legalized there, as pot was Wood's medicine of choice. The house was a no-brainer and Wood bought it back immediately.

It was a perfect summer morning with a light breeze coming over the mountain when a pigeon arrived at Wood's coop. Seeing the attached note, he saw it was meant for Lovey. He took it inside and announced, "You got a bird o'gram."

Lovey was sitting cross-legged on the floor in deep meditation, surrounded by six of Wood's pot plants that had grown to enormous size, when she was aroused by the sound of his voice. As she came out of it, she opened her eyes to see Wood handing her the note from the carrier pigeon.

"Here. Bird o'gram," he said again with a smile. "Who's it from?"

Lovey carefully unfolded the tiny note and read aloud, "Your reluctant to ask you niece in Arizona needs you. Can you come?"

She paused for a moment, then felt a curious urgency.

"My niece, Vera. She needs me for something and I believe I need to go."

"Your niece? Grace's kid? Does Grace know?" Wood questioned.

"I guess not if she used the birds. That is odd. Vera lives in Arizona. You up for a road trip?"

Wood was always up for an adventure.

"To Arizona? Hell yeah! I'll get the birds and buds handled. What do you suppose she wants?"

Lovey closed her eyes and sat on the sofa. She took a few deep breaths and a wrinkled brow appeared on her forehead.

"Wood, I don't know, but all of a sudden I feel something strange. I think she's in trouble and doesn't know it. We need to go tomorrow. If we leave in the morning, we can be there by tomorrow night."

"Oh, shit. You don't think this has anything to do with the amulet, do you? I smashed it, so all that should be over," Wood reminded her.

"No. This is different. It's something else. I don't..."

Lovey stopped mid-sentence and said, "We need to leave today. I feel like something is coming."

"Today?" Wood barked as he realized something must really be wrong.

Lovey had always been clairvoyant, but this was different. It wasn't like her to want to drop everything and go somewhere.

"Today it is," Wood proclaimed. "Here we go again. You want me to call Maggie and Jack? They might be able to help."

Lovey looked around the room and agreed, "Yeah. Mags would be helpful. Let's stop by on our way out. I need to lie down for a minute."

Wood got concerned. "Oh, man. This looks like it could be another big one. I'll roll a couple for the road. Can't be too careful in situations like this."

Wood was trying to act nonchalant over the arrival of the bird. Deep down there was another story. Wood had been tested. He was a warlock and had known that for some time and accepted it, though he didn't recognize his "powers" in a daily manner, as some do, he wanted to live his life with a simpler flair. It was his choice. However, he did concentrate on his marijuana. Each morning Wood attended the plants and gave them "a sparkle." He'd do a slight meditation at each plant and lay his hands around the pots the plants were in. They had grown to enormous size in only a few weeks. Wood was like a proud papa.

Wood secretly worried about his daughter, Maggie. He had accepted his lineage and knew that his ancestors possessed an "advantage" in life. Maggie would prove no different. She was coming into her own with who she was and what she was. Hope Blanch, an evil witch that lived two hundred years ago, had in the past invaded Maggie and made her do things she wouldn't normally do.

"Each generation grows more powerful," came into his mind. He'd been told that by his father, but didn't understand it, until now. He and Maggie were the descendants of Daniel and Hope Blanch. Hope was a Master Spirit that controlled others to do her bidding. Wood shuddered at the thought that Maggie could one day become such an entity and shook his head as the scenario played out in his imagination.

Lovey went into her bedroom and walked over to her dresser. She pulled out the bottom drawer to reveal the envelope she found in the hidden bottom of the old trunk at Maggie Styles Antique Barn, an establishment Maggie and Wood once owned. It was the list of witches and warlocks executed for witchcraft in 1801. She'd gotten it back from Pete, her brother, and had kept it for over a year. Now, for some reason, she felt she needed it for Vera. She was then filled with a sense of dread.

Wood had his van ready in no time. It looked like something you'd see parked at a Grateful Dead concert or in a Scoobie-Doo cartoon. The psychedelic paint job made him stand out wherever they went. He loved it as he'd never really grown out of the seventies. Flower power, love and peace with a finely rolled joint was all he ever cared about. His government paranoia spanning from that era is why he opted for carrier pigeons over conventional communication. "You can't hack a pigeon," he'd say when cornered about it.

Wood was getting his birds ready for his absence and remembering the year before. His daughter is Maggie Styles, whose given name was Abigail Long until she took the name of Wood's 'Maggie Styles' Antique Barn'. It was to throw off the scent of reporters and such who might decide to dog her about a trial in which she was the chief suspect. Four of her students she was close with had gone missing and though it was never proven, there were those who still considered her guilty of misconduct. Hope Blanch, an ancient evil entity, was the real culprit, but no judge alive would agree to that. Maggie had taken the last year to try and erase the images of the four plastic bags that contained the bodies under the tool shed at the Fredericksburg Cemetery. Though they had never been discovered, some day she knew they would be.

Wood and Lovey were once part of a group of people who served Hope Blanch. In the end, Wood decided otherwise in a leap of last-minute faith. Though Wood acted like the events of the year before didn't bother him, deep down he was wanting to hide it all as far in as possible. His pot use helped with that. His happy-go-lucky demeanor made everyone like him. Lovey loved him unconditionally. For a man who'd just turned sixty, it's all he could ever really hope for.

Maggie Styles was sitting on her back deck overlooking a canyon that bordered her property. The Colorado mountains offered her a backdrop like no other and she had lived most of her life there. After the past year in which she lost her beloved Antique Barn to a fire, she was trying to re-build her life. The only constant she had known since then was her confidant, companion and lover, Jack Reynolds.

There was something in the air and she felt it. Maggie had become aware of her cognitive abilities through Lovey. Together they had done a few past life regressions giving Maggie a window to see into her past. It was a door that she regretted opening, and at the same time knew it had saved her life. Until then her world simply held too many mysteries.

The word, "witch," was a big word for Maggie. She knew there was something in her that let her see into dark corners but wasn't ready to take the reins of the stereotypical witch and kept her feelings on the matter to herself. She assumed one day it would all seem commonplace, but until then, she was apprehensive.

Wood blew the horn as he turned into the driveway. Maggie got up and looked through the window then smiled big and wide when she saw her dad and Lovey pull in.

"Jack!" Maggie shouted down the stairs. "Dad and Lovey are here."

"I'll be right up," came a voice from the basement. "Why did they come?"

When Maggie opened the door, the mere sight of Wood and Lovey brought back images of when she and Jack had found the ledger a year before and sent them all into a world of witches, spells and clouded history. She'd tried to forget it all, but voices still haunted her dreams and made her meditations uneasy at best.

Wood walked in with a resonate "Mags!"

They hugged in the doorway as Jack came up the stairs to greet them.

"Wood! My buddy!" Jack exclaimed at seeing the little man with the big beard and shoulder length hair he had grown to know so well.

"Jack," Wood said as he fell into his embrace. "I got a couple rolled. You wanna burn one?"

"Who you talkin' to?" Jack answered with a laugh.

Jack's pot smoking had escalated since meeting Wood. He now realized the medicinal characteristics of the plant and used it daily. He'd never been so calm and sure of himself and was for all purposes drug free now. No alcohol or prescription antidepressants, just a joint or two a day and he was right as rain.

Maggie turned to greet Lovey. Together their psychic abilities had given them light into some very dark places. As Lovey took Maggie's outstretched hands, it was like connecting two broken wires of electricity. Immediately they both were transported to images of a burning church and screams coming from inside. The silhouette of crazed Pastor Jeremiah Bolt clutching his bible and the sound of a gunshot shook both Lovey and Maggie as they saw the scene play out in their minds. Then a voice, "Find me!"

At that they both let go of the others' hands and stepped back in astonishment. Lovey took a deep breath and said, "We have to go to Randall, Arizona. My niece..."

Maggie interrupted her with, "Your niece needs us to help her understand why she is being contacted." Then she paused and said, "Bevan...."

"What is a Bevan, Mags?" Lovey asked looking into her eyes.

"Not what, but who," Maggie answered. "We need to go there. Who is Vera?" Maggie questioned.

"Vera is my niece. She lives with her roommate, Cat. 'Cat' is short for Cathy." Lovey said, not taking her eyes off of Maggie.

And then they both said together, "Everyone calls her that."

"How do you know that?" Lovey asked Maggie. "How did you know that everyone calls Cathy 'Cat'?"

"I don't know. It just was there in front of me like a scene I'd already played out. What does that mean?" Maggie asked.

Maggie's powers of reception had grown far stronger in the last year. She'd learned to strengthen her abilities to where she had become able to see things in her conscious mind that Lovey could only tap into while in deep meditation.

"You're getting stronger, Mags. I can see it. You know where that can lead."

"I know. Believe me, I know," Maggie confessed as she and Lovey acknowledged the obvious.

"We need to leave for Randall, Arizona today," Lovey stated. "I also feel I need to bring the envelope. The one I found in the bottom of the trunk you and Jack found the old ledger in."

"The one from the witch trials? Why do you need that?" Maggie asked, almost afraid for her to answer.

"I don't know why. I just know we better take it. Mags, I have a very bad feeling about this. Vera doesn't ever contact me and now out of the blue she sends me a carrier note from Arizona."

"Does she do pigeons like you and Dad?" Maggie asked.

"No. She knows a guy out there who has a few birds she uses. She must really be in deep to go to the trouble of using someone's birds, only I don't think she gets just how much she needs us. And it's odd she contacted me and not Grace, her own mother. It further makes me think it's something paranormal. I did say...us. Are you ready to do this again, Maggie? This could be far and away more dangerous than Hope Blanch."

Then Lovey and Maggie heard the sound of familiar laughter. It seemed Wood and Jack had done away with one of Wood's "rolled ones." Then in the midst of it all...

"Lovey! Get in here. Gilligan's on. You gotta do her," Jack yelled out as the two women turned towards the living room.

Lovey took Maggie's hand and led her to the living room where they were hit with the aroma of freshly burning cannabis and the sight of two grown men giggling like schoolboys in front of a television.

"Lovey!" Jack blurted out. "Do her, please. Here she is."

Lovey walked around to the front of the television as Gilligan's Island was showing Natalie Schaffer's character, 'Lovey' and Jim Backus' 'Thurston Howell III' discussing dinner. Schaffer's character said, "Oh, I would just adore a bottle of French wine and a scone from that little cafe in Paris."

Wood paused the TV, and everyone looked at Lovey. She took a deep breath, cocked her hip and as flawlessly as one could, she mimicked the Gilligan's Island characters' voice to perfection. Wood and Jack exploded into laughter as Maggie looked on. She couldn't help but smile at her beloved Jack enjoying himself with her father. "Man, I love it when she does that!" Wood exclaimed. "She nails it every time. That's why we call her..." And everyone said together, "Lovey!"

As the giggling subsided and the mood slowly changed to the obvious, Jack took a serious brow.

"Maggie?" he began, "I know that look. I've been trying for a year to forget it."

"We have to go to Randall, Arizona." Maggie began. "Lovey's niece needs to see us. I think we can help her, but I don't want you to go, Jack."

"What?" came the response from the other three. Maggie stepped back and said, "I get a feeling that you'll be in danger if you go. Something's coming and I don't know what it is, only that it will be bad, and I can't risk you putting yourself in harm's way again. This concerns Lovey and me, not you two. Yes, I said you two. Dad, I want you to stay here with Jack."

"I appreciate your concern, kiddo, but where Lovey goes, I go," Wood proclaimed. "I know Jack feels the same way about you."

"Damn right," Jack began. "Where you go, I go. We've literally been to hell and back. If you're headed down that road again, I will admit it scares the crap out of me, but I won't risk saying goodbye to you knowing where you are going. Hope Blanch is gone. If this has anything to do with payback for that..."

Maggie interrupted Jack mid-sentence and said, "No, it doesn't. This is different. This is something else."

"I don't care what it is, I'm going," Jack said defiantly. "And where Lovey goes, Wood goes. Am I right, Wood? Are you going to be able to sit this one out knowing these two are headed to trouble again?" Jack faced Maggie. "I say that, Maggie, because I can see trouble in your face. You wouldn't ask us to stay if you didn't really feel anything. Am I right?"

"Yeah. You're right," Maggie sighed. "Lovey's niece has been contacted and doesn't know why. Jack, Lovey's niece is also Grace Hecker's daughter. I don't think Grace knows we are going to see Vera. I can help Vera see some things, but I'm not sure where all this is going. I'm just getting bits and pieces now. I just know it's bigger than Hope and that's why I want you to stay here."

"I'll get us packed," Jack said as he got up and headed for the bedroom.

As the three watched Jack leave the room, Wood looked up at Maggie and said, "He loves you. I hope you know that. Any man who'd go through hell, again, for a woman is worth hanging on to. And that's your fatherly advice for the day."

Maggie leaned down and hugged the little man and said, "I love you, Dad. You're my hero. Don't forget that."

"Say, how about we stop at the old bitch's place on the way out. She's got pot roast today." Wood's suggestion skated him away from the mushy stuff. "You been to the Grizz lately?"

"No, I haven't seen Grace in a while," Maggie admitted. "She still had my picture up on her goddamn Wall of Shame last time I was in there. It's actually got living people on it now. I'll never live that down. Dad, I don't want you to mention anything to Grace just yet about Vera. We don't know what we are dealing with and a mother could cloud things, somewhat."

"I get it," Wood sighed. "But if you were in some kind of shit, I'd want to know about it. I know this is a little different, but still, your kid is always your kid no matter what. Can't change that."

Wood yelled back to Jack, "Hey Jack! You want to stop at the Grizz?"

"Hell, yeah! It's pot roast day," Jack yelled back from the bedroom.

"See? Wood laughed. "That's my boy!"

Wood's van turned into the Grizzly Beer Trap's driveway. Looking around, the most obvious thing was that nothing had changed. The big blank lot across the street brought back memories of Maggie Style's Antique Barn which had burned to the ground a year before. It had all been bulldozed. Even the storage house where Maggie and Jack took a leap of faith towards one another that lead to their finding the lost ledger of Daniel Blanch; an event that would set the tone for the rest of their lives together, was gone.

"Sad to see it gone, huh Mags?" Wood said as he felt his daughter's pain standing there reliving her favorite moments in the store. "I loved that old place. Never be another."

Wood turned and headed into the front door of the restaurant as Jack put his arm around Maggie. "Hey look, Hecker's Wrecker. Pete's here," Jack commented as they stood by Lovey's brother's wrecker. "Come on. Let's get some pot roast."

The volume of the place had already risen a bit at the sight of Wood and Lovey walking in the door. Everyone loved Wood. Lovey walked over to her brother Pete as he stood up to give her a hug. It was a scene that wouldn't have happened a year earlier when family friction had them at odds. It was a welcomed change for the both of them. Her other brother, Sam, had also seen a reevaluation of what sibling relationships could offer. In the family at least, everything was good.

Wood's eyes widened at the sight of Grace Hecker. She owned the place and was Wood's Achilles tendon. Publicly they had carried an aggressive banter towards each other for years when Wood was the sole owner of the Antique Barn before Maggie, but they'd be first to be at the others' side should trouble occur to one of them. In some odd way they needed each other. Wood called her, "The Old Bitch" and she called him "The Nut Job." It made for many entertaining volleys between the two of them over the years. Of course, in a relationship such as theirs everyone wonders if it had ever gone in another direction, even for a short while. If it did, it will forever remain between the two of them. Neither one was talking. Wood was firmly with Lovey, Grace's half-sister. Though Lovey and Grace had the same mother, they acted like casual friends who barely knew each other. Family shit can get complicated.

"Good lord, look what the dog dug up," Grace said at the site of Wood.

"Speaking of dog, you're looking ugly as ever," Wood bantered as he pulled up a stool at the bar.

Grace let her hand rest for a second on top of his as their eyes met in stalemate. That was enough for now.

"What brings you in? Got a hankering for my pot roast?" Grace asked as she put a roll of silverware in front of Wood.

"You know it. Best damn pot roast on the mountain. You ought to think about opening a restaurant," Wood said as the other patrons laughed at the comment.

Grace got quiet for a minute. She was there when Wood made his choice to smash the amulet they all felt compelled to find under the evil will of Hope Blanch. It had been in their lives for so long they knew nothing else. When it was gone, they had to start over in a lot of ways. Grace secretly missed it. It was a way of life and then it wasn't. They were all still healing from it.

"Something's up, isn't it?" Grace asked Wood. Seeing Maggie and Jack across the room together with Lovey was in some ways frightening. "She okay these days?" Grace asked as she nodded towards Maggie.

"Yeah. She's good. Jack's still with her which gives them both stabilities, I guess. After last year, she's changed, Grace. Lovey says Maggie's psychic abilities have grown a lot. That's both good and bad, and you know what I mean. Now she's seeing shit. Visions and such."

Grace felt a knot in her stomach. She knew where having certain psychic abilities could lead. If Maggie's powers were growing, that meant there was a reason for it. Sometimes nature has a way of dealing with things. It's about balance. But today, Grace felt the scales tipping in the wrong direction.

"Where you headed?" Grace cautiously asked.

At that moment Maggie came over to say hello to Grace. As she walked across the room every eye in the place was on her. Pretty, hot women such as her rarely came into the Grizz and Maggie was well known. Secretly she was an object of desire up and down the mountain, but an unwritten law kept potential suiters at bay. Everyone wanted her, nobody dared take a shot.

"Hello, Grace," Maggie said as she slid onto the stool next to Wood.

"Maggie. How's life down the mountain? We miss you up here. Ain't the same. I get a crazy feeling every time I look at the big blank spot across the road. Didn't realize how much I liked seeing the Antique Barn until it wasn't there anymore. I shut down The Grizz when the dozers came to clean it all up. Didn't want to watch it go, I guess."

"Me either," Maggie agreed. "I got Jack out of it all and now I'd be lost without him. He's good people. I owe you for sending him over, even if it was supposed to turn out differently, you know?"

Grace let her mind go back momentarily to the ritual of sending "potentials" over to Maggie's Antique Barn. Men were chosen to see if any would possibly lead them to the lost body of Hope Blanch, which concealed an amulet of considerable power. The ones that didn't never did anything else. Their pictures were taken while in a makeshift shower behind the bar while they were hungover, then placed on Grace's Wall of Shame. "They looked like hell, then went there," was scribbled over the top of the wall.

"Did somebody say my name over here?" Jack said as he walked over to the bar. He was the envy of quite a few people, and he knew it. Being Jack, he played the role of boyfriend really well. He'd gotten to know everyone on the mountain and liked most. He'd become one of them. He was friendly and asked for nothing but sincerity in return.

"Hey there Miss Grace. Your eyes are sparkling like the first evening star at twilight," he mused as he took her hand and kissed the back of it.

"You men see this shit?" Grace shouted. "That's a gentleman! You guys take note and treat your wives that way from now on, you hear?"

"If we did that, you'd go broke because we'd be home

rolling around in the sack all day." Pete yelled. "I'd rather have pot roast!"

After the laughter in the room subsided, Lovey took her place with the four of them at the bar. "Hello, Audrey," Grace softly said.

"Hello half-sister dear. You know, you, Sam and Pete are probably the only people that still call me that?" Lovey said. "I've been Lovey for so long now I forgot my real name."

Lovey could feel the resentment Grace still harbored towards her and her brother, Pete, for burning down Maggie Style's Antique Barn. Lovey saw the dark magic that came from the Ledger of Daniel Blanch, called her brother Pete and together they saw the need to get rid of anything else related to it that Wood may still have had hidden in the Barn. Though it was ruled a case of faulty wiring, everyone knew who did it and why. Whether it was all worth it or not still remained to be seen.

Grace served up four plates of pot roast, smiled, then went into the kitchen. It felt good having her half-sister and friends there, only she was having flashbacks of Hope's command over them all. It was like an addiction. She'd gotten away free and clear, she tried to tell herself anyway. She still remembered the rituals. Images of the sacrifices she had a hand in raced through her mind. Like remembering a bad series of dreams, she wondered if she would ever really be free of the guilt from killing all those people and then showcasing them on her Wall of Shame, like trophies. The realness of it all was coming back to her a little at a time. Seeing those four people sitting at the bar brought it all back in waves. Especially Maggie. Grace opted to step out back for a smoke, regardless of the people inside.

As she took the first drag off her cigarette she heard, "It's going to be okay up here, Grace."

Startled, she turned to see Maggie standing behind her. "I know you're upset. Seeing us all together brings it all back, doesn't it?"

Grace was caught. She'd seldom mentioned any of the

previous year to anyone. Now, here she was shaken and feeling vulnerable. The crusty outside shell she kept herself wrapped in began to melt under Maggie's mention of the obvious. Grace began to shake and then the tidal wave of emotion hit her as she fell into Maggie, sobbing uncontrollably as Maggie felt the warmth of Grace's tears penetrate her shirt.

"Let it go Grace. It's me. Give it all to me. You didn't do anything, it was Hope. It was Hope, not you."

"What did we do?" Grace whispered. "We killed all those people for her. We are all going to hell, Maggie. We are all going to hell for what we did."

"What Hope did," Maggie said. "We got played. It's all over now."

"Is it?" Grace asked. "I know that look, Maggie Styles. You all are going somewhere to start that shit up again. Wood told me."

Maggie hugged her. "It's not like that. Lovey and I have a feeling…"

Grace interrupted her. "I know what you're feeling. It's been keeping me up nights. Wood said something was coming. It's coming for Vera, isn't it? I've been seeing visions, Maggie. Vera is involved. We can't allow that child to go down that dark street. She knows nothing of Hope Blanch, the rituals, none of it. Why would some evil try and take her? She's an innocent."

"We were all innocents at one time, Grace. You know that. If she's been contacted, we need to know why. We've been here before, she hasn't."

"Has Audrey got the envelope?" Grace looked up and asked. "Has she got the envelope from that damned trunk?"

Maggie didn't say anything.

"She does! I know it. That thing is evil, Maggie. I told Pete to burn it when he had it, but she wanted it back. I have no idea why anyone would want death certificates from two hundred years ago unless they were going to start something back up. I'm telling you, that list of witches is attached to

Hope Blanch. Her fucking name is in it, Maggie. Why do you want to go back down that road? Stay here with Jack. Start a family before it's too late, for God's sake. Leave this black magic out of your life. It consumed me for years, now I'm hollow. Lost. Trying to get through the days without remembering the rituals, the faces of men who stared back at us with looks I'll never forget. Don't go back to that. It's not natural. It's damned. All of it. Let it go before we are all pulled back down with whatever you revive in Arizona. Leave Vera out of it. She has no clue where it can lead."

"We have to go," Maggie proclaimed. "There is an evil that's coming and we need to help. She doesn't understand it."

"What are you now?" Grace snapped. "Some sort of paranormal crime fighters? Modern day ghost busters? Why you? You need to go and watch The Wizard of Oz, Maggie. They dropped a house on one witch, but the one behind it was the real badass. There's a lesson there for us all. Be glad the first one's dead. Leave it at that."

Grace was right. Still, Maggie knew what lay ahead was already in play. There was no stopping it.

"Why didn't she call me, Maggie? I'm her mother," Grace questioned. "I should have been there for her more. It was Hope. She had all my attention when I should have been trying to have a decent relationship with Vera."

Maggie was sympathetic. "If it makes you feel better, it was her roommate who had her contact Lovey. Vera just reluctantly played along."

Maggie tried to reassure Grace in whatever capacity she could, but despite all the warning Grace could muster, Maggie Styles was headed to Randall, Arizona.

Maggie gave Grace one last hug and returned to join the others. Grace watched Maggie disappear into the diner and then glanced over to a box near the back door. Stepping on her cigarette butt, she walked over to it, reached down and took out an old book. A very old book. She closed her eyes and let her hand rub over it as visions began to come and go. She removed her hand and silently looked at Maggie and Jack having pot roast, not knowing about the book she had. Wanting to show them, but conflicted, she opted to return the book to its hidden container then hurriedly began to seal the box up out of frustration. As she turned to rejoin the others at the bar, an envelope fell to the floor. Picking it up, she recognized it as the letter Vera had sent to her telling her she was having her name legally changed to 'Vera Chase' from Vera Chase Hecker. She'd opted to drop her last name, Hecker, and simply be Vera Chase. Grace took a deep sigh, then she heard, "Find me!" rocket through her head. Grace stopped and looked around to see no one near. Shaken, she leaned up against a wall and closed her eyes. A vision of a curved brick ceiling with torches around it came into view, then she heard the word 'Bevan.' Grace steadied herself and then looked around the room. If the rest were going to Randall, Arizona, then she had just received her invitation as well.

Grace and her daughter had a distant relationship. She kept Vera away at school during most of the Hope Blanch era. She wished she knew Vera better, but too much time had passed. Collecting herself and putting the voices behind her, she returned the envelope to its hiding place. She thought of how this might be a chance for them to reconcile their differences as she and her brothers had. Anything down that road would have to wait. Vera had more in front of her than forgiving Grace and Grace knew that too well. She took a deep breath, got back into character and then proceeded to her spot behind the bar.

Maggie had returned to her seat and was listening to the sound of the crowd. It was a good place for her to be. She knew that trouble of some degree was awaiting them in Randall, but at the moment she was simply enjoying her friends. Then, "Find me!" shot through her head. Jolted, she sat silent as she scanned the room. Visions that came and went on a daily basis didn't bother Maggie now as she'd grown accustomed to their coming through. The voice was different. The visions she had were more like echoes and suggestions of what may occur and some of what had. The voice telling her "Find me," was more of an order. Someone or something needed Maggie's attention. At the moment, whatever it was had it in full.

Maggie wanted to talk to Lovey about the voice but opted to wait it out. They had a long drive ahead of them and there would be plenty of time to explore the message. Still, Maggie got the feeling something was coming.

After lunch, the four of them said their goodbyes and after once more reassuring Grace, they headed down the mountain for Arizona. There was anticipation in the air as they all were enjoying the scenery and camaraderie of being together again. Maggie was still sitting on the voice she heard, assuming it was meant for her.

Both Lovey and Maggie knew Grace was having a hard time with knowing there was a chance Vera, her own daughter, would be tempted by an evil she only had glimpses of. They both knew Grace wouldn't be able to stay on the mountain long, even though they knew it was in Vera's best interest for her to do so. Sometimes a mother overlooks her own peril when her child is involved. It's nature doing what nature does.

"Grace is getting visions," Maggie relayed. "She's feeling something, as we all are."

"That old broad needs to stay out of it," Wood directed. "I don't feel right involving her in this. Just don't."

Jack was reading between the lines of what Wood was saying. It was his aggression with the 'protecting the mate' thing that comes out in everyone when someone they feel close to, or even covet, is in peril or becomes threatened. Wood was showing that side of himself where Grace was concerned, and everyone saw it, and everyone loved it. Even Lovey, who admired Grace as well. It was Wood at his best just being himself. He cast quite a shadow at that moment.

Jack understood. "Wood, I know you can't help it. Grace means more to you than any of us will ever know. You two have been through a lot. She's tough. That's a gritty woman up there and she can handle herself. Makes damn good pot roast too. She's like the rest of us, Wood. We manage. You know why you want her safe? You care about her."

Wood looked over at Jack and said, "I owe her for my birds shitting on her truck."

Everyone busted out laughing.

"Damn Wood, I didn't know you were such a romantic."

After a minute Jack resolved, "If Grace wants to chime in on this, we can't stop her. I know you want her to be safe and all, as we all want, but if she comes, she comes. It's mommy/daughter shit."

Jack was thinking of the crusty lady he'd come to know and wondered how things could have soured between her and Vera. Every family has its share of bullshit. That's a given. But to be so far apart was foreign to Jack. He was always into family.

"Why did she and Vera grow apart?" He asked.

"Long story there." Lovey seemed to be drifting back to the way things were when she and her brothers had a falling out.

"Everyone has a long story somewhere," she said. "Count on it."

Chapter 6

WE'RE HERE

Cat and Vera heard the sound of Wood's van pulling into their driveway. Cat looked outside through the curtains and heralded, "They're here! Your Aunt Lovey's here. Act nice. They've come a long way."

Cat went to the door, Vera was tired. She didn't feel like being sociable and her head hurt from reading old documents nobody even knew existed with mostly fine print and faded letters. Reluctantly, she decided to try and talk to Lovey about the regression.

Vera came out into the living room and greeted Wood first, then Jack. When Lovey came in, her long brick-top hair braids were a spectacle to behold. Vera was mesmerized.

Lovey locked eyes with Vera and stood quietly as the others shared small talk. Lovey felt something was coming for Vera. It was an uneasy feeling that Vera would soon be leaving. Going...somewhere.

The door opened wider and Maggie walked in. With her long dark hair and voluptuous body, she was a sight for any sexually active person, man or woman. Maggie looked at Vera and they both were taken with a familiarity that neither could deny.

Vera wanted to say, "I know you."

Maggie fell silent and looked Vera from head to toe. She stepped closer and felt a warmth. She stepped closer still and put out her hand. As Vera's hand slid into Maggie's, each woman fell into a twilight trance like the one Maggie and Lovey had experienced earlier. Images of a torch-lit, rounded brick ceiling in a musty cellar came into their minds. A man in a hood and mask stared straight at the women. Then, "Hi, my name's Cat."

Maggie was jarred from her vision to a sudden return to regularly scheduled programming. She turned to Cat, put out her hand and felt her sincerity, liking her immediately. With a nuclear Maggie smile she softly said, "It's nice to meet you, Cat." Cat was momentarily hypnotized only returning a slight nod.

"Killer house!" Jack was praising the architecture as he looked at the high ceiling and antique woodworking. "You two live here alone?"

Turning from Maggie's smile, Cat answered, "No, only at present. The college owns it and Vera teaches there, so it's kind of a perk. When people come in to see the campus or guest lecture or whatever, the college puts them up here. Vee and I run it as sort of a bed and breakfast for nerds."

"Some perk," Maggie declared. "I taught in Tennessee and didn't get anything like this."

"What did you teach?" Cat asked Maggie, who was now becoming aware of the home's antiquities.

"History. I'm retired now. I decided to make my own history instead of living someone else's."

After giving everyone bedrooms, they all settled into the living room. Wood produced the remainder of the joints he had rolled for the trip.

"Anybody wanna get stoned? I know I do," he said as he lit the slightly curved joint he'd had in his pocket.

"Hell yeah," Cat responded as she looked up at Vera. "Settle down, Vee. It's your relatives for crying out loud."

Shortly after, everyone was comfortably buzzed with Wood rolling a repeater. Lovey stood up and reached down to Vera, tapping her on the shoulder. Vera looked up at the tall woman leaving the room and noticed her slight motion to follow. Maggie watched as Lovey led Vera away from the others knowing what was to come for her. Her world was about to change into something Maggie knew all too well.

"We need a quiet room for your regression," Lovey whispered.

Vera nodded and hesitantly walked Lovey into her bedroom closing the door.

"You want to do this now? I'm exhausted and pretty stoned. I don't think this is a good time," Vera admitted as Lovey motioned for her to sit on the bed.

"It's the perfect time. You're receptive now," Lovey calmly told her. "Your guard is down, so let's do this."

"I need to show you something first," Vera said. She then reached over and got her shoulder bag and took out the newspaper she had gotten at the Courthouse.

"Look at this. This is an article about a fire that happened in 1802. Four women were chained in a church here in Randall and burned alive."

Lovey studied the article. She said, "Why do you have this? Is it because you feel like you are connected to it somehow?"

"Yes, God..." Vera reacted. "I've been telling Cat that I feel like I was there. I was a part of that whole thing. But how could I be? It was in freaking 1802! I can't seem to figure it out. Why do I feel like this? Now, Maggie walks in and I feel like I've known her forever. What is happening to me?"

Lovey could feel her pain. "Maggie and I had a moment when we first saw each other this morning," she confided. "We shared a vision of an old church ablaze with people inside. We saw what this article reads. Is that anything like you're seeing?"

"Yes! Oh, thank God...yes! I've been having visions of it like I was there. I thought at first it was because I do a paranormal ghost tour at the rebuilt church where the fire happened. I opened the door to take a group in and I saw a woman at the front of the church. I swear I did. Then while I was taking them through, I heard a woman's voice ask me why the pastor, Jeremiah Bolt, killed those four women, but it wasn't one of the girls on the tour. It was a voice only I heard. When I responded, those people looked totally confused. I started to get panicked and I don't do that. Now, are you ready for the really crazy part?"

"I'm all ears," Lovey answered in anticipation.

Vera took a deep breath and sat up on the bed so she could directly look at Lovey's face.

"I have been in that church countless times. Last night, a man asked to see the basement. He walks over to a crack in the wall paneling and finds this small door, opens it and there are stairs leading down into a basement I had no idea was there. Me and the two girls go down to check it out and I swear we found a casket. An old antique casket with some sort of foreign writing carved into the side of it."

"A casket?" Lovey asked. "Was it empty?"

"Yes. The people on the tour ran out when they saw it. I was left standing there holding my flashlight with a casket. The crazy thing is, Cat and I were talking about trying to find one for a mock funeral for me. You see, I've always felt there was a man living inside me, so I got the idea that I would have a funeral for my feminine self, then be re-born as my masculine self. See? It was all supposed to be fun, and then there is the casket I said I wanted to find, rent or whatever, to lay in there feigning death while my friends gave the girly side of me a sendoff."

Lovey was fascinated. "You're doing a gender reassignment? You're going to live as a man? Forever?"

"No, not forever, just for a while. I want to see what it would be like to acknowledge my inner male. Just for a while," Vera confessed.

"You do realize you could never really know what that's like, because you were not going to fully commit to it," Lovey advised. "I have experience with transgender clients doing regressions to help them figure out the same thing you're talking about. I'll tell you more about that later, but now tell me, what happened in the basement after you found the casket?"

"Nothing then," Vera recalled. "I came here to tell Cat I found the casket. She wanted to see it for herself because she is planning the funeral for me, so we went back to the church. When I was down there with Cat, I started talking about decor for the funeral and all and I mentioned I was going to change my name. When I was about to say what I was going to change it to, I swear I heard the name 'Bevan' come from a wall in the basement."

Lovey reached out and put her hand on Vera's arm and said, "Bevan? You heard the name Bevan coming from a wall in the basement of the church where four women burned to death in the 1800's?"

"Yes, I swear I did," Vera pressed. "Why do you ask that? Do you know of this Bevan person?"

"I know that name," came from the doorway as it slowly opened. It was Maggie. "I heard it this morning when Lovey and I met. I heard it in thought. What do you know about him, Vera?"

"I don't know anything, Maggie. I swear. It was just was a name I heard. Cat was there. I almost fainted when I heard it, but she didn't hear anything at all. Then, when we were leaving, I was closing the door and a woman ran up to me, touched my face and my cheek turned ice cold. I fell down and Cat had to help me up. Cat was right there and never saw her. I'm not kidding, my face was ice cold. Cat felt it and freaked."

"What happened after that?" Lovey asked.

"We came home. We were both scared to death, but nothing happened. I went to the college this morning to research the fire and then to the courthouse where I found the paper."

"What paper?" Maggie asked.

"Here," Vera said as she offered Maggie the newspaper. "There is an article about Bevan in there."

Maggie reached out and took the paper and immediately dropped it on the bed.

"Where did you get that?" Maggie said sternly. "Where?"

"I got it at the Courthouse. A lady I know there showed me an old storeroom where I found it in a box," Vera explained. "Why? It's all I have on the fire and this Bevan person. What do you know about him?"

Maggie wasn't ready for Vera to ask about Bevan. She was caught off guard but wanted to warn Vera.

"I only have glimpses. Vera, this is dangerous. There are forces at work here that are not to be ignored or coerced. Do you understand? Something wants you. You need to stay close to us so we can try and help you understand, but whatever it is seems to be pointing at you. Let Lovey regress you back and I'll try and go with you. Together maybe we can understand what is happening and why. Are you ready for this, Vera?"

Vera was dumbfounded. She'd always been so on top of everything, now she'd never felt so out of place and frightened. Here she was with two women who wanted her to take a trip into her past where she felt she'd lived before but couldn't be sure. The one thing she did know was that Maggie Styles was different. Vera trusted her hands down, absolutely and couldn't figure out why.

Vera leaned up and said, "I feel like I have some sort of connection with you, Maggie. You took my hand and we were like transported to an old brick cellar. It was so vivid. I know you. I'm telling you; I know you from somewhere. I've never physically met you of late, but we've been together somewhere, sometime before. I know it. I feel it. What's happening to me? To us?"

Lovey didn't like the sound of what Vera was saying at all. She knew that anyone who had any degree of psychic contact with Maggie was in danger. Maggie was now a lightning rod for the paranormal. If Vera had anything to do with Maggie in another life, then it was in everyone's best interest to find out what that connection was. Now was as good of a time as any. Lovey got ready.

"Nothing is happening to you that you can't control, Vera.

What you saw with Maggie is what has already happened to you, but you simply, understandably, don't know why. We need to go back there and tie up the loose ends. That's all. Now relax, lie back and close your eyes so you and Maggie can take a little journey."

Lovey pressed down on Vera's shoulders to push her back on the bed. Maggie closed the door, laid down beside her and closed her eyes. Vera's eyes locked with Lovey's as she let herself go enough to be semi-relaxed.

"Let go now, Vera Chase," Lovey began. "Let go of this time and remember the time when you first met Maggie. Where were you? What were you doing? What were you wearing?"

Lovey watched Vera's eyes close. She herself felt apprehensive about Vera going where she had no control but felt better knowing Maggie would try to be with her. If there was a dark force waiting for Vera, the inevitability of the situation was apparent. She couldn't run from it or stay away. If it wanted her for something, then it was coming and Lovey needed to know why and was scared. She tried not to let that show through, but after Hope Blanch, she couldn't help it. Lovey was determined to help this young woman in front of her, despite any danger to herself or the others. She took a deep breath. They were doing this.

Vera and Maggie lay quiet for a few minutes then Maggie took Vera's hand and softly held it. The marijuana had relaxed them enough to speed up the session, pushing open the door to a point where all they had to do was walk through. Lovey could sense they were close.

"What do you see, Vera? Who are you with?" Lovey was prompting Vera to go deep. The room was filled with the soft white noise of an air purifier that softly whirred in the corner, drowning out any sounds that would keep them from totally relaxing.

"Listen to your heartbeat, Vera. Listen to the room. Go to where you are called to go."

Almost immediately Vera was once more transported to

the cellar with the rounded ceiling where she could see the flames as they danced on the end of crude torches placed throughout the musty dungeon. She could hear the eerie sound of a lynx as it made a moaning cry that echoed throughout. Its eyes glowed a hot green through the mist that rose up from the floor. Muffled sounds could be heard as Vera moved closer and saw a hooded man in some sort of ritual with his hands raised high in the air as if in celebration. Vera was drawn to him. She stepped forward and could feel herself being taken in as the voice became clearer still.

There were four women in the room. One, cloaked and hooded, was strapped to a worktable close to where Vera was standing. The others had fallen lifeless, still bound in shackles that were now obviously unwarranted. Vera turned to look behind her and saw Maggie standing in a doorway that led down a long dark corridor. She nodded to Vera giving her the courage to continue.

"Rebecca Middlebrook," came to her mind as she watched the woman on the table writhe in pain from the restraints and damp coldness. But that didn't make sense. Rebecca Middlebrook was Mrs. Jenkins' friend who died in a sledding accident. Vera was now in Bevan's cellar and she knew it.

The voice of the man at the pulpit suddenly became clear as a bell. The searing eyes burned through Vera as she silently studied him. She was terrified as Bevan got into her head, pointing to something in the mist. Vera turned to see a vision of the room she was in filled with unsuspecting women like herself. The four who were there now weren't the first. There were hundreds who found themselves forgotten and shackled in Bevan's cellar. Visions of unspeakable torture ransacked Vera's mind.

Bevan had been collecting women for a long time. Vera could see the gallows where accused witches were supposedly hung, then revived. Their deaths were a staged illusion to make crowds believe they were punished. Bevan would then claim them, very much alive, for his own.

A woman's raspy voice came into Vera's head; "Find me!

Find me woman and you save yourself. Leave me and be buried with me." It was the same voice she had heard in the church that asked why Bolt burned the four women. "Have you sought the answer?"

Vera stepped over to the woman and reached down to remove the hood. Maggie's hand reached out, took her arm and stopped her. She turned to Maggie and could see her shaking her head, "No," as if to stop her from removing the mask. Vera looked at the woman and then back at Maggie. She had to know whose face was hidden. With one quick pull the hood came off. Suddenly she was back in the room with Lovey and Maggie.

"Holy shit!" Vera let her surroundings soak in. Maggie began coming around as well.

"What did you see, Vera Chase, and where did you see it?" Lovely calmly asked the now shaking Vera. "Tell me now. Don't lose it."

"I saw the cellar. It was Bevan. I saw him with four women in there but only one was alive lying on a table. I pulled her hood back and tried to see her because I thought it would be the same woman from the church who appeared to me when I opened the church doors and later ran up to me and touched my face."

Vera gently let her hand rub across the area where the entity had touched her. "It was a cold touch. Ice cold. She told me to find her or I'd be buried with her. I heard her name as plain as day. My friend Mrs. Jenkins at the Courthouse said she was friends with her as a child, but that can't be the same person. Mrs. Jenkins would be two hundred years old. Maggie, do you know anything about a Rebecca Middlebrook?"

Lovey sat up. "Rebecca Middlebrook? I had a feeling." Lovey stood momentarily silent and then, "I thought this was where we were headed when we got here."

"Why is she there?" Vera questioned, still groggy from her experience.

"I heard it too," Maggie confessed. "Vera's right. I saw

him. Bevan Nicholas, a Master Spirit that controls other spirits to do his dirty work like Hope Blanch, only stronger. He has been collecting women for his own amusement for centuries."

"Amusement?" Vera reacted. "You call what he did to those women 'amusement'?"

"For him, yes," Maggie tried to explain. "He is evil, Vera. Evil incarnate. He keeps who he chooses and then moves on."

"So, why does he want me? I'm not accused of witchcraft or on trial or anything? What could he possibly want me for? What could I possibly have he needs?"

Lovey reached down and with one hand, took Vera's and lifted her up off the bed. Vera looked up at Lovey's tall frame and knew something was dangerous here and that Lovey and Maggie had an insight to what that something was.

"I need to show you something, Vera. Wait here," Lovey said as she left the room.

"Did you see everything I did?" Vera asked Maggie. "Could you hear his voice? Did you hear that moaning sound? Jesus! That was creepy as all hell. Those women. Maggie, he showed me hundreds of women he'd..." Vera stopped at the memory Bevan had given her she didn't want.

"Thank you for going, Maggie, if that's what you call it. Nobody would have believed me if you had not been there."

"Yes, we would have," Maggie said taking her hand. "You're part of us now, Vera. You'll never have to face any of this alone again as long as we are here for you."

When Lovey returned, she had the old leather envelope she found in the bottom of the trunk at Maggie Styles Antique Barn. She opened it and showed the heading to Vera. It read:

Executed in League with The Devil:
Summons and Certificates of Death
Fredericksburg, Virginia, 1801
Witches and Warlocks

Lovey turned to the first page. It was a summons directed

at Rebecca Middlebrook to answer charges of devil worship and witchcraft. The next page was her death certificate confirming she had been hung as a witch on February 20th, 1801. There were pages of other young women whose lives had been cut short from the trials. Most had probably ended up in Bevan's cellar.

Vera was shocked. "Where did you get that?"

Lovey explained, "I found it in the hidden bottom of an old trunk over a year ago," Lovey began. "Maggie and Jack found a ledger in that trunk that changed us all and I think for some reason you have been drawn into that world. Someone, or something needs you. I think Rebecca Middlebrook is just the tip of the iceberg here. What I don't understand is this document says Rebecca was hung as a witch with the execution happening in Virginia. If so, what was she doing in a basement with this Bevan in Randall, Arizona and why did your friend at the courthouse say they were friends over a hundred years later? It doesn't make sense. I know documents were sketchy from back then, but these all were signed by multiple people."

Vera grew defensive. "Well, obviously Mrs. Jenkins knew a different Rebecca. Maybe it's a coincidence that someone named their child that to honor an old relative. That happens all the time. No mystery there. Rebecca is a pretty common name."

Curious, Lovey asked, "What was the next closest date of a paper before the one you have? Do you remember?"

"No. I wasn't looking at other papers when I found the one about the fire. But why now?" Vera asked. "I'm nobody. I just happened into that church and started seeing things I can't explain."

"Then you've been chosen," Maggie said with authority. "Have you seen anything else? Just the woman at the church?"

"Not that I recall. Things just started to happen when I told Cat I wanted to..." Vera then hesitated, let her head drop and almost laughed.

"To what?" Maggie asked her. "To what, Vera?"

"Oh, it all seems so silly now. I explained this to Lovey already. I have made the decision to live as a man. Not to the entire world, but just to my friends for a start to try it out. I was going to have a funeral where my feminine self is pronounced dead, and my new self, my new masculine self, would be resurrected. You see?"

"Go on," Lovey directed.

"I'd have myself made up all girly and my friends would pass by observing me lying there, and then the casket would close, they'd leave for a bit and when they came back, the casket would open and I'd emerge in the guise of a man. I told Cat I wanted to do it while we were at a funeral for a friend of ours. She was dressed so girly and perfect. It was there that I first mentioned it. I got the idea there.

We needed a casket for the illusion and when we went down in the basement of the church, there one was. Like mail order, it was perfect. Down in the basement by that casket is when I heard the name 'Bevan' for the first time. It came out of a wall. In the wake of this spirit thing, I'm almost embarrassed."

Lovey took Vera's hand. "It's a big leap, Vera. Respecting who you really are inside is big magic for anyone. I respect you for it, but there is something more pressing. I believe when you were in the presence of your transitioned friend, you were standing in a doorway to the other side. You announced that you wanted to die. Not literally, but it was enough to kick start this series of events. Our physical death is just a beginning to something else. You looking for a casket and talking of being resurrected made you vulnerable for this evil to move forward through you. If you were already there in another life, this thing was waiting for a way into you. You unknowingly gave it one. I think we need to go back to the church with Maggie to see this casket. When can we go?"

"When do you want to? I have the key. I'd suggest going in daylight. It's pretty dark in that place."

"Is it far?" Maggie asked.

"No, about three miles," Vera calculated.

Maggie stood up and said, "Let's go first thing tomorrow. We need to get a head start on this. Go tell the others. They need to know," Maggie sighed. "They need to know."

As the women walked back into the living room, the sounds of laughter could be heard all around. Jack was standing on an ottoman doing his best Frankie Avalon fake surfing pose, while Cat and Wood looked on and howled with laughter.

The others looked up to see Lovey, Vera and Maggie had come into the room. Something was afoot. Wood and Jack knew that look all too well. They could feel it.

"I have to tell you something," Vera said as she made her way to the couch.

Maggie looked at Lovey and acknowledged what was coming and Vera relived the past two days one more time for Jack and Wood. When she finished, everyone buckled in because things were about to get interesting.

Chapter 7

BEVAN VISITS VERA

Vera and Cat got in bed. Vera was reliving her regression and trying to determine what was real and what she hoped she'd only imagined. Cat put her arm around her and pulled her close.

"This is going to pass, Vee. Lovey and Maggie know this stuff. Let them do their thing."

"I know," Vera responded. "It's just that I feel like I've known Maggie before because she has a bizarre air about her that is hauntingly familiar. Lovey is my aunt, yes, but Maggie Styles is something else. She's got a strength. Right now, that's something I feel that I'm lacking."

Cat could sense Vera feeling vulnerable, which was not the norm because if anyone was together it was Vera Chase. Cat relied on her for stability in many ways but now she was out to lunch. Not focused. There was a scattering of emotions that was coming from her Cat needed to adjust to.

As the time passed, Cat began to emit a soothing snore. Vera was wide awake and focused on it to help her relax and took deep breaths while staring at the ceiling. She took refuge in knowing Maggie was near if something happened, then thought of Lovey and tried to remember her when she was just plain old Aunt Audrey. They both were different people then.

Vera tried to imagine what life was like in 1802. Her regression had taken her to Bevan's cellar where the world outside it must have held a simple beauty. She opened her eyes and slowly tried to move Cat so not to wake her. Getting up, she went to the lounge chair by her window and pulled back the curtain to reveal the desert as the moonlight bathed the landscape in a warm glow. Vera could see well as she lay in the chair contemplating her fate when she heard a laugh coming from beside her window. She raised up and stealthily peered out to see Maggie and Jack on the back deck laughing and looking like they were enjoying life, no more than ten feet away.

Jack kissed Maggie as she fell into him. Vera watched as Jack's hand ran up the back of Maggie's shirt, causing Vera to shudder at the sight of it. Maggie's long dark hair fell down across her face as her mouth locked with Jack's. Vera wanted to turn away, but when Jack removed Maggie's shirt and tossed it to a lounge chair, Vera wasn't about to.

"God, she's beautiful," Vera thought as she watched Jack reach in front of Maggie and unsnap, then unzip her blue jeans. Secretly, Vera wished she was Jack, feeling the faint sweat on Maggie's perfectly toned body as she removed Jack's shirt and threw it to the chair.

Maggie stepped out of her now fallen jeans and stood only feet away as a shade of guilt begin to take Vera. She told herself she should turn away and let them have their moment, but seeing Maggie standing in her underwear was something she couldn't resist as Jack reached around and undid her bra, letting Maggie maneuver out of it and toss it aside allowing her large breasts to sway in the moonlight. Maggie stepped out of her panties and stood naked to the world as a drop of sweat ran down Vera's face.

Maggie unzipped Jack's jeans and dropped to her knees in front of him. Vera watched as Maggie took Jack in her hand, leaned forward and devoured him. Jack closed his eyes as Maggie took control.

Vera glanced at Cat and wanted to wake her to see the spectacle of lovemaking that could fuel many fantasies for them both, but couldn't move as she watched Jack reach down and put his hand behind Maggie's head to hold her still as he began to writhe back and forth, smooth and deliberate. At that moment, Vera envied Jack, as the man inside Vera came alive and wanted the sex Jack was now enjoying.

Jack pulled away to her soft protest as she obviously wanted to taste him further. Maggie stood up and turned around facing Vera, now closer than she originally was. Vera dropped down further in her chair to conceal her spying but couldn't turn away as Jack got behind Maggie and spread her legs, getting into position. Vera had full view of Maggie as Jack rammed into her, causing Vera to gasp unexpectedly to Jack's sensual aggression. Then "find me! Shot through Vera's head."

Vera was shaken back to reality. "No, not here, not now."

Vera looked out as Maggie and Jack began their climactic lap around each other as Vera felt the conflicting circumstance she found herself in. Then again, "Find me!" rocketed through her mind.

As the heat subsided between Maggie and Jack, Vera could hear a lone wolf off in the distance give a howl to the moonlight. Maggie and Jack busted out laughing as Jack let out a wolf howl of his own. Vera pulled back from the curtains and lay in her chair both envious and conflicted feeling she shouldn't have watched them but was unable to turn away. If anything, it was a welcome distraction from the uncertainties that seemed to be ever present.

Vera had never let herself be a punching bag for anyone or anything and she wasn't about to start. Sitting in her chair she again glanced out at Maggie and Jack who had recoiled in the deck chairs in a heap of sweat and satisfaction. Vera closed her eyes and opted to address the voice.

"Find you where?" Vera thought. "Tell me where? Rebecca? Rebecca Middlebrook? Where are you?"

A vision flooded her thoughts she didn't expect. The searing eyes had her. She tried to move but was frozen in place as Vera could feel someone moving in front of her. It was him. She knew it was Bevan.

"Vera," the voice said. Vera tried to run from it but couldn't. Feeling her body react to the fear, she pushed herself further away into a dark void. The harder she tried to move away, the closer she got. Bevan's eyes were on her. She could see the women in the cellar once more, shackled and tormented for his amusement.

"More," came to her. "More!" Bevan shouted at her. Then, "Find me!" Vera was battling to stay together when she felt herself begin to rock back and forth. Then, "Vera, wake up."

Jarred, Vera opened her eyes to see Cat in front of her in the morning light. The night had passed Vera by in an instant.

"Vee, wake up. You okay? You're moaning."

Vera put her hand up to stop Cat from shaking her. She tried to focus her eyes in the morning sun coming through the window.

"Did you sleep here all night?" Cat asked. "Vee?"

"Ah, yeah I guess so," Vera answered as she took note of her situation.

"Why did you sleep in the chair?"

Vera tried to focus. "I was restless and looked outside for a bit and I guess I fell asleep." Then she remembered Maggie and Jack as her heart fluttered at the thought of being confronted with watching them. When she remembered her vision of Bevan a chill came over her. Trying to decide what was real and what wasn't, Vera got up and regrouped. Like trying to remember a dream, she was putting the pieces together as best she could with the word 'more' still echoing in her head. Why did she hear him say that? Did it mean he was coming and wanted more women to torment? And why was Rebecca in the vision wanting to be found?

"Hey, talk to me," Cat coaxed.

"I'm fine except for this chair having my back in a spasm. Let's go downstairs." Vera was avoiding Cat's question. Was she indeed fine? No. Not by a long shot. Vera had a force in her coming to fruition and it was a force that had become ripe with age and wanted to be harvested like low hanging fruit. It was noticeably unavoidable.

"What is it, Vee? Talk to me." Cat was insistent.

"It's Bevan," Vera confessed. "I'm getting visions of him. I see things he did to women. Hundreds of women. He was in league with the witch trials where women would supposedly be hung in front of a crowd. Somehow, he made it look like the hanged women were dead, but they weren't, like in a magic show where people were made to believe something happened, but it didn't. Papers were done like the ones Lovey has. Death Certificates stating time and place of their hangings, then Bevan would get the women, revive them and have them for himself like his own personal playthings. Nobody would ever think to search for someone hung as witch, so graves were filled with those he'd already killed while the actual person whose name was on the tombstone was being tortured by Bevan, who was indeed a monster."

Cat was trying to take in what Vera had just unloaded.

"But if that were true, then he'd have to have had help. Some people along the line would need to be aware of what he did so it could continue, but why?"

"Why indeed," Vera sighed. "That is the hundred-dollar question."

"Vee, how do you know all this? I didn't think Maggie and Lovey had put anything like this together yet. You need to explain to them what you told me."

Vera looked back at Cat and with a sharp snap replied, "Maggie and Lovey know everything they are goddamn supposed to! Stay out of it, Cat. It's not your problem."

Cat stepped back and tried to take in what Vera said, and how, but it was Vera's mannerisms, her tone that spoke volumes that something had stirred deep inside her. This wasn't her. It was her voice, but nothing like Cat had ever heard Vera say before. Somehow, she was different.

Vera caught what she'd let out and how she said it. She placed her hand over her mouth momentarily and then lowered it.

"Cat, I'm sorry. I don't know why I said that."

Cat tried to readjust. "Look, if I had slept in a chair all

night, I'd be cranky too. It's all good. Let's go downstairs. I hear people."

As they moved to join the others, Cat reassessed Vera. Something was indeed off.

Maggie was up early and once more admiring some of the girls' antiques. Her Antique Barn had been her haven and now that it was gone due to a fire, she really missed the surroundings of old things. Jack awoke to an empty bed and came out to find her.

"You okay, Maggie Styles? Ex-owner of Maggie Styles Antique Barn?" Jack asked as his hand slid across her shoulders.

Maggie nodded. "Yeah, Jack Reynolds, ex-cabin salesman from Ellijay, Georgia. I have a feeling that something is coming. It's not like last year with Hope. It's different. I can't control it."

Jack tried to help. "You can't control it because this time it's not wanting you, it's wanting Vera. She has to handle this, Maggie. You can help her where you can, but Lovey knows this shit and she said it was Vera's journey. We are on the side lines this go-round."

"I can't accept that, Jack. I feel something here. It's like we were brought in for a reason. That little lady in there has got a big job in front of her. I knew her before, Jack. I felt it. We have been together somehow, some way before. I know it and she felt it too, all too clear. Those old newspaper articles, it was like I was re-living it when I read them. When she first handed me the paper, I got a flood of images coming from it. That old parchment is not meant to be here because there is something unworldly about it. I can't describe why I feel that way. Call it paranormal instinct. I wish you and Dad would go back home so you won't be drawn into this anymore than you have to be."

"You tell Wood you want him to go home and you'll get a boot thrown at you. You know that. Where Lovey goes, he goes. He beat the beast last time, remember? He was slated to be Hope's boy, but in the end, the little guy came through. We aren't going anywhere. We love our women and that means I love you. Don't forget that."

Maggie glanced up at Jack and took his hand, pressed it to her face and sighed, "What in the world I did to deserve you, I wish I knew. Us finding that old ledger was a shot in a million, yet there it was. It's fate, Jack. You're here to give me strength."

"I think you do pretty good on your own, darlin'. Oh, I think Wood's up," Jack noticed as he heard a rustle coming from the back room.

Maggie turned to watch her dad waddle into the room.

"Morning folks! Anybody want to go on a ghost tour?"

"A ghost tour?" Maggie and Jack said together.

"Yeah, Lovey said she and Vera were going over to see the casket in the basement of the old church. Sounds like an occasion. Let's burn one."

Both Jack and Maggie had to laugh. If there was ever a person in their lives put there to provide comic relief, it was Wood. Their comedic moment was short lived as Lovey came into the room. She looked worn out, like she'd been up most of the night.

"Good morning," she muttered as she went straight for the coffee pot. "Today, we see what is going on here. You ready for this?" she asked as she looked across the room at her counterparts.

"This won't be like last time. It'll be different. It'll feel different. I don't know what to expect so keep your wits about you and don't get stoned yet. It's important. I need... Vera needs us all on this. Stay sharp."

"Got it!" Wood barked. "Jack, Maggie and I are on the job." They all grinned as Wood gave a salute to Lovey.

Vera and Cat came into the room and Wood proclaimed, "Uh oh. Looks like some serious girl talk about to happen here." Wood then motioned to Jack to go outside. Now alone, the girls gathered in conference. Vera immediately let her mind go to her memory of Maggie and Jack hours before in a state of heated sex. She had to turn away from Maggie for fear of blushing as she remembered Maggie's nakedness in the moonlight.

Lovey confessed, "I have been up all night re-reading the contents of the envelope and the newspaper and I don't see any other names pertaining to the Randall fire of 1802. I know names changed a lot back then, a lot of miss-written texts and such, but as for clues into why Jeremiah Bolt did what he did to those women, I can't find anything more, other than Rebecca Middlebrook's letter of Summons and Certificate of Death from Fredericksburg. There are some names that are barely legible on it where some people verified her death, but no leads. We need more information from somewhere. Maybe the casket in the church will hold some clues as to what this is."

"Vera had a restless night herself," Cat added.

Maggie and Lovey turned to Vera and got a, "Oh, I'm fine. Just nervousness. It'll pass."

Maggie looked at Vera and casually smiled. "I know you had a restless night Vera. It's alright. Take your distractions where you can. All this will be behind you soon enough."

Vera went cold. Was Maggie hinting that she was aware of Vera's voyeurism? Did she know she was watching Jack make love to her?

The girls then heard laughter coming from outside and turned to see Wood and Jack exhaling a big cloud of smoke.

"Where did you find those guys?" Cat asked. "Girls are better. Trust me."

Not wanting to know exactly what Maggie did or didn't know, Vera blurted out, "I have something." She then told Maggie and Lovey how Bevan used the witch trials to acquire women for his own amusement. She explained the grave rotations and how he had to have had help. Maggie and Lovey listened intently.

When Vera finished, Maggie sat down and Lovey wrapped her arms around Vera.

"My sweet little niece. You are indeed special, in so many ways."

Maggie was quiet for a minute. She let the explanation Vera had given them soak in. It all made perfect sense. Years of executions added up to hundreds of women. The ones Bevan chose, he 'hung.' The men and women he didn't were burned at the stake all nice and tidy. It seems they were the lucky ones as the rest faced a fate far worse. Now this force was awakened and wanted back in the world of the living through Vera. Maggie knew she and Lovey were the only ones standing in its way.

Chapter 8

IT'S A TIGHT FIT

As Wood's van pulled into the church parking lot, Maggie got a cold shiver. She looked at the now sprawling cemetery behind the church with the feeling of returning to the scene of a crime. The church gave off its own energy like it wanted to swallow her. For the first time that day she'd drawn her psychic battle sword and held it tightly, feeling something in the church knew she had come, and was waiting for her as well. The stage was set for war.

"Here we go. Ladies and gentlemen, I give you Bethel Church," Cat announced mockingly. "Suddenly, the creepiest place on the planet."

"Get ready," Lovey said as she looked back at Maggie. "You're stronger now. You know that. Go with your inner self and be careful. Whatever this is, it's not happy."

Wood turned around and looked at Jack who was also feeling apprehensive and said, "Here we go again. This is some real Hardy Boys shit here."

They all had to laugh. Lovey looked at the little man behind the wheel and secretly said to herself, "God, I love that man."

As they got out of the van, Maggie took in the warm sunlight. It was a beautiful day. It seemed out of the ordinary they would be walking into anything but an old standing relic from days long gone. Still, she knew there was another story to be told waiting for them all. Vera walked forward as the sound of her rattling keys made everyone go on alert.

The church doors opened. As they walked in, Maggie had the sensation of standing in front of the building ablaze. She could hear the screams of women and see townspeople through the windows. It was all reliving itself on fast-forward.

"I first saw the woman standing at the front, there," Vera said as she pointed forward. "She came up to me later as Cat and I were leaving. The doorway is behind the pulpit."

They all felt every step as each sound reverberated in the small structure.

"This is cool," Jack said as he looked around. "I can see the appeal of this place. And you said its two hundred years old? I hope I hold up this well when I'm two hundred years old."

"Don't worry. You won't know it if you don't," Wood said with a laugh.

Vera found the small entrance and pried it open. The creaking noise made Wood cringe. "I hate that noise," he said trying to keep a chill away. Six faces took their place at the top of the stairway as they all peered into the darkness.

Wood was spooked. "Man, you sure you want to go down there? I say we just stay up here and use our imaginations as to what's down there."

"This is a tight fit, buddy," Jack laughably warned Wood. "You think you can fit through there?" He had to chuckle, acknowledging Wood's belly.

Vera turned herself sideways and stepped forward putting her foot on the first step. She shined her flashlight down below bringing the dirt floor into view.

"I don't like this," Wood said. "I'm going in, but I'd rather be back on the mountain."

The six people found the bottom of the stairs with Maggie sweating profusely and her eyes widened. Visions flooded her mind to the point she had to lean against the scorched wall so not to fall. As her body landed against the mortar, she saw

Bevan's cellar in her mind. The torches, the tables, it all came flooding back. She pulled away and glared at the light as it swirled around the room, landing on the casket that was now far too real. It was just as Vera had described.

"There you are. A casket," Vera said. "How it got here? Your guess is as good as mine."

They walked up to the curious box and each let themselves be transformed by it. They thought of a time when this was the norm for the dead to rest in. Crudely dug graves under the hot desert sun awaited some of the finest carpentry of the day.

"Look at the hinges. They look like they are made of gold," Jack observed as he let his fingers rub across the antique. "They sure don't make 'em like this anymore."

Wood was fascinated. "How did a coffin end up here? You say nobody's home in there? No vampires or anything weird?"

Vera looked up at Wood and said, "It's not a coffin, it's a casket. A coffin has four sides. This has six. See?" Vera then counted each side, "One, two, three, four. Five and six are the ends."

"Now I'm educated. Can we go now?" Wood mocked.

Looking at Lovey, Vera said, "The writing on the side is here." She shined her flashlight down the side of the casket. "I think it's some sort of Aramaic. I don't know how anyone from this area two hundred years ago would know that language. Latin I can see, but this? I know a guy that teaches at the college who might be able to tell us what it says. Jason King is the man when it comes to old texts and such. He'd be thrilled to see this, I'm sure."

"You think he needs to come down here and see this thing?" Jack questioned. "The less people that know about this, the better."

"I totally agree," Lovey sighed. "We need to figure this out between us, for Vera's sake."

"Why don't we just take a picture of it?" Cat asked. "There's a camera in my phone."

"From the mouth of babes," Wood remarked. "The

government listens to those things, you know. I heard they got cameras in a cloud somewhere. I'm not kidding here."

Cat rolled her eyes at Wood and walked around to the writing on the casket as Vera held her flashlight up. Cat then took a few pictures of the writing. "We can show your guy these pictures, Vee. He doesn't have to know where we took them."

"Somebody is thinking," Lovey said as she scowled at Wood and Jack.

Jack shrugged and pointed at Wood. "His fault," he said with a grin.

"What now?" Wood asked. "We've seen the casket, the basement and the church. We need more info. Mags, you got any ideas?"

Maggie was quiet. She kept staring at the wall she had leaned against and seen the vision of Bevan's cellar. She needed to find out more about Bevan Nicholas. She remembered the newspaper that Vera found with the article from the fire and needed to know more about where it came from.

Turning to Vera she asked, "Can we go back to where you found the newspaper? I need to know more about it. We need to see into the whereabouts of Bevan's house and find out where he lived. There is a chance the cellar is still there. It was underground. If it was in a remote area, then we might get lucky."

"Still there?" Vera questioned. "It's been two hundred years, Maggie. This town has grown leaps and bounds since then. I wouldn't know where to start."

Jack spoke up and said, "Wood and I found an old house last year that wasn't supposed to exist, yet it still stood by a reservoir in what is now a big graveyard. If this place was indeed underground, then two hundred years isn't that long. Look around you. Where we are is that old and here we stand. It's worth a shot, so why don't Wood and I go scout around for some old pictures from 1800. You never know, there may be some reference to where people lived. We may indeed get lucky. You girls go to the Courthouse and look for more info in the newspapers and we'll meet back in here in what, two hours?"

"Sounds like a plan," Wood agreed. "Let Jack and me do some bird doggin' on this thing. If it's in town, we'll find it."

Lovey agreed and they all left the church. Maggie was relieved to be out of the basement. There was something there that was evil. She knew it and it rattled her down to her soul, but she didn't want Jack to know that. In typical Maggie fashion, she remained her cool, calm self once outside.

The girls walked a short distance to the Courthouse and the boys headed for McDonalds.

"You think they'll find anything?" Cat asked.

"Yeah. They'll find a hamburger and a milkshake," Lovey laughed.

"Don't underestimate those two. They helped save my life in more ways than one," Maggie reminded them.

"I still say girls are better," Cat laughed as she watched the two disappear into the McDonalds.

The girls all filed into the Courthouse. Cat and Vera had been in there many times before, but Lovey and Maggie needed a minute to catch up. There were pictures taken from an airplane that tried to get the entire town limits in a single shot. Compared to Denver, a few hours away from Maggie's home in Colorado, Randall wasn't that big. Lovey studied the architecture while Maggie casually admired the antique wooden frame housing the directory. She nodded in approval.

Vera recognized the mayor coming down the hall and acknowledged him with a wave and, "Hello Mr. Mayor."

Vernon Collier, Randall's mayor, gave a friendly smile back as he passed. Maggie stepped away from the directory and ran into him.

"Oh, excuse me!" she said as she clumsily collected herself.

Stepping back to see who had just run into him, the mayor got a good look at Maggie, who immediately turned on the hot sauce. She let her eyes cool into his while stepping just a little too close.

"Oh, I had no idea you were so important. The mayor! I'm so embarrassed," Maggie said shyly.

It didn't take a genius to see the effect she had on him. He quickly looked her up and down and was a little taken aback himself.

"It's quite okay, no harm done," he said. "Can I help you nice people with anything?"

"No thank you," Maggie answered. "We are here with Vera. She wanted us to see the Courthouse, but I had no idea we'd meet the mayor. I look a mess."

"You look..." and the mayor caught himself about to say something un-mayor like. "...Ah, like you may need some refreshments? Vera, show your friends to the kitchen and let them help themselves to some beverages."

Collier didn't take his eyes off Maggie.

"Thank you so much," Maggie said as she stepped into him letting her breast push into his arm. "I was hoping for something to cool me off."

"Glad to help, Miss..." the mayor stammered.

"Styles. Maggie Styles. I'm here from Colorado. Thank you for your kind hospitality, Mr. Mayor."

Maggie then released herself from Mayor Collier and did a "he's watching me" walk down the hallway. Vera and Lovey followed her a few steps behind. The mayor turned and walked away shaking his head.

At the end of the hall there was a small kitchen with a refrigerator for the staff. Maggie turned into the room as Cat joked, "and the Golden Globe goes to Maggie Styles for her performance in Turn on The Mayor."

"That was crazy," Vera had to say. "Why did you fluff that guy up?"

"Something told me we might need him. You never know. It pays to be nice to people," Maggie replied in a tone that suggested she was proud of herself.

"We might need that guy?" Cat bantered. "He used to hit on Vera until he figured out she was gay."

"Yeah," Vera agreed. "Now he hardly does anything but wave."

Vera took three bottles of water from the refrigerator and gave Lovey and Maggie one.

"I want you to meet Mrs. Jenkins," Vera said. "She's the real deal. That woman has worked here fifty-three years. If anyone knows more about the fire than her, I can't think of who that would be."

"Is she here?" Cat asked.

"Let's find out," Vera said as she led the others out of the kitchen.

An Information Desk was coming up with a teenage girl sitting behind it. As they passed, Vera recognized the girl and said, "Hello, Sophie. You good today?"

"Hi, Miss Chase! I'm taking your class in the Fall. Don't fail me, okay?" she said with a smile.

"I won't if you won't. I need to speak with Mrs. Jenkins. Is she around? I need to ask her something."

Sophie's manner changed to serious. "Mrs. Jenkins that worked here? Oh, don't you know? She passed away. I'm sorry. She was the nicest person."

Vera was startled. "She passed away? When?"

"About a week ago. She died in her sleep. Her daughter found her. I sort of got her old job," Sophie said sitting back in her desk. "It'll take a while to learn all she knew, I'll say that. She was a walking encyclopedia about this town. We all miss her."

"Wait, you say she passed away when? A week ago? That can't be right, I saw her just three days ago. She showed me the old Records Room downstairs. She told me about..."

Vera felt Maggie's hand on her arm and looked up as Maggie slowly shook her head.

"No," Vera began. "I came in here and saw her. We had a conversation about Rebecca Middlebrook. She walked downstairs with me."

Sophie was perplexed. "You have to be mistaken. She was buried over in the cemetery near the street on Friday. They put her marker up this morning. We all went to her service."

"I have to see this," Vera said as she began walking fast towards the door.

Vera left the Courthouse with the others in tow. The Randall Cemetery was just across the street behind Bethel Church.

"Will you slow the hell down Vera. Vera!" Cat insisted as she ran behind her.

They reached the Randall Cemetery and Vera began reading the tombstones by the street. She saw a fresh grave and went to it reading the name, "Olivia Marie Jenkins. Born January 31, 1928, died April 28th, 2022. April 28th? I saw that woman on Friday and we talked about Rebecca Middlebrook. She told me about how Rebecca died in a goddamn sledding accident. The horse bolted for some reason and she was thrown into a rock and broke her neck. She told me all that. I'm telling you I talked to her. She led me down the stairs and let me in the Records Room. When I turned to thank her, she was gone. She didn't say good-bye or anything, she just wasn't there. I heard a door close down the hall so I thought she went to the bathroom. I'm not shitting you; I saw Mrs. Jenkins after...she...died."

Vera looked at Cat, Maggie and Lovey. "I'm not crazy. I saw her!"

"I believe you, Vera," Maggie calmly said. "I believe you. You did see her; just not like you were used to."

Cat was speechless. She was literally shaking. "Babe, you saw a ghost. You really, really saw a fucking ghost. I'm freaking out here. You had a conversation with a dead woman."

Lovey stood towering over the three. She quietly reached out and pulled Vera to her large frame and held her. "It's okay, Vera. It's okay. You just made a big leap forward; we just need to figure out why. Let's go back to the Courthouse and go through the old papers. Surely there's something else on the fire or Bevan. Come on, let Mrs. Jenkins rest. Looks like she's earned it."

Vera began to slowly walk, still in Lovey's embrace. "She said she would go and visit Rebecca soon and take her wildflowers. Wait! She said she was going to take Rebecca flowers and it 'would be nice'."

"Vera turned to run back into the cemetery. "We have to find Rebecca Middlebrook's grave. It's here, somewhere. We have to find it!"

Vera was like a woman on a mission, running into the cemetery with the others following. "The old section is back here!" she yelled as she began studying the stones, reading aloud the names as she flew by each one.

"Vera," Maggie said calmly. "Vera, look there."

Vera and the others looked at Maggie pointing to a corner plot. It was an old stone, gray and weathered. There were fresh wildflowers laying on the marker.

"No, I don't believe it," Vera stated as she approached it. She walked around to the front and read: Rebecca Middlebrook. Born: July 5th, 1784, Died: February 20th, 1801. She was seventeen. Mrs. Jenkins told me that Rebecca was seventeen." She stared at the flowers. "Mrs. Jenkins said, 'I should visit her soon and take her wildflowers.'" Vera then looked to the sky and yelled, "What's happening! What the fuck is happening to me!?"

"Wait," Maggie said, as she kept studying the flowers. "You say Mrs. Jenkins told you she should take Rebecca flowers and here are flowers on a grave that has Rebecca's name on it. She wanted you to come here because she marked this grave site for you to find. Your Mrs. Jenkins wanted you to come here for something. Look around. There has to be something else here."

Vera had to agree. "Maggie, that makes perfect sense. I think you're right. There is something we're missing. Has to be."

The women began scouring the surrounding stones and old mausoleums. Nothing else was there that was out of the ordinary.

"I'm telling you, there is something to all this," Vera

began. "We are supposed to be here. I know it. Maggie's right, Mrs. Jenkins wants us here."

"Maybe she did, Vee, but not now. There's nothing here. Just wildflowers on a rock. Let's go back," Cat prompted. "This is a bust."

Giving up, Vera let herself be taken back to the Courthouse. She felt emotionally exhausted. She and Cat had joked about seeing a ghost, now here she was having conversations with one. They stopped on the Courthouse steps for a moment.

"When I went to see Mrs. Jenkins, I noticed there weren't many people around. It's because they were all at her service. They were burying her while I was having a conversation with her. Jesus, Maggie, you know something you're not saying. You have to know something here. During all this you've been too quiet. What the hell is happening to us? I know you. I feel I have known you forever and yet during all this you seem to just be watching it all roll on by. You knew I saw a ghost, didn't you? You didn't even blink when Sophie told me Mrs. Jenkins was dead. It was like you expected it. Why are we thrown back together to find a woman whose name is on a tombstone here in Randall with fresh wildflowers on it? Why am I seeing what I can't rationally explain?"

"The answers are coming Vera," Maggie said as she sat down on the step. "We have to wait it out. Look where we are now. Events will unfold as they are supposed to and we can't question their sequence. I will tell you this, I don't believe we need to go back to the Records Room. I have a feeling Mrs. Jenkins led you to a place that only she could have. You said the Records Room was in the basement. I looked at the directory when you were talking to your student. Vera, there is no Records Room downstairs. It's all office space and a copy room."

Vera stopped and faced Maggie. "You are wrong there. I know I spent hours in that room going through all kinds of shit to find that paper. You can't tell me there's no room. I was in it!"

"And you also had a nice conversation with Mrs. Jenkins before you went in there. Tell me, when you went into the room, did she open the door, or did you?"

"What? I don't know. We were talking," Vera replied.

"Think Vera. Did she open the door?" Maggie questioned her as her long hair blew about her face.

Vera closed her eyes and remembered in detail walking up to the records room door and then... "She did! Mrs. Jenkins opened it."

"That's what I thought. Vera, if you go back there now, you won't find that room. I have a feeling it, like Mrs. Jenkins, were aberrations meant for you. Just you."

They all stood silent. Vera looked back at the Courthouse.

"No. I don't believe it."

Vera ran back into the Courthouse. Cat started to follow her, but Lovey called out and stopped her.

"Let her go, Cat. Let her go. She needs to see it alone and believe it by herself."

"You mean it's true? Vera actually spent hours in nowhere?" Cat asked as she watched Vera run down the stairwell.

"Not nowhere, but somewhere meant only for her," Maggie explained. "This is her quest, Cat. You have to remember that. We are only helping her. That woman in the church spoke to her. She said, 'Find me.' A voice spoke to me too, but it's Bevan I want. There is a connection between Bevan and me that I can't seem to figure out. It will come, I'm sure of it. I just can't see it yet."

"You talk in convenient circles," Cat sighed. "None of this makes any since to me. I love Vera. She means everything me and here I am watching her go crazy. I have to do something."

"You are, darlin'," Lovey began. "We can't know why these situations happen to those we love. Last year we almost lost Maggie and Wood to something dark. It took all of us to figure it out. Wood was faced with turning into something sinister, but lucky for us his goodness came through and defeated it. Now, here we are again with Vera being tempted and we can't let that happen."

"I'm sorry, I need to know," Cat said as she turned to go into the Courthouse. Lovey started to stop her, but Maggie said, "Lovey, let her go. Vera needs her right now."

Cat found the stairs and headed down. As she made the final turn, she saw Vera standing there, staring ahead. She stopped and then slowly continued down. "Vee? You okay?"

As she reached the bottom stair she stood by Vera and looked where she was looking. It was a copy room with Xerox machines and shelves of office supplies. "Is this it? Is this the room you found the paper in? Vee?"

"Yeah," Vera said hesitantly. "That's the space. It was there, Cat. I was in a room right there full of old parade stuff and boxes of junk. In the back, where that stack of paper boxes is, is where the newspapers were in an old filing box."

Cat said the obvious. "Well, maybe they moved them somewhere else. They just did this, right? This stuff just got moved here. Right? Vee? Is that what happened?"

"There's no door, Cat. Look at it. Look at the walls. The entrance has been redone so no door was needed. Look at the edges. There are smudges from dirty hands and chips in the plaster. There hasn't been a door here in years."

"Didn't you ever take a ghost tour down here? Didn't you see this place before now?" Cat asked while desperately looking for answers.

"No. Never. I've never had a reason to come down here until Mrs. Jenkins led me here. Cat, I'm certain you need to get away from me. I'm afraid I'm losing my mind. This is taking me down a path that I absolutely have no idea what could happen. If I put you in harm's way, I'd never forgive myself. This is like nothing I've ever known."

"What? You want me to leave you? Now? How can you say that? I love you, Vera Chase. I'm not going anywhere. Come ghosts, graves or wildflowers on tombstones, I'm in it for the long haul."

Once more Cat saw a tear fall from Vera's face. She

wrapped her arms around Vera as she felt her began to shake in a well needed release of emotion.

"I'm so scared, Cat. I'm losing it. I feel it. I'm falling apart."

"No, you're not," came Maggie's voice from the stairs above. "You're not falling apart because we won't let you. You have a purpose in all this and together we are going to find it. Let us in, Vera. Let us help you while you help me against Bevan. He hasn't gone anywhere. We need to back up, regroup and beat this thing and that takes time. Just trust us. We've been here before. You haven't."

The girls were leaving the courthouse when they heard a wolf whistle. They looked up to see Jack and Wood walking towards them.

"Hey ladies. You looking for a good time?"

Wood and Jack saw the emotion on Vera's face.

"Holy moly, what's going on? Did something happen?" Wood asked. "You look like shit."

Jack went to Maggie and took her hand. "Babe, you okay? What's up? Did something happen?"

"I'll tell you later. Let's just say Vera has been around a bend," Maggie explained as she fell into Jack. "I'm glad you're here, Jack Reynolds. I need you now."

Jack looked at Maggie in his arms and whispered, "Oh, you do huh? Well, let me get you back to the homestead and we'll fix you right up."

Jack looked at Lovey and his glance was met with a scowl.

"I don't suppose you two found anything useful, did you? Other than a burger and fries, that is," Lovey asked with a big dose of sarcasm.

"Well, actually we did," Wood heralded. "There's a bunch of stuff on the fire, old man Bolt's bible and the Sheriff's gun in the museum. We had to pay five bucks each to see it, but hey, it's what we do."

Vera stopped cold. "Oh my God, yes! The Randall Museum. Why didn't I think of that? I mention it on my ghost tour, but I only went in there once when we first moved here. What did you see? Bolt's bible and the gun that shot him? We have to go!"

"See? You got a couple real Hardy Boys here," Wood said as he tilted his head in triumph.

Chapter 9

THE RANDALL MUSEUM

The Randall Museum sat on the edge of town in an old warehouse renovated to house the historical artifacts associated with the history and founding of Randall, Arizona. It had a lot of interesting things about its past, along with pictures, maps and such that depicted old Randall in a time long before today's modern era.

Pictures of dirty miner faces hung on the walls telling their silent story well. It was a time of work, toil and trouble with very little law governing the lands. Tales of wild west shootouts were popular with tourists who happened into the museum.

As they approached, Maggie began to get flashes and pieces of a vision trying to come through. Something in history happened there. Maggie stopped and looked at the seemingly innocent warehouse that housed the museum as Lovey got wind of Maggie's peril. Something was up.

"Mags? You okay?"

Jack took note of Maggie's state as well. "You feeling okay, doll?"

"I'm not sure," she replied.

Lovey began to feel uneasy herself and scoured the landscape for anything out of the ordinary. Looking at the rest, she asked, "What was here before the warehouse?"

Vera froze. She, like Maggie, was in a throw of visions. Nothing she had done prepared her for the onslaught of emotions she suddenly found herself vulnerable to. Anguish, confusion, loneliness, all flooded her at once. Understandably, she fell to the ground.

"Vera!" Cat cried. "Vera, holy shit."

Wood seemed uncharacteristic as he too felt faint. He leaned up against a telephone pole and rode it out.

Cat and Lovey knelt down by Vera and lifted her head off the ground. "Hey, you," Lovey said softly as Vera opened her eyes. "It's us. Hey, come back."

"What happened?" Vera was questioning everything at the moment. "I heard and saw things. Aunt Audrey, what is happening to me? I've been through this town a thousand times and never felt anything like I'm beginning to feel. Is it like this for you and Maggie?"

"Sometimes we get visions," Lovey answered awkwardly, not prepared for the realization her niece had now become a full member of their sorority. Lovey had known there was a chance Vera was special, she just wasn't ready to admit why.

"You've turned a corner, Vera," Lovey told her as she began to help her up.

Maggie was getting herself together with Jack. She said, "Gallows. This place is where the gallows were."

"Ah, shit," Wood moaned. "I was having a good day."

"That's what this is," Maggie continued. "Two hundred years ago some bad things happened in this town that we are only starting to realize. I'm afraid this is only the beginning."

"Are you girls okay?" Jack curiously questioned. "Can you go in there? It's only a museum now."

"Yeah, I'm good," Maggie assured him. "It was this place. It has a dark history. It has a memory all its own and I'm afraid we tapped into it."

Vera stood up and collected herself as well. They all were on alert as their situation began to come clearly into view. Realizing she could have a vision of history at inopportune moments wasn't something Vera had counted on as she had now become susceptible to things she'd only heard tales about.

Maggie went to Vera. "You good? What did you see?"

"It was like I was reliving it, Maggie," Vera began. "I could feel the pure pain, the anguish and fear that hangs like a shadow over this place. Why now? I've been here before and felt nothing. Now I can barely stand. Am I...?" Vera stopped and slowly backed away from the others.

"Are you what?" Cat answered. "Crazy?" Cat glanced at Maggie. "She's not crazy. Tell her that."

"No, not crazy," Vera continued. Looking directly at Maggie she asked her, "Tell me Maggie. Am I a witch?"

"A witch?" Cat let out. "You're no witch, Vee. Maggie, tell her she's not a witch. Now this is crazy."

Maggie and Lovey both wanted to comfort Vera and take away all doubts that she was in danger, but both knew it wasn't so. Unexpectedly, Maggie and Lovey had both a lamb and an accomplice in a war they knew was coming and to tell her anything else was detrimental to the cause. They needed her now as she needed them.

"That's big word, Vera," Lovey said. "Having clairvoyance doesn't make you a bad person. You are still the same as you were before the visions began. Back in the 1800's people discarded what they didn't understand labeling it evil. It wasn't always. There are good people in this world who have been given access to a window inside them that shows the world as it was. They are able to harnesses echoes of the past and put together visions. We don't know why it happens, we only try and make sense of what we are shown. Don't be afraid of it. It's a strength, Vera. Soon you'll see that."

"Say it," Vera said coldly. "Am I a witch?"

"What's in a label?" Wood posed.

"Like Lovey said, that's a big word," Maggie confirmed as she scoffed at Wood. "Let's see what we can find in the museum. You're fine now. Think of it like you jumped into a pool and you simply needed to get used to the water. Soon, all this will seem normal."

"Normal?" Cat snapped. "Maggie this shit is anything but normal."

"Let this happen, Cat. You're fighting it and that doesn't help us now. Vera has something she needs to do, and we need to help as best we can. Telling her all this is not happening is confusing her. It is happening and we are here to help her get through it. She's still your girlfriend, but more."

Cat looked at Vera and shook her head. "'Confusing' is a good word, here."

"If you ladies are ready, we need to go inside the museum now," Jack advised. "People are beginning to notice us."

Jack was right as he could see people beginning to take note of what was going on with them on the street. "This is a public place, you know."

"Ah, yeah," Wood agreed. "Time to mosey."

The six of them walked into the Randall Museum and had to listen to Wood complain about having already paid the admission fee. Maggie had collected herself and gave the young attendant who took the money a fifty-dollar bill and told him to "Keep the change," in a wonderful Southern belle accent. They might be a while, so she wanted him on her side. A wink from her would have done the trick because not too many women that look like Maggie came through the museum. He shoved the bill in his pocket and nodded as he watched her walk away.

"Where's the bible?" Lovey asked, still standing at the doorway.

Jack slightly pointed, "Over there, under all that glass. That's some tough glass for an old town museum. The gun is there, too."

Jack then nodded up at the security cameras. Lovey looked back in agreement.

"I got to say, somebody wants to keep all this stuff in here," Wood began. "I bet I could get to that bible if I had a brick."

"It's bullet proof glass, buddy," Jack explained. "I've seen it a lot. It's the norm for security systems these days. Insurance companies give you a break if you keep your valuables in unbreakable glass cases. It's all computer controlled locks and such. Looks like they get a pretty good break here."

"We need to see that bible," Lovey stated firmly. "If Pastor Bolt took down notes on those four women in the church fire, chances are they'd be in that bible. At least the names or something. Whatever is in there it would help, I'm sure of it."

Lovey walked around the corner of the cabinet and approached the Jeremiah Bolt's Bible display. Lovey could see the Bible still had blood stains on it as it lay untouchable in front of her. She reached out her hand and laid it on the glass above the bible and closed her eyes. All she could see was darkness. A sense of lost hope ran through her as she pulled away and wiped her hand down the side of her pants. Looking up, she said, "Maggie, can you...?"

Lovey stopped as Maggie was already ahead of the game.

Maggie looked at the fresh-faced attendant in his mid-teens and unbuttoned the top three buttons of her shirt. She fluffed up her hair and got into character.

"What's she doing?" Cat asked.

"Getting us that bible," Jack answered.

Cat glanced back at Maggie and had to admit, "Damn, she looks good, doesn't she?"

"Hey, that's my kid there. And yeah, I guess she does," Wood admitted.

Maggie catted up to the counter where the young man sat and bent over slightly, revealing her abundant cleavage. She watched his eyes go there quickly and then back up to hers, which were hypnotic and crazy hot when they needed to be.

"Excuse me, I have a favor to ask you," Maggie whispered.

The young man gulped. "What sort of favor?"

Maggie found her sultry self and cooingly whispered, "I'd love to get my hands on your... your...bible over there. I just wanna see it for a second or two. You see, I think it belonged to a distant relative of mine and I'd really like to...touch it? I'd do most anything to...wrap my hands around it. Maybe you could show it to me in the back room?"

Cat admitted, "Oh, she is good. You taking notes here, Vee? We got to remember this shit. She could get a new car doing that."

"That's my girl," Jack whispered loud enough for each one to hear.

"I'm sorry," the kid stammered, still glancing down at her unbuttoned blouse. "I can't unlock those cases because it's all computer controlled from the insurance company. If we need to clean any of the locked artifacts we have to call, then they send someone here to watch the whole process or we get the mayor to be here. It's unlocked from their mainframe. I just take tickets."

"That seems like a lot of trouble for a bible and a gun," Maggie stated.

"You haven't seen all the rooms. There are gold nuggets in there worth a lot. I understand they are insured for a mint, so that's why all the security is in place. I'm sorry, but I'm tied up here and can't open the glass cases."

"Thanks anyway, I guess," Maggie sighed. "Say, just out of curiosity, what insurance company do you use? I may need a system of my own and this one is really something. Do you know?"

"Now that, I do know," the kid admitted. "Elliott Security in Tucson. They are the best we have out here. They do the bank's security as well."

"You're a doll," Maggie purred as she walked away to rejoin the others.

When she got back to Jack, Cat announced, "and the Oscar goes to Maggie Styles for her performance in The Randall Boner Museum."

Jack chuckled. "That poor kid is gonna have to take five after we leave. What did you find out?"

Maggie explained what she knew to Jack:

"The glass is controlled from Tucson by Elliott Security. The kid has no way of opening it because they do it from their headquarters. There are gold nuggets back there that are insured big time. I think the glass cases the bible and gun are in came with the system. Did you see the cameras? They are thorough here; I'll give them that. We need Paris. Is she still with The Snowman?"

Paris Frances and Steven Winters, AKA "The Snowman," are two computer hackers that helped Jack and Maggie find the lost Blanch house in Virginia last year. Paris and Jack worked together in Ellijay, Georgia at Holiday Cabins. Their boss, Seth Holiday, was murdered to insure the destiny of the Blanch ledger. Paris is very dear to Jack and he wanted her out of harm's way.

"Yeah, as far as I know Paris is still with Steven," Jack said walking away from the camera. "He could get us in here, no problem. Paris could too for that matter, but I gotta tell you, Paris was really shaken up over Seth's death. I don't think she wants anything to do with ghost stuff and I want her out of this one. It's too soon for her."

"Seems like old times, doesn't it?" Maggie said looking at Jack. "Some ghosts, a hack, Lovey and Dad. Makes a woman tear up."

"Tearing up is not what you made me do watching you with that kid. I got a little semi going there for a minute," Jack confessed.

"Oh? That could very well be an area for concern after a while, Jack Reynolds. Last night was good, but I got another one in me if you do. Just keep your eyes peeled. I may be back under ghost patrol but I'm still a horny old history professor. Don't forget that," Maggie reminded him as she made him look down at her still unbuttoned shirt.

"This is insane," Jack had to say. "Yep, just like old times."

Maggie had to laugh. Jack loved to hear her laugh. There was a slight cackle she made when she got tickled that really touched Jack where it counted. He remembered the first time he saw her in her old Antique Barn. He had wandered in looking for a present for his boss and there she was. He broke a vase in his first attempt to shake her hand, as his sleeve caught the handle as he reached for her. It was a vivid memory he kept reliving fondly. Now, almost two years later, they were inseparable.

Cat said, "While we're here, what do say we have a look at the golden boulders. I don't see gold nuggets every day."

"Golden boulders?" Wood remarked. "Sounds like a strip club."

With that they walked in the back room that had a long glass showcase with mining artifacts in it. There were two really impressive gold nuggets that were the highlight of the town museum's offerings.

The museum had the nuggets showcased in an old treasure chest which made it look like more of a pirate's haul than a happened upon gold find. It was a small display, considering the nuggets and the college were pretty much all the town had to attract outsiders. Still, the rustic appeal to the set showcasing the gold was staged well. There were more pictures of dirty miners hanging on the wall as well as handmade shovels and pick axes the miners used to find their bounty. Most never found anything. The few that did usually drank it all away or lost it to gamblers and shifty businessmen.

"Now that's a pretty rock," Lovey said. "Wood, you need to find us some rocks like that back at our place."

"You mean there's gold in them thar hills?" Wood answered. "I'll get right on that."

Jack was busy being casual as not to attract attention while he studied the back door of the museum which was well locked with bars running across the windows. It resembled more of a jail than a museum. "I have an idea," he said. "Let's get out of here. We have some planning to do."

After dinner everyone settled in. It was like a commune where people shared what they had. Sitting in the floor in front of Cat, who was online, Vera was still shaken from having seen into a paranormal universe she'd only read about. Her ghost tours revolved around legends she never bought into, until now. It made her wonder how many of the tales she heard were indeed true.

The flowers on the tombstone really shook Vera up.

Seeing Mrs. Jenkins and realizing she was a for real ghost was bad enough, but for some reason, that simple bouquet of wildflowers lying on the tombstone would not leave her head. The room where she found the newspaper was still haunting her as well. "I was there, I know it," kept running through her mind. This and her experience on the way to the museum was not supposed to happen. She had become unique and felt it. Vera Chase had touched the paranormal.

Jack and Maggie were re-reading the old paper when Jack posed the question;

"If Vera went into a room that was shown to her by a ghost, and the room itself was a room between worlds, so to speak, why is it that we have this paper from 1802 that came from a room that didn't really exist? Vera says the room was not there, yet the paper is. Anybody want a shot at figuring that one out?"

Lovey got the question.

"It's not that uncommon for people to find things from another time in places where unworldly occurrences are said to have happened. I think the paper is like that. People have found old pocket watches, all kinds of jewelry, coins and random stuff that literally fell out of nowhere. Some of it even gets taken back, eventually."

"You mean ghosts take back what they give? That's not right," Wood began. "I have to get all this down."

Wood took a pen and paper off the coffee table.

"Help me out here. When we looked for the amulet last year, I had a list of what to look for and where. We don't have that now. What we do have is that Vera heard a voice that said, 'Have you sought the answer?' and that pretty much kick started this whole thing. Then she finds a casket in the basement of the church where a woman touches her face and freezes it. The next day at the Courthouse, more craziness with Mrs. Jenkins and this newspaper from ghost land. We have the names, 'Bevan Nicholas' and 'Rebecca Middlebrook.' We had an experience on the square at the site of the old town gallows. We have a bible we need to look at to see what the relationships were pertaining to the girls in the fire if there is anything there at all. We have a cellar with a rounded ceiling that Maggie said she and Vera saw in a vision. What connects all this stuff?"

"At the moment, I do," Vera said like she was to blame for it all. "This is all connected to me, somehow."

Maggie stirred. "You're not to blame for any of this no more than I was to blame for what happened last year. It's just fate. That's all I can attribute it to. There are forces that want to be in this world whether they belong here or not. Who they pick to come through is unexplainable at best. It just happens and the people caught in the middle have to simply go with it."

Lovey patted Vera on the shoulder and offered, "She's right, Vera. Don't blame yourself. You are just living your mortal life and theirs is over, but they didn't get the memo. We will fix this. Give it time. It'll all work out. You'll see."

Vera was trying to see anything. "Wood, you just said that when I heard the voice in the church is when this whole thing got kickstarted. Lovey told me that when Cat and I were at Shelia's funeral and I said I wanted to 'die and be reborn as a man' is when a door opened and Bevan Nicholas, or whatever came strolling in. I said I wanted to die, then I find a casket in the church offering me the chance to at least act like I did. What if the casket is like the room where I found the paper? What if it, too, is unworldly and it is the key to this whole set of circumstances?"

Maggie glanced over at Lovey and they together understood exactly what Vera was saying, and it made perfect sense. The casket could be a doorway to some other place and time, and it was offered to Vera to go through when she had the mock funeral. She was going to be put in a state of unconsciousness for a short while. In that state she would be vulnerable to whatever influences were around her. She'd be exposed from the inside out.

Jack and Wood looked at Maggie and she nodded. She got it.

"Go on, Vera," Maggie said.

Vera began to pace. "If Bevan Nicholas is a man, and I said I wanted to be reborn as a man because I've always felt a man alive inside me somehow, then maybe if I go through with the funeral and let him out, Maggie and Lovey can talk to him face to face and figure out what the hell he wants."

Cat jumped in abruptly. "Are you out of your lesbian mind? You are saying you want this guy to possess you? Here we've been trying to figure out how to get you away from all this and you want to jump into the fire with it? Vee, this can't be the way to end it. It's dangerous and you may never come back. I don't want to lose you to Bevan Nicholas, Saint Nicholas, or even Nicholas fucking Cage! This is crazy talk. I'm throwing the funeral thing away right now. I will not sit by and allow you to be possessed so Lovey and Maggie might be able to calm this thing down. It's too big of a risk."

Vera saw where Cat was coming from. "It's staring us in the face now, Cat. The casket has to be the key. Why else would it be there?"

Lovey was curious about the markings on the side of the casket. "Do you still have the picture of the letters?"

Cat said they were on her phone and reached in her pocket to get it. "There is a guy at the college Vera knows who maybe can tell us what it says."

Cat turned on her phone and went to her pictures. The others watched her face as a look of confusion came over her.

"What the hell?" she exhaled. "They are black. Gone. They aren't here. I looked at them down in the basement. They took. You all saw me take them, now I have three black pictures of nothing. How can that be?"

"Because the basement is unworldly," Maggie answered. "It's like the room Vera was in. It's a place between worlds, or it's acting like it is while the casket is there. The paranormal force of that casket is affecting the whole place. You said a man showed you the basement. He opened the door at first, then you and the two teenage girls went through it. Am I right?"

"Yeah, that was it," Vera confirmed.

"Who was that man? Who was the man who showed you the basement? Do you know?"

"I don't remember. I met them at the Courthouse where the tours begin then we walked around town, full circle, ending at the church."

Lovey asked, "How do they pay you? Is there a charge for the tour?"

"Yeah, it's ten bucks a head and it goes to the city. Why do you ask that?"

"Do they sign in?" Jack asked. "Is there a page somewhere that has their names on it?"

Realizing the names may help, Vera realized, "Yes, there is. It's for insurance purposes in case something happens. People sign a waiver saying that the city isn't liable. It's bullshit, really. I always thought it was, until now that is."

Jack confirmed they needed to see the list for the name of the man who opened the door.

Vera tried to remember their faces.

"I can get that easily enough. It was May 6th. There were three of them. You don't think those people had anything to do with this, do you? They were tourists, I think. They took the tour for something to do,"

Jack was wondering, "How do you know if there are people wanting to go on a tour? Surely it's not every day people show up to see ghosts."

Vera sat down. "I do the tours on Friday nights. It's more during Halloween week. I go by there and see if anyone shows up. It's random numbers. I went by last Friday night and those people showed up wanting the tour and I wasn't busy, so I took them out. The city gives me twenty bucks a tour, so there has to be at least two people to pay for my extensive knowledge of the legends of old Randall," she said mockingly. "It all seems like a big joke now. Oh, and I get a tip if I'm lucky. It's hit and miss. Gas money, that's about it. Besides, I like doing it."

Cat was still staring at the phone. "I took those pictures. I did. I saw them after I took them and now, they aren't there. They could be in the Cloud, I guess."

"See?" Wood said as he jumped up. "I told you there was a cloud that had pictures in it! Didn't I? And you think I'm crazy for having birds. I don't know which is worse, this Bevan thing or knowing that clouds can take pictures. It's a messed up world."

Jack walked over to the window and looked out across the desert. "I guess you know what this means now."

He then turned to the other five people in the room.

"If Maggie is right, and the basement at the church is indeed unworldly, like she said, then that means we've all been invited into this thing. We went down there. We saw the casket, we saw the writing on it, and we stood on that dirt floor. If the room at the courthouse was meant for Vera to find on her own, because she was invited, then we've all been handed an invitation by being able to go down there. You following this? We are all subject to whatever is down there wanting to come through us. This Bevan fucker is after us all now."

"He's right," Lovey reacted. "If that place is indeed a haunted place between worlds, it has our scent on it now. All of ours, not just Vera."

"Now I'm scared," Cat admitted. "You're saying Bevan wants all of us?"

"We all are indeed candidates for something," Maggie concluded. "We need to find out if there is a history of Bethel Church having a basement. Are there floor plans we can see at the Courthouse?"

Vera huffed. "Floor plans? The last time I looked for anything at the Courthouse I walked into a room that didn't exist. How are we to trust anything from there? We need answers, yes, but quite frankly I don't trust that place. We could be seeing what Bevan wants us to see."

Jack agreed. "She has a point. We need a less haunted source of information."

Vera said she thought the basement was legit. "The

scorched walls. That's the giveaway. There is soot and burn marks on those walls that were obviously made by a fire. I'm thinking that when it was re-built, that space was used to hide things. Maybe even people, and that's why there is no record of it anywhere. Whoever re-built the church the last time needed to hide something down there, so no mention of it was ever put on paper.

The casket? That casket is meant for me. In order to really figure this thing out, I need to go through that door."

Cat put her phone down and left the room.

"I'm done hearing about you going through ghost doors. I'm in the back should you need me for something else. I'm going to look for those pictures online."

"Who do you need to see to get the list of people who took the tour?" Lovey asked Vera.

"The list goes to the same place where we need to get access to the bible; Mayor Collier's office."

Lovey looked at Maggie and smiled. "Well, I think fortune just smiled down on us a bit."

"What's that mean?" Jack asked.

"You'll see. We've already met the mayor," Lovey smiled, still looking at Maggie.

The next day was going to come with an element of fun.

Chapter 10

MAGGIE AND THE MAYOR

The following morning, Vera and Maggie were waiting on Lovey to come down. When she did, she looked more than in the just-woken-up state, she looked borderline exhausted.

"I'm going to hang back here a while with Cat," she said to Maggie. "You two go and do your thing with the mayor."

No further explanation needed to be said. Lovey and Maggie understood each other on many levels. Maggie nodded, not wanting to alert Vera that anything was wrong. "No problem. We got this."

In the driveway Vera questioned why Lovey was staying.

"She needs to focus," was all Maggie replied. With that, the two turned their focus on the task at hand.

Taking advantage of their alone time, Vera wanted to ask Maggie about her life and how they may have a connection. She didn't know where to start. She was still feeling embarrassed about her spying on she and Jack on the deck and got the impression Maggie knew. Maggie sensed Vera wanted answers and pulled the van over.

"I know you saw Jack and me on the deck. It's okay. Jack and I have been together now for two years and I still feel like a schoolgirl when I'm with him. When he wants me, I respond."

Vera dropped her head. "I shouldn't have watched you, but I was hearing the voice again. The "find me!" voice. I got up to sit in my chair and heard you on the deck. You have a beauty that is hypnotic to me. I see you and I feel I've known you forever. I can't say I'm sorry I watched you because it did help me at the moment. I needed something real, and there you two were, something so wonderful."

Vera felt like she was a child again having been caught doing something wrong. Maggie faintly blushed and reached for her hand.

"Let it go," she coaxed. "We have far bigger things to deal with."

Vera seemed relieved her dirty laundry had been put away. She leaned back in her seat and asked, "How did you handle it when you realized your world had changed?"

"It came to me in flashes, just like you, Vera. This magic. I keep getting stronger, as Lovey keeps reciting, and yes, I do feel different but that's not a bad thing. Don't let it scare you. You're young, strong and smart. Your mother is one of my dearest friends and there is an unwritten mountain law that clearly states that when your best friend's daughter is being invaded by a spirit from the 1800's, you do what you can do to kick its ass. You hearing me? Nothing will harm you as long as we are here."

Vera had to smile.

"There it is!" Maggie heralded. "Keep that smile around. We may need it."

With one deep breath Vera asked, "Are we witches, Maggie? Are we? Are people like us why all those women died? Because we have visions that are naturally coming to us? You think I wanted this? Why now? I'm sorry, it is so much to swallow. I'm not doing very well."

"Vera, you're doing fine. It's the rest of us that are fumbling over ourselves now. We will figure this out. Give us a chance. Remember, we've been here before."

Maggie tried to regroup.

"A long time ago people didn't understand things like they do now. They called the women all sorts of names and yes, 'witch' was one of the stones they threw. It didn't matter if you were a good witch, or an evil one. Witches were different from the rest of them and that was enough. Crazy religious people came to show they had the power to do away with such evil but what they did was bring out the worse in the townspeople. Hangings became sport. It was entertainment for the masses to come and tell themselves they were validated for watching their friends and neighbors meet their ends on the town square. You ask me, 'Are we witches?' To tell you truth, I haven't come far enough to believe that yet, so I'll say this; To the outside world we probably appear to be. To us, we're just people dealing with the hands we were dealt, trying to live our lives like everyone else. Is that good enough for now?"

Vera nodded and took in a deep breath. "For now," she acknowledged.

Vera and Maggie got out of the van in front of the courthouse. Vera started to get quick glimpses but couldn't make sense of what she was getting.

"I'm sensing something," Vera cautioned. "The courthouse knows I'm here. This is weird. How can a place know you're there?"

"Vera, you're more receptive now. Every day that passes you become more aware. Soon, you'll be able to control it, but now, don't fight it. Your receptive self is evolving really quickly. You'll be aware of a lot more in days to come because it's who you are now."

"Who I am now?" Vera echoed. "I liked who I was just fine."

"Didn't we all?" was all Maggie could muster as they turned their attention to the job at hand.

Maggie wore her faded blue jeans that clung to her hips like Velcro and a white halter with nothing on under it. Vera commented on how hot she looked.

"You know, if we weren't getting a bible, I'd think about taking you to dinner."

Maggie faintly blushed again. Though she was bisexual, Maggie had not been with a woman since she and Sue, an unsuspecting insurance investigator and a member of the

Hope Blanch cult, had a moment in her old house a year earlier. Vera's remark reminded her that she was indeed still desirable to both sexes. It was an option Jack had replaced. He was everything to her and she liked it that way as she truly needed his stability.

Maggie did indeed know she looked like a sex kitten and, for the moment, wielded a degree of power. People tend to respond to a woman who carries herself in a mood. Maggie had "HORNY" written in neon above her as she moved through the courthouse. Vera just smiled like she was exhibiting a prize.

They got to the doorway of the mayor's office and could hear him talking to his secretary as Vera walked up and softly knocked on his open door. His secretary looked up and said, "Hello Vera. What can we help you with?"

Vera stammered over a "Hi. Have you got five minutes Mister Mayor? I have a small request that needs your assistance."

"I'm pretty busy today. What sort of assistance?" he responded in a flat tone.

"My friend and I are doing some research on the church fire of 1802 and we..." Vera was interrupted as Maggie walked through the door. "Oh, excuse me," Maggie whispered. "Am I too early?"

The mayor looked Maggie up and down. His eyes widened as a puppy dog demeanor came over him.

"This is Maggie Styles," Vera said to the mayor. "You, ah, ran into her yesterday? We are doing research for a possible documentary and we need to see the bible in the museum."

"Bible? What bible?" the mayor said stumbling for words.

"I feel foolish asking you, really," Maggie began. "I know when we met yesterday you were in a hurry. If you have a minute, I'd love to fill you in on what we need? Is that possible?"

His secretary began reciting the mornings agenda when the mayor's hand went up and silently stopped her from continuing.

"I have a few minutes for the ladies." He smiled as he gestured them into his office with the secretary rolling her eyes as Maggie sashayed passed her. The mayor sat across the room behind his desk as the girls sat down in the high-back leather chairs in front of him.

'Now, what's this about a bible?" he asked Vera, while trying not to look like he was looking into Maggie's see-through white halter.

"It's in the museum. We are looking into the church fire of 1802 and we believe that Pastor Bolt's bible may hold some keys as to why he did it."

Maggie leaned forward and went into her Southern Marylin Monroe character. (Her weapon of choice) She used the halter as a means of subtle hypnosis.

"It's really one of the only pieces of evidence from that time period available to us." Maggie took a deep breath and stretched slightly. "If we could get the book, we could see if Bolt left any text at all in it pertaining to the fire. The book is currently in a glass case we need to have unlocked by the insurance company in Tucson in order to see it. They don't open the cases often because they have to come here and have a guard on hand. However, you are the exception to that." Maggie reached for the mayor's hand and her cleavage moved to eye level, revealing enough 'food for thought' for the mayor to have a preoccupied afternoon.

"If you were to call them and sanction a quick unlocking of the cases with you there, we could get the bible and look it over. It would add to the knowledge base Vera has for her ghost tours and a possible documentary, as well as serving the community with factual accounts of one of their most regretted, but still highly publicized incidences."

Maggie noticed the light coming through the window. Casually, she walked over and stood between it and the mayor so the light outlined her breasts through the thin halter as she slowly writhed under the rays of sun.

She turned and caught the mayor with his mouth hanging open and asked, "Could you please come to the museum with us, call the security people and get the case unlocked? It would be a big help."

The mayor almost leaped out of his chair saying, "Of course I can go! I have some time for you nice ladies."

"Score!" Vera thought to herself. Then she remembered the waivers.

"Oh, yes, one more thing. Can I see the waiver form from last week for the ghost tours? I need to get in touch with one of the women who signed a form. It was from last Friday night when I saw you ride by and you waived. Remember, I was with three other people?"

"Three other people? I didn't see you with anyone, Vera. You were alone," the mayor confirmed.

Maggie jumped in and said, "Vera left us at the saloon and we were coming up behind you when you drove by. One of the ladies on the tour borrowed my reading glasses for a minute and I forgot to get them back from her. She lives here in Randall, I believe."

Vera was caught out in the open with the news that the mayor hadn't seen anyone with her. She got cold chills and temporarily couldn't speak.

"You were on the tour with her?" the mayor asked.

"Yes, that's how we got interested in the bible and the history. Vera is good at what she does," Maggie explained, trying to give Vera some breathing room.

The mayor then pushed an intercom button on his desk and asked his secretary to bring in the tour log. She came in, handed it to him and he gave it to Vera, not taking his eyes of Maggie who was still working the sunlight.

Vera took the logbook and slowly turned to the past Friday evening. There were indeed three names written. As she read them, she closed her eyes as if to hide from the reality of the moment. She heard Maggie's muffled voice still talking away, but all her focus was on the names in the log. She opened the binder and took out the sheet of paper and confidently closed it as she laid the logbook back on the desk. The mayor, at the moment, wasn't even aware Vera existed.

"We ready to go?" Maggie asked glancing over at Vera, who was looking like a ghost herself.

"Ah, yeah," Vera answered as she got up.

"Let's walk," Maggie suggested. "The museum isn't far and it's a gorgeous day."

"Okay, let's do that," the mayor responded, still not taking his eyes off Maggie's scandalous figure.

The walk to the museum was short. Maggie took the mayor's arm as they walked through the town with patrons, store owners and little old church ladies taking a scandalous view of he and Maggie walking so close as Maggie's halter almost caused a car accident along the way. The mayor held his head high in a state of defiance.

The museum was at the end of Main Street. The intensity of the vision Maggie had due to her proximity to the site of the old town gallows still haunted her. Vera was affected as well and walked a step behind Maggie and the mayor as she fought off any reoccurrence that could expose their intentions.

At 11:15 AM the museum had just opened for the start of the day when the mayor and the girls walked in with the same kid at the door. His eyes widened at the sight of Maggie. She smiled one of her nuclear Maggie smiles at him as he too succumbed to the power of the halter.

They walked over to Bolt's bible and Maggie proclaimed, "Here the little bugger is. If we could get that for a bit, Randall would thank us."

The mayor cocked his head back, tried to pull the coat he was wearing around his protruding belly, walked over to the counter and took out his phone as Maggie and Vera stood there smiling and gazing around the room. Vera glanced into Maggie's eyes with a look that said, "I have something to tell you." Maggie just whispered, "Hold on," and kept floating around the artifacts as the mayor and the kid watched her, entranced like two kittens watching a butterfly.

The mayor walked over to the case housing the bible and read the small label at the bottom, recited the number over the phone, and then again. He thanked the voice at the other end then hung up and walked over to the girls.

"It'll be 11:30. We have ten minutes," the mayor said. "The locks are on half hour timers. They are programed to open on the next half hour when needed."

"Can you show me your nuggets?" Maggie asked.

The mayor took a step back, swallowed hard and replied, "Excuse me?"

"The gold nuggets in the back," Maggie reminded him.

"Sure!" the mayor said, as he awkwardly headed toward the back room.

Vera stood by the bible and pulled out the page she'd torn out of the logbook. She re-read the names as she listened to Maggie doing her small talk routine with the mayor. The kid at the front desk was staring at Vera like she was about to turn into something.

"Why do you want the bible?" the kid asked.

"It's for research. I'm looking into the church fire of 1802 and I believe Bolt's bible might hold some clues as to why he did what he did to those four young girls."

"Oh, that's pretty dope," the kid said with a swagger. "Why do you think he did it?"

"I can't really say, that's why we are here getting the bible. I think he may have written something down in there to explain some things."

Vera then got a flash. It almost knocked her off balance as she grabbed the side of the counter. Vera noticed the kid's reaction to her sudden instability and countered with a reassurance that she was trying some new medications. Luckily, Maggie was coming back in with the mayor and all the kid's attention went back to her. She had taken the mayor's arm to again be escorted by the now sweating man as they re-entered the main room of the museum.

"It should be just a few minutes," the mayor said as he rubbed his elbow as high as he could toward Maggie's halter.

Vera pulled a large baggie out of her pocket and unzipped

it. The kid at the counter began a countdown from five down to zero as the case in front of them magically unlocked. The mayor marked the moment with, "There you go. Right on the mark."

Vera opened the case and let her hand touch the bible. A surge of images flooded her as she let her hand slip under it and slowly lift it from its long resting place under the glass. Maggie saw Vera's expression and immediately went into spin control. Reaching around behind her she untied her halter and let it fall freely forward for a split second, flashing her breasts at the mayor and the kid.

"Oh, my goodness!" she squealed while holding the cloth over her chest in an effort of feigned modesty. "I'm falling apart all of a sudden."

Maggie brushed the mayor, turned around and said, "Would you please help me tie this thing. It keeps slipping."

With shaking hands, the mayor fumbled with the two ends of Maggie's halter and managed to tie them back together. The kid was frozen as he put what he'd just seen to memory but would need to stand behind the counter for the rest of the morning while doing so.

While the mayor and the kid were entranced with Maggie, Vera scooped the bible into the large baggie and zipped it shut. She didn't want anyone, especially herself, touching it unless they had to. After getting her halter back on, Maggie announced they needed to be running along.

"Vera, we need to give these wonderful men time to get back to their day. Thank you so much for helping us out with this. We will only keep it a few days," she said as she took Vera's arm and headed for the door.

The mayor and the kid didn't say a word. They only nodded as they both watched the last of Maggie's tight blue jeans disappear through the doorway. The mayor then looked at the kid and said, "I think we need to keep this between us."

"No problem," the kid replied.

Maggie and Vera headed straight for the car and got in. Maggie took the bible from Vera and was hit with a flood of images going back to the fire and the cellar. She laid it down on the seat with it still sealed in the plastic. She told Vera that it would be better to wait on Lovey before they did any deep exploration of the bible. Vera agreed.

"So, what names were in the log?" Maggie asked in a matter of fact tone. "I have a feeling they weren't names you'd expect to see."

Vera reached in her pocket and pulled out the sheet of paper from the logbook and handed it to Maggie. She unfolded it and read the names. Her eyes widened. She then read aloud, "Olivia Jenkins, Becky Middlebrook and Bart Campbell. Bart Campbell? As in Bartholomew Campbell? Holy shit! Bartholomew Campbell is a name in an old ledger Jack and I found last year. He was a landowner in the 1800's. A witch named Hope Blanch was accused of ruining his crops using witchcraft. Daniel Blanch, my great-great something grandfather, wrote all of it down in an old ledger and started us all on a path we could only imagine. Olivia Jenkins," Maggie continued, "Well we know who that is. And Becky Middlebrook. AKA Rebecca Middlebrook. You said Mrs. Jenkins said they were friends and Becky died at seventeen."

"Yeah. She said Rebecca was killed in a sledding accident that broke her neck, saying, 'We were all so very close then.' Maggie, after she said that she took a long pause like she was re-living something. I think Mrs. Jenkins felt responsible for Rebecca's death somehow. The Rebecca she knew, anyway. There was a touch of guilt and fear about her, now that I think about it. We will never know what really happened to her."

"I can see where those two might show up here because you said Mrs. Jenkins told you she was going to take Rebecca wildflowers. Becky Middlebrook and Mrs. Jenkins ghosts were young. Those were her flowers on the tombstone, but a landowner?" Vera questioned. "What's a landowner from the 1800's doing taking a ghost tour?"

I don't know," Maggie confessed. "I really don't know. We need to show this to Lovey. Maybe she can shed some light on it."

Vera took a long gaze into the oncoming lines on the highway. She and Maggie sat silent until Vera quietly said, "Maggie, my great grandmother's maiden name was 'Campbell.' I think she was directly related to Bartholomew Campbell."

"Vera!" Maggie said as she sat up. "Vera are you sure? Are you sure her name was Campbell?"

"Yeah, I'm sure. I did one of those lineage things online once to see where I came from. It's pretty cool, actually. I only went back a few hundred years, but I remember the name 'Campbell.' Maggie, it makes sense. I am a direct descendant of a man I took on a ghost tour last week and I think I just peed."

Maggie sat and stared at Vera. It was all coming back to her now. It was all pointing back to Hope Blanch, but Hope Blanch was dead. Her powers were erased last year when Wood broke the amulet. Could all this be her? Could all this haunting be related to Hope Blanch even after her powers were supposedly smashed in the old cellar under the tool shed back in Virginia? Maggie wasn't sure of anything anymore. She wanted to talk to Lovey. She had finally swallowed the idea of Vera's relation to Bart Campbell when, "Oh my God!" Maggie sat up in her seat and slammed on the brakes.

"What the hell, Maggie?" Vera exclaimed.

Maggie turned to Vera and said, "If you are related to Campbell, then that means...." and they both said together, "That Lovey is related to Campbell."

This was indeed about to get interesting. As they turned into the driveway of the old house, Maggie got out first. She handed the list back to Vera, took the bible and headed inside.

"Maggie, wait! Let's talk about this," Vera pleaded as she flanked Maggie, who was in a tear to get to Lovey.

As they walked in, everyone looked up at Maggie walking straight to where Lovey sat on the couch. Maggie reached down, took her hand and began pulling the tall woman up from her comfort.

"What the hell are you doing?" Lovey snapped as she felt herself leave the cushions.

"We gotta talk. Now!" Maggie snapped.

Jack and Wood just looked on not knowing what to think.

Maggie dragged Lovey back to the bedroom where Vera did her regression. Maggie looked up into Lovey's eyes and said, "Bartholomew Campbell."

Lovey slowly looked down at the floor and sighed. All she could say was a barely audible, "Shit."

"You kept the envelope with the summons letters because Bartholomew Campbell's name is in it. Not because Hope's name was there, but it was Campbell. You knew you were a descendent of his back when we searched for James Monroe's body and you never mentioned it. Pete knew it, too. Your own brother. He told you to destroy that envelope, but you couldn't because it was a connection between you and your family's past. You want to open up a bit here? Why didn't you mention that you were a relative of the person who had Hope Blanch hung as witch; fucking Bartholomew Campbell?"

"I told her not to tell you," came a voice from the door. Maggie turned around to see her dad.

"Sorry kiddo," Wood began. "We never thought it would matter. We served Hope back then. It was you and Jack that opened the whole Hope thing up when you found the ledger. See, it wasn't coincidence that Jack happened to be the one to find it. We tried everyone on Grace's 'Wall of Shame,' trying to see who would be the one to be the key to find Hope's grave."

"What do you mean 'no coincidence?'" came Jack's voice from the hall.

Jack and Cat walked into the room and stood beside Maggie. "What do you mean, buddy? What do you mean, 'no coincidence'?"

"Ahhh, shit," Wood began. "We never thought any of this would matter after Hope was put to rest last year, but that ledger you both 'found' was not the only book related to Hope Blanch. Grace has another one with all kinds of stuff pertaining to Hope, the amulet and people involved. One of the people was Bart Campbell. Hope supposedly put a curse on any woman descendent of his."

Lovey looked up from the floor and softly said, "Any woman having the blood of Bartholomew Campbell running through her veins is hence forth cursed to find an invitation to the shadow world."

"The shadow world?" Cat barked.

"I didn't think it would matter, Maggie," Lovey sighed.

Jack spoke up and asked, "Now, what do you mean it was no coincidence I was the one who found the ledger with Maggie?"

Lovey stood up and said that in the book Grace has, there was a passage about a man traveling from the South to the North to peddle his wares. He would be the key to opening the lock of the ledger and finding the amulet, leading to a new era of the rule of the High Priest. That was supposed to be Wood, but as we all know, Wood had a change of heart and smashed the amulet, releasing us all from Hope's grasp from the grave."

Jack interrupted Lovey when he realized it all in hindsight. "That's why Grace made me stay the night at the bar. She thought it might be me. Sam shot my tire out because he saw my car tag was from Georgia. I was 'a man traveling from South to North to peddle my wares.' My cabins."

"You've gotta be shitting me!" Cat said in a look of disbelief. "This reads like a crazy ass ghost story book."

"I'm afraid it's all true Cat," Lovey said turning to her.

Vera was silent and hearing all this from a dream-like state. She was waiting to wake up when Jack said, "You mean I was always chosen to find that old ledger? Like some destiny thing? Because I was from Georgia?"

"I guess," Lovey said. "It was last year and we were all different then. Jack, we didn't know you. We barely saw Mags because were in Florida. Keeping all this from you was deceitful, yes, but it wouldn't happen now. I wanted to tell you about my connection to Bart Campbell, but after the amulet was smashed, I just let it go. Bad water under a rotten bridge long gone."

"Wait a minute," Wood said. "You come running in here out of the blue and suddenly you want to know about Bart Campbell. What happened? How did you find out about that?"

"Show him," Maggie said with a direct voice. "Show him the names on the waiver list from the ghost tour."

Vera reached in her pocket and took out the list and handed it to Wood. "These are the names that were on the list."

Wood read the names to himself and then, looking up, recited them as he looked at Lovey.

"Olivia Jenkins, Becky Middlebrook..." Wood paused, took breath and said, "and Bart Campbell."

Jack spoke first. "We are all so fucked. This is the glue on the envelope, people. This seals it. We have been given an invitation to go beyond what we know. By us seeing these spirits have invaded Vera's, and now our lives, our destiny is pretty much laid out for us. We are still dealing with Hope Blanch. That curse of hers apparently didn't die with her and the amulet. She's pissed off and wants anyone having anything to do with Bart Campbell. That's us. Lovey, is there anything else that you and my buddy here chose not to tell us about the events of last year?"

"Nothing," Wood stressed.

"Is there an expiration period for curses?" Cat asked. "I mean, if Vera is cursed for being related to the guy who had this Hope lady hung as a witch, then as long as she, what was it, 'has the blood of Bartholomew Campbell flowing through her veins?' she's going to have to deal with the fallout of this pissed off witch? Well, that seems like it's going to take some time."

Wood looked at Maggie and Jack. "We've been through a lot in the past year. Secrets between us are nonexistent these days and I think you know that. I am really sorry about not telling you that Lovey was related to Bart Campbell, but damn man, it was last year and we were making decisions on the fly. I wasn't myself and Lovey was in as far over her head as we all were. The thing is, now you know. There is nothing else, that I know of anyway, that we would ever keep from you two now. You gotta believe me here. We need you two. Lovey and I are nothing without you guys. It was you two that eventually made me see the good side of where the Hope thing was headed. Let's get past this for Vera's sake. Like Jack said, we are all low hanging fruit for this Bevan thing now whether Hope Blanch is a part of it or not. Let's burn one and put the Bart Campbell thing to bed. It's not worth the shit that is obviously coming from it."

Chapter 11

BOLT'S BIBLE

Lovey was really upset that her best friends saw she and Wood as being deceitful. Yes, she and Pete, her brother, had known they were related to Bartholomew Campbell and now Vera was also reaping that disadvantage. For Lovey to see her great relative's name written beside names of the accused in the witch trials was fascinating to her. She let it be her secret between she, Pete and Wood until now, because now she understood it's importance. Glancing up, she got why Maggie was so upset, then she noticed what was in Maggie's hand.

"Oh my God, is that Bolt's bible?"

Maggie had almost forgotten about it. She was so lost in thinking that Lovey and Wood had been lying to her she forgot she was holding it.

"Yeah, we got it. We didn't open it yet. We had to wait on you."

It was then Maggie was catapulted back to the reality of finding out if Jeremiah Bolt had left anything in there about the four women he burned in Bethel Church. Lovey reached out to take the book and then stopped. She looked at Vera and asked, "Do you have any rubber gloves? I don't want touch this thing if I don't have to."

"Good idea," Vera said as she left the room.

"How did you manage to get it?" Lovey asked.

It was then she looked directly into Maggie's halter and had to suppress a chuckle.

"Oh, never mind." She looked up into Maggie's eyes and said, "Tramp," and for some reason started to laugh. "Was the kid there?" she asked.

"Yeah. He was," Maggie replied, still stern faced.

"Did he get a boner?" Lovey questioned now starting to laugh harder.

Now Maggie's temper was beginning to cool. It had been a long time since she had seen Lovey laugh on her own because Lovey was always reaching out for anything psychic coming her way. Yet, here she was, laughing at a schoolboy's simple reaction to a woman's breasts.

"Hell, I don't know," Maggie answered. "I was in character. I did have to flash him and the mayor my tits to take their eyes off Vera when she first touched the bible. She had a reaction."

"I bet he had a reaction, too!" Lovey said back, now laughing harder.

"I bet that kid is still in the bathroom," Jack jumped in and said.

Lovely howled louder.

Wood added, "I bet he's setting off smoke alarms from the friction in that bathroom!" Then Wood started laughing.

Maggie could contain it no more and said, "That poor mayor is gonna need mouth to mouth!"

Lovey fell on the floor holding her stomach.

"Oh, God, I wish I'd have seen it. It must have been an Oscar performance."

There are times in people's lives when holding something back can be a burden, and those secrets can become really heavy if they are kept from certain people. Lovey and Wood had obviously been burdened with not telling Maggie and Jack the reality of Lovey being Bart Campbell's relative, hence tying her to Hope Blanch's curse. To release that load of guilt can sometimes come with a release of emotion. In Lovey's case, the ticket kid and the mayor being in a room with Maggie in a halter did the trick for her. She was relieving herself of the strain through simple laughter.

Vera came back into the room with Cat and the rubber gloves to find Lovey on the floor in hysterics. Wood had leaned up against the wall with his face in his arms laughing and Maggie had halfway gone that direction herself. Jack was just watching it in disbelief. He'd seen Wood laugh many times, but Lovey rarely let herself go. Maggie looked up at Jack and they both realized the significance of the release. It must have been quite a load off their minds.

Jack looked over at Wood and said, "Ahh, screw it. Let's go burn one and give these ladies minute with the good book. I think Gilligan's on."

With that, Wood and Jack left the girls alone with Bolt's bible.

Lovey collected herself and got up off the floor. Vera handed her the rubber gloves and she put them on her hands like a doctor about to touch a patient. Maggie, Vera and Cat sat down on the bed and watched as she slowly took deep breaths and calmed herself for the task at hand.

Lovey unzipped the baggie and poured the bible out onto the bed. Bolt's blood stains were still on the ancient bible from where Sheriff Jonathan Carriage shot him through the heart in front of Bethel Church all those years ago. Lovey looked up at the others and said, "Here we go."

Lovey slowly opened the old book. There were faint scribbles of verses that had been written in the front, probably to mark for sermons he gave as he waved the bible like a sword in front of his cowering congregants. It was another time when Hellfire and damnation were common topics in small churches throughout the old towns. Religion was either black or white; you believed in God and went to Heaven or you didn't and went to Hell. That was it, not too much in between out there. Jewish people tended to migrate to the larger cities where they could worship in more sophisticated places. Other religions simply weren't tolerated.

After the first few pages rolled by, there were no other notes written. Lovey picked up the book and let her thumb flip through the pages. There were wildflowers between a few of the pages used as bookmarks.

"He must have done some of his reading outside," Cat said. "He'd see a passage he liked and mark it with a flower. That's kind of cool."

There were three wildflowers in all. Lovey left them where they were in an effort to preserve the original condition of the bible. As they got to the back, there was a note which read:

> *If you have found this book and are reading this, I am with Jesus now. My mortal life was ended more than likely by Sheriff Jonathan Carriage for ridding this world of the darkness that has grown here. He and his own daughter, with three others, are in league with evil. I plan to end their reign in our town this night.*
>
> *Lord have mercy on my soul for the act I plan to carry. Give me strength to defeat the Sheriff and the Waechter family from Germany who brought the plague to us from afar. They are evil with rich pockets. May the Sword of God win out tonight against what plagues our little town. It ends tonight.*
>
> Pastor Jeremiah Bolt,
God's servant in Heaven,
Amen

The girls sat silent for a moment. Maggie flashed back to when she and Jack found the ledger Daniel Blanch had written. His broken English and bad spelling still translated his intent. It had been a year and she still could remember it perfectly.

Lovey looked up from the bible and said, "I think we've been accusing the wrong guy. According to this, Bolt wasn't the bad guy, Carriage was. Holy cow, this doesn't play out like we thought. Maggie help me out here. Do you think Bolt was okay and Carriage was part of Bolt's 'darkness that plagued our little town', as he wrote?"

"I can't say. I'm as taken aback by this as you are," Maggie replied as she stared at the book.

Vera spoke up and said, "I don't believe it. For three years now I've been telling people that Bolt was crazy and Carriage was the hero. Now, according to Bolt, Carriage was in cahoots with Bevan and Bolt did the town a favor by burning the women, who were supposedly witches, I guess. But if Carriage was the bad guy, why didn't Bolt try to take him out as well? Why only kill the girls?"

"Look at the wildflowers in there," Cat said. "Any man who's sat in a field marking passages with wildflowers can't be someone who'd carry a gun. Think about it. This bible paints Bolt in a whole other picture. I think he was a passive guy who realized his town had a bad seed growing and took action to fix it. Sometimes taking out someone somebody loves can do more harm to them than killing them."

"I can see that," Maggie agreed, "But it appears that now we need to find out what we can about the Waechters from Germany. I've seen that name somewhere. I remember it from... the cemetery! Wait a minute, when we were at the cemetery by Rebecca's grave there was a mausoleum behind it with 'Waechter' written across the top in gold letters. It must be the same Waechters because it was a family mausoleum. It takes money to have one. That's what Mrs. Jenkins was trying to show us. It wasn't about Rebecca's grave; she marked that tombstone with those wildflowers to show us Waechter's mausoleum. That's where we need to go."

"Wildflowers," Cat said. "She marked it with wildflowers. If she marked a grave with them, then she may be trying to tell us that wildflowers themselves mean something. Bolt marked passages in his bible with wildflowers. Maybe there is a significance there."

Lovey, Vera and Maggie looked up at Cat and then at each other. With a shrug Lovey then went back to the beginning of the bible and slowly turned the pages looking for wildflowers. The first flower she found was Luke 13:16; *Then should not this woman, a daughter of Abraham, whom Satan has kept bound for eighteen long years, be set free on the Sabbath Day from what bound her?*

Maggie repeated; "Whom Satan has kept bound for eighteen long years. There it is. Bolt was certain these young girls who were all around eighteen had to be set free on the Sabbath day. That would be a Sunday night to him. Do we know if the fire was on a Sunday night? Vera?"

Vera was caught unsure of the exact day. It had never come up.

"I don't know. If Bolt is using scripture, then I guess we can assume so."

"Wow, looks like Pastor Bolt put some thought into killing those girls," Cat observed.

Lovey turned to another flower. Job 1:7; *The Lord said to Satan, "Where have you come from? Satan answered the Lord, "From roaming through the earth and going back and forth in it."*

Maggie stirred and said, "Going back and forth in it. That could refer to reincarnation. People who are possessed or cursed die and get reborn. Their new incarnation carries the evil that their previous lives did."

"Holy shit, Maggie," Vera said. "That means that it's hard to kill evil if it keeps being reborn. *'Going back and forth in it.'* That's going into the ground and back out again in some form. How do you do it then? You kill one bad seed and they come back as another? Is that right?"

Maggie shook her head. "I'm out of my league here. We need to go see the Waechter mausoleum because Mrs. Jenkins took us there. These wildflowers mean something. Is there another?"

Lovey turned the bible to the last wildflower. Mark 3:26; *And if Satan opposes himself and is divided, he cannot stand: his end has come.*

Lovey concluded, "I guess we have Bolt saying that someone good is invited into the dark fold, so to speak and their goodness defeats Satan, or whatever, by some means."

Lovey, Maggie and Cat stopped in their tracks and slowly looked up at Vera. She was basically good but now it seems she'd been invited into the 'dark fold.'

"Oh, come on, people," Vera began. "I have no idea how to defeat a demon or anything else. It's not me. I'm scared to death here! If I'm supposed to be some kind of hero, we are really all screwed."

Lovey took a leap and observed that, "Bolt is referring to bible passages that say 'Satan.' Bevan is not Satan, he's an evil unto himself. Bolt assumed that anything evil had to be a part of Satan, the go-to evil guy in the Bible. I think the word 'Satan' here is simply an old pastor's interpretation of something he didn't understand. Back then there was good and evil. If it wasn't good, then they threw it to a satanical influence. Open and shut."

Cat agreed. "Bolt was up against something he interpreted to be textbook devil stuff. That scans. Anything evil was from hell back then. The good book says so. If you didn't believe that, or say you did, you'd end up at the wrong end of a rope. Churches were fat with hypocrites that were there so their neighbors wouldn't accuse them of witchcraft."

"We need to go to the cemetery," Maggie prompted. "Where are the guys?"

Lovey, Maggie and Vera went out into the house looking for Jack and Wood. They heard talking upstairs and went up to see what had taken them up there. Out on the deck, in the lounge chairs, Jack and Wood had reclined and were watching a desert fox pursue a jack rabbit.

"What are you doing?" Maggie asked.

"Shhhh!" Wood barked. "Look at the fox. See him? He's frozen. He's waiting on the rabbit to come closer. This is some real National Geographic shit here."

Jack agreed. "This is cool! He's been sniffing him out. He's about to get him, watch."

Cat said, "I'm not watching a fox eat a bunny." She yelled, "Run mister bunny!"

The rabbit ran when Cat yelled, startled by her voice. The

fox leaped up in the air and landed on the helpless rabbit then carted him away across the barren landscape.

"Man! That was cool!" Jack confessed. "We've been watching him for twenty minutes stalk that damn rabbit. Cat, if you hadn't yelled, we'd be here another twenty, I know. Wanna burn one?"

Cat sighed, "I guess I should have kept my mouth shut."

Maggie was adamant. "We need to go to the cemetery. We think there is something at one of the mausoleums we need to see. You think you two can pry yourselves away from foxes and rabbits long enough to go?"

"No prob!" Wood said, looking up from the lounge chair. "You find anything in the bible?"

"Yeah, actually we did. It turns out we got our bad guys mixed up. Bolt, we think, is the good guy and Sheriff Carriage had other motives other than being the Sheriff."

Jack was surprised. "No way! Now that is bizarre. We always thought Bolt was the crazy one."

"Yeah. So did everyone else," Vera agreed. "Half the tourism in this town is based on it. Old legends die hard."

"Really hard," Cat added. "Do you really think people who live in Randall are going to want to hear that Bolt wasn't the bad guy here? Think about it. That story laid a foundation for right and wrong in this town. What happened back then is basically all this town has they can put a finger on. We go digging up dirt on Carriage, there are people here who won't agree and will ask for proof. Hard core facts. Is anyone going to believe any of this Bevan shit? I say we leave the dead, dead. It's going to ruffle too many feathers. Right now, that's something we don't need."

"She has a point," Lovey agreed. "We'll be exposing a lot more than just a compromised Sheriff. Let's go to the mausoleum for now. Finish this. We need facts we don't have before we go changing the moral history related to Jeremiah Bolt and Jonathan Carriage. We are far from ready to do that."

Chapter 12

THE WAECHTER MAUSOLEUM

Wood parked the van in front of the cemetery off Main Street. This time the approach was far more tactical than Vera's tear earlier when she was looking for Rebecca Middlebrook's grave. The six people walked silently to the back of the cemetery. When they got to Rebecca's marker, the wildflowers were gone.

Maggie looked up at the writing on the mausoleum behind Rebecca's grave. "Waechter," she read aloud.

"Let's check it out," Jack suggested. "Maybe there's a doorbell."

Maggie was starting to feel something and was uneasy. Lovey didn't want to approach the huge granite structure.

"I don't like this," she admitted. "Mags, you okay?"

Maggie stood silent, then responded, "There's something here. I've been here before."

She looked at Vera and said, "So have you."

"I know," was all Vera could mutter.

Jack walked up the front steps and looked at old inscriptions he couldn't read. A dragon's head was to his right and seemed to be hung as a warning. "You see this dragon here? I have a feeling he's hiding something."

Wood walked up and agreed. "Yeah, I'll go there. I just hope he's not hiding the rest of the dragon."

Jack began putting pressure on the sides of the sculpture when it moved to one side, revealing a keypad. It was made of stone with nine symbols on it forming the shape of a triangle. A row of four with one of three underneath, then two. "Woah!" he said as the stone symbols revealed themselves. "Anybody want a shot at this one?"

Maggie walked up to the structure and examined the letters in three rows of three. "Looks like it's some sort of lock, like a gate or something."

A rush of images flooded her head as she started to fall backward into Jack. He caught her with a "Maggie!"

Lovey went to her. "What did you see, Maggie? Was it the cellar?"

Maggie collected herself. "It's Bevan. He's here. We have to open this somehow."

Cat was standing back looking at the letters. She then recalled, "The letters! Those are the same letters that are on the side of the casket. Look, it's the same style and everything. Damn, I wish I had those pictures." She then took out her phone and opened the file where she took the photos down in the basement. "They're back! Look! They were black back at the house, now here they are again."

"Proximity effect," Maggie said. "This place is like the Records Room and the church basement. It's connected to someplace between worlds. I believe we've been invited in."

Wood took a step back. "You sure you want to go in there?"

"That's where the road leads," Maggie confirmed. "Cat, let me see those pictures."

Cat handed Maggie the phone and she began trying to push in the symbols. They didn't budge as she became flustered.

"This is not working. Why would we be here if this isn't right?"

Vera was standing on the ground in front of the steps watching it all in a dream state. "Let me try," she offered as she slowly ascended the marble steps.

Vera laid down her bag, approached the stone pad and took the phone from Maggie. She looked at the order and pushed the first symbol. It slowly submerged into the rock wall.

"Score!" Jack heralded. "She's got this."

Vera slowly pushed in all the symbols in the correct order until the last one awaited. She turned to her friends and said, "I want you to leave now. This is not meant for you. It's an invitation for me and Maggie. We have to go. You don't."

"We are here," Cat said calmly. "We are part of this now, just like you. Where you go, I go."

"Ditto," Wood replied.

Maggie looked at Lovey, who was standing back on the ground. The look on her face told her what was to come.

"Not this time," Lovey said, still with her eyes on Maggie. "This is not our place. It's meant for Vera and Maggie, not the rest of us."

Jack looked at Maggie and said, "What the hell is this? Where you go, I go. I'm not standing here while you go into some goddamn tomb."

"It's not a choice, Jack," Vera tried to explain. "We've been invited, not you. This is ours. Maggie's and mine. We've been here before."

Maggie looked up into Jack's eyes and he could see what had to be done and didn't like it at all. But here, in front of this odd mausoleum in this little desert town, he knew he had to let her do this.

"It'll be okay, Jack. Trust me," Maggie said with a confidence that Jack was trying to see through but couldn't. This was indeed their fight.

"You sure about this?" Jack asked.

Maggie looked up and smiled, then turned to Vera. "Push it," Jack and Wood joined Lovey on the ground in front of the structure. Vera looked back at Cat and smiled as well, then turned, raised her hand to the keypad and pushed in the last letter. The wall began to move sideways.

"It's alive!" Wood said as he took a step back into Lovey.

Vera started to move towards the door, then stopped, looked at Maggie and remembered, "My bag. It's got my flashlight in it."

Maggie turned and saw the bag at the foot of the steps. As

she took a few steps towards it, Vera stepped inside the mausoleum with her eyes fixed on Cat. The door immediately closed.

"Vera!" Maggie yelled, as she turned to see the slab of door close.

Maggie ran to the door, put her hands on the cold stone as it fell still and silent.

"Shit! Why did she do that?" Cat yelled as the others stood in silent disbelief.

Lovey was stunned as well. "What on Earth!" she shouted as she turned to meet Maggie's frustrated gaze. "She's alone in there."

Cat put her hands on the structure and began to yell, "Vera! Vera! Can you hear me? Vera?"

Only silence returned. The five people felt helpless as they'd seen their friend become out of reach.

Vera stood on the other side of the door in total darkness thinking this was a bad idea when a torch that remained from a previous time ignited itself, letting her see around the mausoleum's walls. "What in the world…?" she said aloud as she studied the flaming light. Reaching up, she took the torch out of its holder and held it as five marble containers, each with a golden plaque with engraved inscriptions, were revealed to her. The last one she read aloud; "Bevan Nicholas Waechter. Well I'll be. Bevan Nicholas is really a Waechter. Why didn't I see that?"

The walls were closing in on Vera in her mind as she was by nature claustrophobic and this place was really working that. In frustration she yelled out, "I'm here goddamn it! What do you want me to do?"

Turning to the wall behind her, Vera found the same door Mrs. Jenkins showed her in the Courthouse that seemed to have arrived out of nowhere. Slowly she moved towards it in the light of the torch. Reaching down, she found the doorknob and this time, she turned it. Pulling it to her, the hinges were like those on the casket in the basement of the church; silent and golden. Standing at the top, she peered down a stairwell that had not been seen for what looked like centuries.

"Well, here we go," she said to herself as she took the first step.

Vera descended twenty feet until at last finding the bottom of the stairs with a long pathway stretching out in front of her.

As Vera walked slowly down the corridor, there were old shovels, wheel barrels and other artifacts from mining that lay broken and discarded. A large number "8" hung over the shaft as she walked under it.

"This was once a mine shaft," she said aloud.

She remembered the story of gold mines in the town that went abandoned after nothing was found. This must have been one. A lost entrance to dreams of riches and a better life.

Vera made the last turn that lead to a chamber with a rounded brick ceiling. "Bevan's cellar," she whispered.

It was like the vision in her regression with Maggie and Lovey, only there were no tables with bound women or any sign of Rebecca Middlebrook or the hooded figure she'd seen before. Something, or someone had summoned her there, now there she was, waiting for anything.

Feeling a sickness in her stomach, Vera put her hand out and tried to steady herself as a feeling of vertigo began to take her. She closed her eyes for a brief moment and when she opened them, she began to hear a crowd. As her surroundings came into focus, she realized she was on the gallows as Bevan put a noose around her neck. People were shouting at her and throwing things as Bevan's hand reached for the lever. Vera was fading out of consciousness when she realized, "The holy water. I drank the holy water. The drugged..holy...water."

Bevan stood looking back at her and said, "My sweet Rebecca, be a good girl and die for the crowd."

The lever was pulled, and Vera felt herself in a free fall as she awaited the jolt at the end of the rope that never came. Vera opened her eyes and she was outside the mausoleum leaning up against Rebecca Middlebrook's tombstone. Looking around, still in a haze, she tried to get up but slowly slumped back down. Closing her eyes, Vera fell into a deep sleep only yards away from Cat, who was now growing frantic and had no idea Vera was on the other side of Rebecca's tombstone, sound asleep. It was done. Bevan wanted Vera to know that it was her. Vera was the reincarnation of Rebecca Middlebrook.

"Damn it Maggie, we have to do something," Cat stated out of frustration.

Lovey was trying to remain calm. She closed her eyes, trying to reach beyond the concrete wall and felt nothing.

Maggie was still standing in disbelief. "The keypad didn't budge when I touched it, it moved only for Vera," she said, studying their situation. "Now that she is in there, we have to put this in a different frame of mind. The door was meant for her. Just her. I feel what is in there, but it's apparently Vera's fight."

"One she's going to lose without us," Jack acknowledged. "That little woman is a tough cookie, but she is way out of her league with all this."

Lovey spoke up. "I agree. Vera is no match for Bevan and somehow we need to be there for her."

Wood looked around the outside of the place. "I don't see a backdoor on this thing. Unless you've got a tank, I don't see..."

Maggie interrupted him. "Backdoor! That's it!" She looked at Jack and said, "This is about doorways. Vera said she saw a doorway in the Courthouse when she went in and found the old paper on the church fire. This is the doorway into this mausoleum. Where it leads, I can't say for sure, but I have an idea. There has to be another doorway someplace, here."

"The church!" Cat said in a hurried voice. "The casket at the church. That has to be a way in. Maggie you said it could be a doorway to someplace. What if it is the other way in?"

"Vera found that casket, Cat," Lovey confirmed. "Not you. I believe it was meant for her."

Cat was perplexed. "But if this door is the door to Bevan,

where is she now? Her needing two doors doesn't make sense."

Maggie had to agree. "She's right. We need to go to the church. That's where this all started so it has to be connected somehow. What I felt down there was too strong not to be."

Lovey was still in disbelief that all of this was happening so easily. Something wasn't right. It was as if they were being played and didn't care. She remembered last year when she had the same feeling that took her back to the trunk where Daniel Blanche's ledger was found. There, concealed in the bottom, was the envelope from the witch trials and the death certificate of Rebecca Middlebrook.

"We need to go home," she coldly said.

"What?" everyone said in chorus. Then they turned to her and Wood said, "Home? You mean back to Colorado?"

"No," Lovey said beginning to pace. "This is too easy. Something isn't right. Everything is falling into place too easily. If we go back to the church, we will be right where Bevan wants us to be. He knows that. I have a feeling we are missing something useful in Bolt's bible or somewhere else. There is something there. I know it. I feel it. I need to get it and go over it again."

"Vera is in there, Lovey!" Cat stated coldly. "Did you just forget a wall just swallowed up my girlfriend? We don't have time for you to play twenty questions with a dead preacher's bible."

Cat turned to Maggie and pleaded, "Tell her Maggie. Tell her we need to go to the church and see if we can get to Vera through the casket. It's our only play."

Lovey was calmly looking at Maggie, slowly shaking her head as her long red dreadlocks swayed back and forth. "This is not right, Mags. This isn't right. Feel it. Everything is falling into place too fast. We need to stop and see if there might be anything else there, in the bible or somewhere. Bolt was trying to tell us something. What it is, I don't know, but it's there. I know it."

"This is crazy!" Cat insisted. "We need to go to the church."

"Cat," Maggie said as she turned to face her, "I've known Lovey to be right when I questioned her judgment. If she says we need to go and have another look at Bolt's bible, it's in Vera's best interest to do so."

Jack agreed. "She's the real deal, Cat."

Wood sympathized with Cat. "I feel your frustration, kiddo. Let this play out the way we want it to. We have been here before, you haven't. I know you hate hearing that, but it's true. Let us work. If Lovey wants to go see Bolt's good book, then I'm behind her."

"Ditto," Jack agreed. "Let's get in the van. Vera went in the doorway from an invitation to her. Apparently, just her for now. We may find out we have all we need to get her back, but just don't know it yet."

Cat hung her head and looked at the big stone mausoleum. With a sigh she said, "Okay, we go back for Bolt's bible. But if there is nothing there, I'm coming back here as soon as we get that. Understood?"

"I'm with you, Cat," Lovey soothed. "She's my niece, remember?"

The five people turned and walked to the van. As they passed Rebecca's grave, no one noticed Vera was asleep on the other side of the tombstone.

Chapter 13

LOOKING FOR JEREMIAH

Cat opened the door to the big Victorian house and led the group back in. Lovey went straight for Bolt's bible and cautiously began to thumb through it, leaving the wildflowers in place.

"Come on Jeremiah, give me something. There's a reason you want us to look in here, now spit it out, what am I missing?"

Two hours passed and Lovey was still at it. Cat was pacing. Frustration had taken its toll with her ready to go back and try to help Vera, if she was able to at all. "This sucks," she said with a sigh. "If there was something in that bible you would have found it by now."

Lovey could read Cat's frustration and glanced at Maggie who assured Cat, "These things take time, so why don't you go up on the deck with Wood and Jack? Relax a little. This is taking a toll on you. Everything is as it should be here and this is playing out the way it's supposed to. Let it ride."

"Fine," Cat snapped. "But I don't like this at all."

Cat went up the staircase leading to the deck where Jack and Wood had been enjoying the scenery, along with a couple of joints of Wood's crazy great pot.

"Ho! Can the dirty jokes, a lady's on deck," Jack shouted mockingly at Cat's arrival.

"Lady, my ass," Cat snarled.

Seeing the back third of a joint on a roach clip in the ash

tray, Cat reached down, picked it up and looked at Wood. "You mind?" she said as she reached for the lighter.

"Go for it," Wood said, glancing at Jack. "I like this kid. She's got potential."

Cat lit the end of the joint and took a monster hit. Holding it in, trying not to cough, she gave a thumbs up sign at the guys. She exhaled a huge cloud and went for seconds.

Jack laughed. "That's some good weed there little darlin'. Be careful you don't end up out there chasing bunnies with the fox."

Cat stood up and began to pace. "This waiting is driving me insane. My girlfriend is in some tomb, her aunt and Maggie are down there trying to squeeze God knows what out of that fucking bible and you two are up here watching foxes chase rabbits again. It's just another day in paradise. And holy shit, this is some good pot."

Jack and Wood laughed out loud. "We told you, it's my own recipe," Wood proclaimed. "Handed down for ...what about six months, Jack?"

"Yeah, about that," Jack agreed. "Look, I know you're bothered by all this waiting, but Maggie and Lovey are the pros here. We are just the...what are we Wood...the.." Jack was shaking his hand in the air trying to define their relationship to the girls.

"The brains!" Wood answered.

Cat and Jack both busted out laughing.

"That's it!" Jack heralded. "We are the brains."

"God, how did we get here?" Cat asked the sky. "One minute I was eating popcorn on my sofa downstairs, Vee walks in and announces she found a casket, we go see it in that damn dirt floor, burnt brick wall, smelly ass basement and here we are. There has to be a connection to all this, but the rest is buried, and we don't have the shovel. Shit! Man, this pot is nuts! Have you got any more of this I can...?"

"Shovel!" Jack said as he stood up. "That's it!"

"Shovel?" Cat said looking more confused.

Jack began moving towards the stairs. "Come on, I got an idea."

The three came down the stairs and into the kitchen where Maggie and Lovey were still pouring over the book.

"I have something," Jack announced.

Maggie and Lovey looked up and saw their condition and Maggie offered, "Yeah, you have buzz and a half, and we're not watching Gilligan's Island again."

"No, listen," Jack began. "Something has bothered me this whole time about the basement at the church. When we went down there and saw the casket, I was noticing the construction. I was a cabin salesman, remember? The stone steps that we came down on, I noticed it then, but it didn't hit me until now. The last step was partially buried. That church was rebuilt after the fire. Why would they go to the trouble of rebuilding it leaving a dirt floor in the basement? Those walls are the original mortar brick from when it was built. The scorched walls from the fire tell that, but the floor is dirt. I'm telling you; those steps go down farther than we can see. Maybe a lot further. Maybe there is something buried down there that no one was ever meant to see again. It doesn't make sense they'd rebuild that place and leave a dirt floor, unless it was to cover something with the dirt. It's in a cemetery."

Jack paused and waited for his logic to hit home. Maggie looked at Lovey and said, "We got nothing here, Lovey. Maybe he's on to something."

"We need a shovel, I guess," Lovey said. "Cat do you have a shovel?"

Cat was staring out the window.

"Cat?" Maggie said.

Cat turned around with a more than stoned look on her face and said, "Holy shit. Have you tried some of that pot? It's amazing!"

Lovey looked back at the boys and quirked, "Looks like you got yourself a prodigy there."

Wood agreed, "Yeah. She's got potential!"

Jack ran out to the garage and found a shovel, then they all poured back into Wood's van and went to the church. Cat handed Maggie Vera's bag and said, "Her keys are in there, somewhere."

Maggie found the keys and flashlight and unlocked the door. They all entered and went to the doorway at the back of the church.

"I hope nobody saw you come in here with that shovel," Maggie said. "We don't need a crowd here."

"What? You've never seen anyone christen a shovel before?" Jack asked as he slipped through the small opening.

The five stood at the bottom of the steps and turned to see the casket was still there.

"There's your other door, Lovey," Maggie said. "It's still here."

Lovey gazed at the casket and corrected her with, "No, it's still being offered. That means if the casket was meant for Vera, she's still alive. If she wasn't, the casket wouldn't still be here. That much I see. That is if the casket was indeed offered to only Vera."

Jack went to the steps. "Shine the light here," he said as Maggie pointed the light down at the bottom step. "See? I think this place has more to offer than it seems."

"I see your point," Maggie nodded as she studied the step.

Jack steadied himself. "Let's see just how far down this thing goes."

One shovel full at a time, Jack removed the dirt from around the bottom of the steps. He cleared out a six-foot area. It went deeper and deeper.

"I'm amazed," Lovey said. "I'd have never thought to do this. How far down are you going to go?"

"Until I hit bottom," Jack answered, never looking up.

"The foundation has to be coming up soon. I'm running out of space. If I dig out here more..."

Jack's shovel hit something making an uncharacteristic sound in the dirt. He hit it again.

"Pay dirt," he said. "I hit something hard."

He began clearing the dirt away from the bottom.

"It's wood," he said. "It seems hollow." Then, "No! I don't believe it."

The five people stood around the hole Jack had dug. Wood

broke the silence. "Congratulations Jack. You found a casket in a cemetery."

Jack looked at Maggie. "You seeing this? What is a casket doing buried in the bottom of a two-hundred-year-old church?"

"I guess it depends on whose casket it is," Maggie answered. "One way to find out."

Jack cleared the dirt off the top of the casket. "It's locked. Why would a casket be locked?" Jack looked up at Wood. "Any ideas, buddy?"

"Well," Wood started, scratching his head. "You lock a door usually to keep something out. Locks work two ways, to keep something out or to keep something in."

With that they all looked at each other. It was the "keep something in," part that bothered them.

"We've got to know what's in there," Cat said, still trying to focus through Wood's pot. "If it'll help Vera, we've got to know."

"Everybody cool with this?" Jack asked as he raised the shovel back.

Everyone nodded, then Jack looked at Maggie who offered an expressionless, "Hit it."

Jack let the shovel come down hard on the lock which crumbled in front of them. Jack leaned down and opened the lid to reveal the ancient corpse of a man in antique clothing wearing a string tie with blood stains on his vest. His grey skull, old and withered, was bent forward, making him appear to be looking down. A dark velvet cloth was at one time wrapped around him, but now had fallen to the side.

"Who is this guy?" Wood asked.

Jack saw a piece of parchment sticking out of his vest with an envelope. He reached down, removed them and handed them to Maggie who read the parchment aloud:

> *"I will yield the Sword of God tonight against the*
> *evil that has taken this town. At midnight I will*
> *send them home. I give my soul to the Lord, God*

*this day. It will forever live on to fight the evil
that lives in the world."*
Jeremiah Bolt, Servant of God

Maggie held the old parchment as once more visions of Daniel Blanch's ledger came to mind and could see it in her photographic memory as clear as day. She nodded to Jack, who understood her perfectly.

They all looked at each other.

Maggie concluded, "So this solves the mystery of whatever happened to Pastor Jeremiah Bolt."

Cat stared at the open casket. "Vera is going to freak out when we tell her we actually dug this guy up. I'm just saying. I wish she were here, damn it!"

Maggie then opened the old envelope with "Carriage" written on the front. "This says 'Carriage.' As in Sheriff Carriage, I presume." She unfolded the paper and studied it. "It's a deed to a gold mine. It's a claim that says that Carriage has ownership of Mine Number 8. It was given to him by B.N. Waechter. As in Bevan Nicholas Waechter. Well, Bevan is a Waechter. That explains a lot. Apparently, Carriage was indeed in bed with Bevan. Vera said she saw old mining artifacts in the shaft when she went through the mausoleum in her regression. She said she saw 'Mine number 8' on a sign. This has to be the mine the sheriff got."

"Why is it here?" Wood asked. "What would the deed to a gold mine be doing buried with Bolt?"

Jack was studying the situation. "Probably so no one would ever know the transaction was made, but why bury it with Bolt? Why not just burn it? If Carriage was trying to hide something, why is it here?"

"Maybe he was putting it away for later," Lovey assumed. "You have to admit, someone went to a lot of trouble to hide this. He didn't destroy it because he thought he might need it again and let Pastor Bolt here keep it like a safety deposit box. Everyone thought Bolt was buried out in the desert somewhere, remember? I guess the good sheriff killed him and then put him down here to hide his claim. It's weird he'd go to all that trouble. Why would he do that?"

"Payment," Wood sighed. "It's written that Carriage shot Bolt because his daughter was in the church. That drove him over the edge and made him kill Bolt with a single shot through the heart, so the legend says. We have a deed to a gold mine to Carriage from Waechter. Is there any mention of payment?"

"Payment?" Maggie asked as she looked at the deed once more. "Nothing here about payment."

Wood had his moments, and this was one. Jack and Maggie were stumped. Wood looked down at the ground and kicked some of the loose dirt.

"What if his daughter was payment? What if Carriage struck a deal that he'd get the mine if Carriage gave Bevan his own daughter for something. Maybe he thought Bevan was taking her somewhere for a wife. She was what, eighteen? People got married a lot younger then. He was rich and Carriage must have supposed she'd be taken care of. It makes some sense, but it still doesn't explain the fire and why the girls were in there to start with."

"Payment?" Maggie sighed. "Good lord, how could anyone do that? Give away your own kid for some degree of riches? Not cool. It's obvious that Carriage still loved the girl because it was his grief that made him shoot Bolt."

Maggie put the deed aside and looked at another page in the envelope. She unfolded it to find a long list of women who Bevan had apparently taken for his own.

"Hang on, I got a list of names. They are broken down into first middle and last. Lovey needs to see this because she…" Then Maggie stopped cold. Her eyes widened and she lowered the page.

"What's up?" Jack asked. "Any names we don't know, as if I have to ask."

Maggie was just short of trembling.

"Mags?" Wood said. "You good?"

"I'm afraid life just threw us another curve ball," Maggie

began. "This is a list of names and addresses of some of the women he executed."

Lovey turned to Maggie and asked, "Is Rebecca in there somewhere?

"Yes, only we have more information now." Maggie handed the list to Jack. "Read the fourth name," she coaxed.

Jack took the paper and counted "one, two, three, four...holy shit! Are you kidding me?" Jack turned and looked up to ceiling and shook his head. Wood was confused.

"What's on the list, buddy?"

Jack handed the paper to Wood. He read it to the fourth name. "No way!"

Lovey was standing stoic and quiet. "And it says?"

Wood re-read the paper. "This is a list of women executed. It's broken down into first, middle and last names. It says here Rebecca's name isn't Middlebrook. Her full name is Rebecca Brook Blanch."

Lovey jumped. "What? Rebecca is a Blanch?"

Wood was trying to rationalize. "Over the years her last name must have smudged off. They used what they had. First name: Rebecca. Middle: Brook. Last name: Blanch. Rebecca is really a Blanch. As in Hope Blanch. I think Rebecca is Hope's daughter before she married Daniel. They would have taken his name after marriage. Over time her death certificate must have erased the last name, somehow. A quick fix was just to say Middle-Brook. Bam! Middlebrook. That's why we couldn't find anything on her. There were no other Middlebrooks because that wasn't who she was. Rebecca is really a Blanch."

Maggie began to pace, then explained, "That's the connection we have. Back in 1802, Vera and I were family. Lovey and I did a regression and confirmed that I am the reincarnation of Pamela Blanch, Daniel and Hope's daughter. Daniel Blanch married Hope back before 1800. Pamela was Daniel and Hope Blanch's daughter. Rebecca must have been Hope's daughter from another marriage or somewhere.

Blanch married Hope despite her already having a kid from someone else. Hope's first husband who fathered the kid more than likely died of anything from smallpox to the flu back then. If that scenario is right, then my connection to Vera is verified. At one time, we were half-sisters. Hope Blanch was our mother. That feels right. Rebecca must have gone somewhere else at some point. Maybe she got married. The ledger only has Daniel talking about Pamela going to live with Bart Campbell. It never mentions Rebecca. She had to have been somewhere else. Maybe that's how she ended up in Randall in the first place; Daniel Blanch sent her away to protect her from the trials, knowing she was Hope's daughter. He must have found out she was on the list to be hung somehow, or at least suspected it. That's how her name got on the list and maybe that's where Middlebrook came in, to hide her real identity as a Blanch."

"Look," Jack jumped in. "I can see all this is important here, but we have found a big piece of our puzzle. Vera said Bolt was buried out in the desert in an unmarked grave. That must have been a smoke screen to throw people off, but why? Vera said a sandstorm covered up the grave so no one would ever go looking for it. Someone must have brought him down here, but who? Who would want this old man hidden from the rest of the world?"

"Someone who feared him," came a voice from the top of the stairs.

Maggie shined the light up the staircase. "Grace?"

Wood was surprised. "Holy moly. The old bitch herself! Why aren't you back at the Grizz cooking pot roast?"

"Who the hell is that?" Cat blurted out.

"Cat, she's a friend," Lovey whispered. "That's Vera's mother."

Cat was freakin'. "Oh, God! I never met her. I can't meet her now, I'm baked!"

Jack stepped up. "Oh, Grace, I wish you hadn't come here."

"My choice," Grace coldly responded as she made her way

down the steps. Looking around the room she asked the obvious: "Where's Vera?"

Jack turned to Maggie and nodded toward Grace in an "explain where Vera is" motion. Maggie sighed and dropped her head. She took a breath and said, "Grace, Vera is in the Waechter Mausoleum. She went in by herself, against all of our wishes because she thinks she's endangering the rest of us if we went in. She's a lot like you."

Grace was stunned. "She's in a mausoleum? Where? Here somewhere?"

Wood walked closer to Grace. "We need all of us to figure out why in the world she went in there and how to get her out. It's good you want to help, but now you've been down here and seen all this. Your scent is on this place now. Whatever evil shit comes out of all this, you are a possible target now. You good with that?"

Grace huffed as she landed on the dirt floor. "Well, since I'm here I need to see it." She turned to see the casket that had started this whole thing when Vera found it. "It's still there. I've been seeing visions of that casket for days. There, like it sits. Plain as day."

Grace looked at Maggie and held out a curious book. It was old. Very old. It resembled the ledger they had found the previous year, big and dirty.

Maggie asked, "What's this?"

Lovey looked at the book and reminded Maggie, "It's the book I told you she had. It's got things in it I never did understand."

Jack looked at Maggie and said, "Great, another book."

"I've been studying this since you left," Grace began. "I've had a feeling that has kept me up for days. I've been getting visions, Maggie. Dark visions of a fire, chains and people that can't get out of a burning building. I went to see if there was anything in this book and I had a vision of you. This book wants you. There is something here you need. I can't even look at it anymore. Did I hear you say, 'The Sword of God?'"

Maggie handed Bolt's parchment to Grace and said, "Give her some light." Grace took a moment to study the parchment.

"It's in there," she said gesturing towards the book, now in Maggie's hands. "It talks of an evil man of European decent. His whole family carried the heart of the un-holy."

"What's the heart of the un-holy?" Jack asked. "Do I want to know?"

"I have no idea," Grace confirmed. "It sounds like someone, or some…thing evil for sure."

"Ya think?" Cat said looking at Grace.

Grace could tell everyone was ragged. "I think you need to get out of here for a bit. You need to see what is in there."

Grace then looked over at Bolt's casket and noticed Jack was holding a shovel. "Holy Lord, Jack. Did you just dig that guy up? Why did you do that?"

Wood spoke up. "I was just thinking I needed to take a break. Watching Jack dig up that casket wore me out." Turning to Grace, he understood her. "Come on upstairs and I'll fill you in. You girls got more homework to do, looks like."

They all began to ascend the stone staircase to see what Grace's book offered, if anything. Cat was last in line and kept studying their situation. Vera was inside a mausoleum with no way out, as far as Cat knew. The casket Vera found was still there in the shadows of the basement as an offering to somewhere. Cat had had enough of Lovey's bible searches and needed something more. Looking up at the rest exiting the small opening, Cat walked over to the casket, lifted the lid and let her foot step in the center of the aged wooden box. She could hear the conversation upstairs as she slowly laid down and closed the lid. Darkness came over her.

Grace's truck was parked by Wood's van.

"How did you find us?" Lovey asked.

"Wood's van is easy to find," she said as she put her hand on the hood of the psychedelic paint job.

They got in the van and regrouped to what Grace had found in the book.

"Here," she began. "The Sword of God. It says here that the evil can be returned to the underworld by The Sword of God. It's here." Grace leaned down to show a drawing in the book. "The Sword needs to be forged from gold, using the mold...here."

Grace turned the page to reveal a drawing of a small box with two halves. It opened like a suitcase and showed the image of a sword in both hemispheres.

"It needs to be forged from gold," Jack observed. "That sucks. I'm fresh out."

Grace continued. "The Sword of God has to be forged on a holy site. Ninety-six ounces of molten gold is poured into each half, left to cool for a short time, 'until the two halves are ready to be joined' it says. Ninety-six ounces is what? Six pounds? Apparently, what you did was pour the gold in the mold. While it's cooling, close the case quickly and the two halves will fuse together, forging the Sword of God. It is then 'used against the evil that has taken the souls of the innocent, until that which is evil has been confined. The mold and Sword shall be the lock and key to banishment from this earthly plane.'"

The group fell silent. It all seemed so out of reach. Gold, a mold of a sword, trying to decipher images in an age-old book that may not even be true. They all thought of Vera and imagined what must be happening to her.

"You got any ideas?" Wood said to Jack. "I'm all out."

Maggie was quiet. Deep down she knew that all eyes were on her. She was their secret weapon. If anyone could figure it all out, it had to be Maggie. Still, the uncertainty of it all was incredibly heavy. They all needed time to think.

Wood was the first to notice Cat's absence. "Where's Cat?" he asked as he looked around the van. Grace's presence in the van had occupied the space Cat would have taken, so she was easily missed.

Lovey looked around and said, "She was here a minute ago when we were coming...up." She then glanced at Maggie and said, "No. She didn't."

Maggie understood immediately. "Oh, God."

Jack bolted out of the van and headed straight for the locked door of the church. "Keys!" he yelled back at Maggie behind him. He unlocked the door and ran to the back, opened the panel and squeezed through the small opening.

"Cat!" He yelled down the stairs. No answer. Slowly making his way down the old steps he reached the bottom, turned to see the "offered" casket and found nothing but empty space.

As the others made their way down the steps, they saw Jack standing in a hypnotic stare.

"Jack?" Maggie called out. "Is Cat...?"

Reaching the bottom of the steps and turning to see Jack, she stopped mid-sentence.

"She's gone," was all Jack could say.

The rest descended the staircase and became aware of Cat's decision to go through in search of Vera.

"Oh, my goodness!" Lovey exclaimed at Cat's initiative. "She went through."

"Through to where?" Wood asked. "Do you think she found Vera?"

Lovey was as stunned as the rest of them were. "I don't have a clue. Maggie? What now?"

Maggie was looking at the empty space as well. This was indeed a game changer. Now they had two people to worry about instead of only Vera.

"We need to go back to the mausoleum," she directed. "If Cat went through to there, then we should be able to tell."

In agreement, they all ran out of the church and headed to the mausoleum. While on the way there, Lovey looked up to see a woman walking towards them.

"Vera!" Lovey shouted.

As everyone gathered around, Vera had an odd reaction. She stretched a little, as if she'd just woken up from a nap.

"I'm fine," she said softly. Realizing Grace was there she stepped back and said, "Mom? What on Earth are you doing here?"

Grace wanted to reach out and hug Vera but didn't know how. Their journey had not been the perfect mother/daughter relationship. Grace lived most of her adult life serving Hope Blanch. Her daughter was to be initiated into the coven when fate intervened and lured Vera away to school. Grace let her go. Vera was a good spirited person who would have reacted badly to the rituals associated with Hope Blanch. Grace knew that and never questioned her to stay. Now she was feeling that Vera was the recipient of an invitation to the shadow world because she was a descendant of Bart Campbell's curse:

> *"Anyone woman having the blood of*
> *Bartholomew Campbell running through her*
> *veins will receive an invitation to the shadow*
> *world."*

Grace stammered, "I came to bring Maggie and Wood something I thought may help figure out the purpose of some things."

"What things?" Vera questioned.

"How did you get out?" Jack asked, as he bypassed the mother/daughter reunion. "Did Cat get out? Where is she?"

Vera turned and looked at the mausoleum and back at them.

"Cat? I don't know. I have not seen Cat. Why do you ask that?"

Everyone looked at each other. They had one back with one still missing.

Jack was anxious. "What do you remember, Vera? What happened in there?"

Vera readied her explanation. "I remember it was pitch black. I was frightened. The walls were cold and rough as I made my way around the room, then out of nowhere a torch ignited itself.

"Ignited itself?" Jack asked.

"Yes. It simply started burning. It let me see, at least. I then went into the front room where there were five coffins."

Wood scratched his head. "Well, it is a mausoleum."

Lovey scowled at Wood, "Go on Vera."

"A door appeared that looked like the one from the courthouse Mrs. Jenkins showed me. I remember the same knob. I opened it and saw it led into a corridor to . . . somewhere."

She looked at Maggie and said, "It was Bevan's cellar. I'm sure of it, but that's all I remember. I was seeing it, and I woke up sitting against Rebecca's tombstone like it was a lounge chair. Where is Cat? Is she at the house?"

They all stared at Vera looking for anything different. She seemed calm about the whole thing, not shaken at all.

Lovey looked over at Maggie and they both shrugged at the other in a "I don't have a clue," response.

Once more Vera asked the question; "Where's Cat?"

Maggie stepped in and took a breath. "Vera, Cat was frantic about your going into the mausoleum alone, so we went back down into the church basement to see if anything had changed. When we left, we all went upstairs. When we did, Cat was alone and got into the casket. I guess she thought it was a direct line to you."

"In the casket? I'm not following you," Vera confessed still starry eyed.

"After she got in there, the casket left," Maggie explained.

"Left?" Vera's response was curious.

Maggie looked to Jack with a "help" expression on her face. Jack was as lost as she was. "Vera, the casket went somewhere with her in it. She laid down in there and when we got back down the stairs, the casket was gone and there was no sign of Cat."

Vera was semi-shocked. She was trying to understand what Jack was telling her but couldn't wrap her head around the 'gone' part.

"So, the casket I found, that Bevan offered to me, I assumed, was actually being offered to Cat? Not to me, Lovey or Maggie?"

"It wasn't offered to Cat," Lovey explained. "It was offered to you and Cat took your place."

Vera's expression changed to one of casual acceptance. She seemed to be pondering the moment of Cat's departure and wasn't having the reaction the others expected.

"If Cat got into the casket on her own, without any prodding or intimidation, then the casket was always meant for her, not me. It is as it should be, we can't change that."

Wood asked the obvious question; "Vera, do you know where Cat went?"

Vera took another long stretch and looked around the old cemetery and seemed to be reliving it. The town had a dark past and Vera seemed totally emerged in it and accepted everything, even Cat's disappearance. This wasn't right and both Maggie and Lovey knew it.

Jack felt helpless. "Can you tell us anything at all about what you saw that could be of use?"

Vera paused and said, "Yes. I noticed the name on one of the coffins was Bevan Nicholas Waechter. He's a man of many names."

Maggie nodded. "Yeah, we figured that out. Anything else?"

Vera closed her eyes and shuttered. "I heard the lynx. It was moaning from the end of the corridor. Jesus, that's a creepy sound. It's haunting. That's all I remember."

"Close your eyes and walk down the passage you took," Lovey said softly as she took Vera's hand. "See it again, new. What's there?"

Vera closed her eyes. "The light is from the torch I was given. The shadows are all moving with the flames. There are buckets and shovels in there with old wheel barrels. There's a big number '8' hanging over the passage. I think it was a mine shaft to Mine Number Eight at some point."

Lovey jumped in and said. "It leads under the cemetery to the church, I'll bet. Wait a minute. It can't be that easy. What if Bevan's cellar is on the other side of the basement wall? We could break through and see."

"I heard something coming through the wall the first night I went down there," Vera reminded them. "Cat said she didn't hear it. It said 'Bevan.' It was when I was talking about the mock funeral and being re-born as a man. I was going to tell Cat I was going to change my name to something when I heard the word 'Bevan" come out of a wall."

"I felt the same wall," Maggie added. "I felt we were close to something."

Lovey was adamant. "Before we go breaking down walls, we need to spend some more time with Bolt's bible and Grace's book. I'm telling you, there is something there. This is all too easy, I'm telling you. We need time."

Everyone was studying Vera. She went into a place where no one expected her to return, yet, there she was. She seemed okay, but not a soul in the group felt good about her being back.

Vera looked around at her cohorts who wanted to help. She understood that all too well but wasn't ready to disclose her vision of being with Bevan on the gallows. That was something Maggie and Lovey would have wanted to know, but Vera decided that vision was for her.

"What now?" Grace asked. "We need to figure out some things to go with all the other stuff we don't know."

"I'll say," Wood admitted. "But we can't forget that we have a missing person. Cat went somewhere and we need to find out where that somewhere is, or questions are going to come we don't have answers to. As of now, Cat is MIA and we are the suspects. No one is going to believe Cat just laid down in a casket and vanished into God knows where. We gotta find her for all our sakes or major questions are going to come up. Enough questions have been asked concerning Abigail Long over the years."

Wood was looking at Maggie whose real name was Abigail Long before she took the name Maggie Styles from Wood's Antique Barn. Any missing person surrounding Maggie, who was under suspicion already from the trials in Tennessee, would be looked at hard. This was not where they wanted to be.

Chapter 14

BACK TO THE GOOD BOOK

They all filed into the house with an uncertainty no one saw coming. Even Wood was quiet as everyone tried to see angles they were convinced were right in front of them. This was the frustration that goes with searching out the paranormal. To most of the world, if you can't touch it, it's not real.

Grace looked around the large Victorian house with a fascination. "Great house! You get this house for free?"

"It's a perk," Vera said straight faced.

"Some perk," Grace replied as she continued to roam the house.

Lovey took her position at the kitchen table with Bolt's bible. With rubber gloves on her hands like a surgeon, she carefully turned the pages looking for anything she may have missed. Grace had brought her book that had some references, but nothing conclusive.

Jack was laying across the couch with his head in Maggie's lap with Grace's book standing open on his chest studying the part about the Sword of God. Maggie's fingers were playfully rummaging through his hair in a fidgety motion that largely went unnoticed. She herself was trying to imagine what Vera had seen inside the mausoleum. Maggie knew she should have gone in with her but was tricked, and what led to Vera getting out? Maggie wasn't easy with Vera's statement that she simply woke up sitting on Rebecca

Middlebrook's grave. It was all too convenient. There was something else she wasn't saying.

Wood was at a standstill as well. Instead of rolling a joint, as normal, he too was staring off into space trying to see what wasn't there. He counted on Lovey for this sort of thing, but he now was invested in trying to figure out the mystery.

Jack was commenting on the mold for the sword. "It says here that you take the gold, pour it into the mold, close the box, lock it and wait. When it's opened again, behold, The Sword of God. Just like Creepy Crawlers but bigger. It's pretty straight forward, really. Only thing we need is molten gold and the mold to pour it in. After we have the sword, I am clueless as to what comes next."

Wood was listening to what Jack had read and was restless.

"If you had the mold to create something to kill you with, where would you put it? The bad guys obviously hid it wanting it long gone and forgotten, like our buddy Bolt down in the church basement. He was pretty much put away until our bird dog Jack here started...to...dig."

Wood stopped mid-sentence like he had realized something. Everyone turned.

"You got something?" Jack asked Wood.

Wood began to pace and get his thoughts in order.

"It seems to me that we need to forge what Grace's book says we need from a mold. This is obviously an ancient mold to bring a gold sword into fruition with the instructions there in the book. It's an old book, so we are obviously not the first people to have to do it. I think the sword has already been made at some point because of the instructional literature. If that sword already exists, and we have every reason to believe it does, then where would it be and is there anything anywhere that references it? If we find it, we won't need to forge one, which will be darned convenient."

"How old is that book?" Maggie questioned. "It looks old, yes, but where did it come from? Grace, where did you get that book of yours?"

"Nobody knows its origin," Grace answered. "It was given to me. I was told I'd need it."

"By who, Grace? Who said you'd need it?" Wood asked.

"My grandmother," Grace confessed. "She had it in her attic and one day she gave it to me and said I'd need it. Three days later she died. I never got to talk to her about it. She was dying and we were all shell shocked, so I didn't push it. I wish I had now."

The room grew quiet and now everyone was looking at Grace.

"What?" was all she could muster as she felt the sting of everyone's gaze.

Maggie was surprised. "Grace, what was your grandmother doing with that book? How long ago was that? How long have you had it?"

Grace felt uneasy. She didn't like being put on the spot and here she was up against a wall she didn't understand. Looking down at the hardwood floor she answered, "When I was ten."

"When you were ten?" Jack barked. "Grace, your grandmother gave you a book dealing with the paranormal when you were ten? Why did she give it to you?"

"Beats me. She was on her death bed when my mother told me to go see her in her room one day when we went over there. When I walked in, the book was on her bed. She said she knew I'd need it one day and told me it was rightfully mine and to always keep it. I'd know when the time came to use what was in there."

"Use what was in there," Jack echoed. "Not read but use. She said 'use.'"

Everyone looked at the book and Wood said, "I believe we need to spend a minute with Grace's book, there. Sounds like some destiny shit going on in it."

"I hear you, buddy," Jack agreed.

Lovey took the book from Jack and began slowly turning the pages. Page after page went by until the chapter on the sword.

Wood wanted to know, "What does the book say exactly about the Sword other than how to mold it?"

Lovey began to read:

> *The Sword of God shall be used to rid the physical world of evil. When the light of hope shines no more, it is that which will keep the Sword in this world and protect the living from its magic. It is this magic that will contain the darkness for another one hundred plus ten years. Under the Sword, windows will open, and deaths are erased.*

"There," Lovey finished. "That's what we have. It doesn't say where or how, just that it's got magic."

Wood walked to one of the big windows and looked out over the desert. Everyone was still letting the information Lovey read soak in. After standing a moment he turned to the others. "I believe I know where the Sword is. What's odd is I have read that page before but never saw it until now."

"Saw what?" Jack asked curiously.

"That book says, 'When the light of hope shines no more,' what was it? It is that, that will protect it? I have a feeling we have had the answer all along, people. Anyone want to go to Fredericksburg, Virginia?"

"Virginia?" Maggie asked. "Why there?"

"It's been staring us in the face all along. That line, 'When the light of hope shines no more.' I smashed the light of Hope Blanch last year. The amulet. It's taking us back to where that happened. I think Hope Blanch is protecting the Sword somehow. It's with her in Virginia."

Silence took the room. What Wood had offered made perfect sense and Virginia was a long way off.

Jack spoke up and determined, "Wood and I need a red eye out tonight. Lovey, can you book us a flight?"

"On it," she replied as she turned her laptop on and headed for the net.

Jack calculated, "We can be in Virginia by morning,"

Wood laughed. "If we are taking a red eye my eyes aren't near red enough. I got some work to do," he said as he sat down at his rolling tray.

Jack went to Maggie. "You okay with this? Sounds like Wood may be right. You remember what we left under that tool shed in Virginia?"

"Yeah, I remember," Maggie sighed.

Jack got serious. "You need to stay here, doll. You don't want to be around that baggage."

He was referring to the four bodies in the basement of the tool shed that were tied to the Abigail Long (Maggie's former name) trails in Tennessee. It was assumed they'd never been found, hoping that was indeed the case.

"You and Dad go. I'll stay here with Grace, Lovey and..."

Before Maggie could complete her sentence, Vera stepped forward and proclaimed, "I have to go to Virginia."

Lovey and Grace turned to question her when Maggie held up her hand in a 'stop' motion. They both looked at Maggie and remained silent. Slowly they turned to Vera whom they had just realized was indeed headed to Virginia.

Lovey was curious. "Why do you want to go, Vera?"

"It's not a 'want to go' situation, I assure you. Something is pushing me there. I hear Rebecca saying, 'Find me,' again. I think I have an answer there."

"Answer to what?" Maggie asked.

Vera sighed, "Why I'm here. All of this points to me. I think the answer is in Virginia, or at least a big piece of the puzzle is. I need to go. If we can find a way to bring Cat back or we can see any sort of endgame in all this, it's what I have to do."

Lovey was on the fence as to whether or not to be intensely proud of her niece or be worried to death for her. It was indeed the curse of Bartholomew Campbell. Vera's invitation to the shadow world had taken another turn.

"You sure?" Lovey asked in an attempt to seal the deal.

As Lovey studied Vera, there was a distinct difference in

the Vera she'd encountered only days ago and the one she was looking at now. What awaited Vera in Virginia, Lovey could only guess.

"You know I'm sure," Vera answered as her eyes burned into Lovey's.

Yes, Vera had indeed turned a corner. "I have a feeling I will find something there. It's like being caught in a river and you can't get out. I feel movement. I turn left and I get pushed in another direction towards something. I don't want to cause a panic, but this needs to happen."

Maggie needed answers as well. "Can you be any more specific, Vera? We need answers here and quite frankly we are still figuring out the damn questions. Everyone here is tapped, including me. If you have a revelation you want to share or anything, we'd appreciate it."

It was time. Vera wanted to tell Lovey and Maggie about her encounter at the gallows but kept it to herself. Suddenly she felt the need to release it.

"When I went into the mausoleum, I was petrified. I was in total darkness. I reached out and felt only the cold concrete of the mausoleum walls. Then out of nowhere a torch lit by itself. It was up in a bracket and I took it down."

"It just came on?" Wood asked.

"Shhh!" Maggie directed at Wood. "Go on Vera."

"I turned around and could see the coffins and that's when I read the plaques and saw Bevan's name on one. It's his family mausoleum so it makes sense his body at least would be there. When I turned around, I saw a door like the one Mrs. Jenkins showed me. I opened it and went down a deep staircase. At the bottom was a long corridor with 'Mine Number 8' hanging over it. I walked under the sign, turned a corner and I was in Bevan's cellar. I knew it was where I was, Maggie. It was just like our regression."

"Go on," Lovey coaxed.

"I remember feeling sick all of a sudden. I got dizzy and grabbed something. I remember I had briefly closed my eyes and when I opened them, I began to hear a crowd chanting and booing. When I focused, I know how this must sound, but when I focused, I was on the gallows in front of a crowd in 1801. Bevan was there and put a noose around my neck. I was fading. Like passing out fading. Then I looked down at the bottom of the steps and saw the women with the bowl of water. I was made to drink Holy Water that had been drugged. We had all been starved for three days to purify us. That poisoned water was the first water we'd had in days, so it hit us fast. Maggie, I could hear Bevan's voice whisper to me, 'Now Rebecca, be a good girl and die for the crowd.' He called me Rebecca. I know now that I am the reincarnation of Rebecca Middlebrook Blanch."

Everyone sat there in silence. Now things, as outrageous as they seemed, were starting to make sense. If Vera was indeed the reincarnation of Rebecca, then it was in everyone's best interest to find out all they could about it. If that meant Vera was going to Virginia, then that was that.

"Vera, or Rebecca or whoever you are, we are behind you," Jack offered as he stepped forward and wrapped his arms around her. As he did, Vera lost it. She sobbed in his arms for minutes as everyone tried to console her. If anything was coming for Vera now, the defense was just amped up. Nothing was going to harm that woman if they had anything to say about it.

Chapter 15

UNDER THE TOOL SHED

Jack, Vera and Wood landed in Virginia. Jack was staring out the window as the plane taxied to its resting spot outside the terminal. He was remembering the events of last year when they were all tested. He didn't want to be going back, but for Vera's sake, he knew there were simply no more options.

"We need a car," Wood said as he raised up from his seat.

"On it," Jack assured Wood.

Jack glanced over at Vera who didn't look good. He secretly worried for her as he had for Maggie a year earlier. Jack wasn't as used to the paranormal aspect of life as Maggie and Lovey, but knew he was representing those that were. Vera needed him and he only hoped he was up to the challenge, whatever it was.

The drive to Fredericksburg Cemetery was a long one. It was four thirty in the morning, so traffic was tolerable.

Wood was trying to see where Vera's head was. "Have you gotten any knocks on the door from the other side?"

Vera looked back at him curiously and asked, "The other side of what?"

Wood clumsily adjusted. "I don't know. The other side of the place Cat is?"

Vera closed her eyes and sat still. Opening them once more, she said she didn't feel Cat anymore. "Cat is someplace else. She's where she needs to be."

Jack was listening. "Is she cool?"

"Cool?" was all Vera mustered.

"Yeah, you know, okay?" Jack answered in a back slide.

Vera casually responded, "Cat is not in danger nor out of danger. She is where she should be, whether that's a good thing or not."

Wood looked worried. "Why don't I like the sound of that?"

"Same reason I don't, I guess," Jack sighed as he once more began to wonder about Cat's fate.

At last the three arrived in front of the Fredericksburg Cemetery. Wood and Jack looked at each other as memories surfaced from their experience here before.

Jack admitted, "I gotta say, I never thought I'd be coming back here."

Wood agreed. "I hear you, buddy. This place creeps me out."

Wood had been tested here. This place was like a crossroad for him as he was chosen to go down one path then did an about face and went the other way, to the good fortune of everyone involved. Now here he was again.

Vera studied her surroundings. "You say you found a witch here last year?"

"Yeah," Jack answered. "We did at that."

"Well," Vera sighed, "I'm here now. That means there are two witches on the premises. I don't know if that is either good or bad."

There's a strength in owning who you are. Vera had just admitted to Jack and Wood that she was now seeing herself as a witch. That can be a powerful revelation to someone in denial. What bothered Jack was that only yesterday Vera as skating the idea, now she was acting like she'd known about that side of herself forever. She was changing and Jack and Wood could see it. With every turn Vera Chase was coming into her own as a chosen lady of vision.

As they walked to the front of the cemetery in the early morning light, a foggy scene of tombstones was laid out before them. The three were reverently quiet as the graveyard came into view and Jack stopped and turned to Vera.

"Vera, do you know this place? Look around you, have you been here before?"

Vera took a deep breath and scoured the landscape. The layout of the land had changed dramatically in two hundred years, but Jack wanted to see what Vera's reaction would be. He and Wood watched her feel her way around the fields of marble markers and statues. She took a step forward, stopped and turned to Jack.

"In answer to your question; 'have I been here before?' I'll tell you what I believe. I think I have been here many times before. This land has a distinctive familiarity. It's been my home and it's also been my destination from afar when it wasn't. I have lived many lives, Jack. As have you, Wood, Maggie, Lovey, Grace and yes, even Cat. It's all coming back."

Jack glanced at Wood who was taking in the same revelations as he was. A look resting somewhere between amazement and fear had taken him and he really missed Lovey at that moment.

"Where are we going, Vera?" Jack asked. "If you have been here before, do you know where we're headed?"

Vera looked ahead to the concrete pathways that snaked through the graveyard. Cautiously, she began to walk. Wood and Jack flanked her as they scanned the property for anyone who wouldn't want them there. With each step they drew closer to the tool shed, at last stopping in front of it.

"Home," Vera whispered.

Alerted, Jack asked, "Home? Did you say, 'home', Vera?"

Vera scanned the area. "I lived here once."

She opened the thankfully unlocked door and slipped inside as Jack and Wood followed, sharing uncertain glances as they too disappeared into the tool shed.

Vera walked in immediately taking her gaze downward. "It's down there, under us."

Jack walked over to the closet and took out rakes, brooms

and odd landscaping equipment so the floor was clear. He found the release lever and pulled up on it revealing the way into the hidden room below. Jack looked down into the shadows and got a knot in his stomach. He looked up at Wood who was also in a state of reliving his own events in the bottom of the tool shed. This was to Wood 'ground zero.' Everything he was before changed here. Now Vera had returned home to the same place, only she was reliving a past life's experience.

"Shall we?" Wood casually asked as he offered the entrance to Jack and Vera.

Vera moved to the small opening and began her descent down the ladder as Jack and Wood followed. At the bottom of that ladder, Jack hoped they would find answers.

Vera walked around the small, musty room that had a dirt floor and stone walls sealed with old river mud. Jack and Wood watched her as she walked over to the four plastic covered bodies that lay against the far wall. This was the baggage Jack wished would go away as they could lead back to Maggie, who under the spell of Hope Blanch put them there as a gift of souls to Hope. Vera walked to the repaired wall where stones had been replaced to keep the body of Hope Blanch hidden. They watched as Vera put her hand on the wall, closed her eyes and a faint smile came to her face.

"Vera? You getting anything we need to know about?" Wood asked. "We need to know if the Sword is here. Do you know if it is?"

Vera seemed almost about to break into laughter. She looked around the room and closed her eyes as if she was reliving a moment of fondness, then turned to a distant wall. She raised her arm and pointed. "There. That wall. Something is behind that wall where it could be watched."

"Watched?" Wood answered. "By who?"

"Hope," was all Vera said. It was enough. Jack and Wood went to the stone wall.

"Got a shovel?" Jack asked Wood.

Walking over to where the bodies were, Wood picked up a shovel and gave it to Jack.

"Keep an ear out for anyone coming in upstairs. We don't want any company down here," Jack instructed as he took the shovel and found his target stone on the old wall.

"Amen," Wood agreed. "Let's get this done."

With that, Jack hit the rock wall until a hole was made at its base. Clearing out an area in front of it, Wood leaned down and shined the light into the darkness.

"We got something," Wood said. "Looks like somebody else is down here."

Vera began a noticeable change of demeanor. She went from a faint smile to one of anxiety. Jack stooped down and looked up into the wall at Wood's discovery.

"Yep, looks like we got company. Better see," he said as he glanced back up to Wood and Vera.

Wood and Jack reached into the dusty wall and pulled and tugged until an adult size roll of cloth was freed from the darkness. The three looked at the wrappings and could only wonder what, or who lay inside.

Jack pulled down the cloth and the face of a woman came into view. Withered from age and time, she saw the first light of day in two hundred years.

"Who do you suppose this..."

Before Jack could finish Vera interrupted him with, "It's Rebecca."

"Rebecca Middlebrook Blanch?" Wood asked as he stepped back.

"Holy shit, people," Jack began. "You sure, Vera? If this is Rebecca, who is out in the Cemetery in Randall in Rebecca's grave?"

"One of the unfortunate many," Vera answered. "I need to see her."

Vera bent over the woman and slowly stroked her face. There was something there that seemed familiar as well as needing something. Vera closed her eyes and held the body close. Jack and Wood had seen Maggie and Lovey go into a deep trance meditation, but nothing like this. It was as if Vera was absorbing her.

Wood had learned from Lovey, "When they're in the zone, leave them alone," so he opted to keep his distance. He motioned to Jack to let her do what she wanted to.

Vera raised up and let her hand run under a chain around Rebecca's neck. She lifted off the chain and a locket emerged from the ancient dress. Wood was reminded of last year when he removed an amulet from the neck of Hope Blanch.

Vera held the locket tightly in her hand and once more closed her eyes. Expressions of wonderment, question and fear all came to her face. Finally, sentiment. She had touched a part of herself deep down. Jack and Wood could see it.

Vera got up and walked to the far corner of the room where Hope was entombed. With her back to Jack and Wood, she opened the locket and seemed to be studying it.

"We need to look for the Sword," Jack whispered to Wood.

Wood was ready to leave. "You do realize we are in a tool shed with six bodies and a witch, don't you? Hope, Rebecca and those four bags over there are trouble we can't afford to cash in. We got to get this done and get out of here. It's daylight big time outside."

"I know," Jack answered. "But we came all the way out here for the sword, not Rebecca and whatever Vera found around her neck. Last time somebody removed something from someone dead down here you smashed it. Remember? Shit, I'll do it."

Jack began to frisk Rebecca's body looking for the sword. He cautiously went up front and back and felt nothing. Wood rummaged the old cloth but still the prize evaded them.

"Vera," Jack called in a loud whisper. "We need to find the sword. I think it's here, in this room. Do you know where it is?"

Vera slowly turned around with a tear running down her face. Jack and Wood were taken back from this uncharacteristic display of emotion.

"The Sword of God? Remember? Is it here?" Jack coaxed.

Vera lowered the locket and became stoic. She stood expressionless in front of Jack and Wood. "Vera?" Jack said as he tried to get through.

"I'm taking the visions now, Jack. Before, on the street at the old gallows I was overcome by them, but now they seem comforting. I seem to be caught in the same paranormal vortex as the casket, the room Mrs. Jenkins showed me and the Waechter mausoleum. We are between worlds now, Jack. This room, the church basement and the mausoleum are all connected. I can see in front of me and behind me in time. I can't explain it, but I know soon the answer will come."

"Vera, I'm glad you're coming into your own witchery or whatever it is, but we need to find that sword or all this will be for..."

Vera interrupted him with a sharp, "Don't say 'nothing'! Don't you dare say finding Rebecca wasn't worth coming here."

"Holy shit, Vera," Wood said with an attempt to calm the situation. "Jack didn't mean anything like that. He just wants to end this thing like we all do, right? We want to end this thing? The haunted thing? Vera?"

Vera collected herself and walked to the place where Jack and Wood had discovered Rebecca. She reached inside the dusty hole and recoiled with a small roll of cloth, slowly turned to Jack and offered it to him.

"This is it," Vera stated as she held it out.

Taking it from Vera, he slowly began to unroll it as Wood stepped forward to see as well. With one move of his hand he uncovered the handle, then he slowly let the cloth fall. Jack was holding a small golden sword.

"Holy moly!" Wood exclaimed. "Behold, the Sword of God."

"Looks like it," Jack agreed.

They took a minute to examine it and both agreed it was the real deal.

"Now what?" Jack sighed. "Now I'm lost again. I knew we had to find it. We have. Now what? Vera, you got any instructions from beyond as to what to do with this blade here?"

Vera studied the sword from a distance. She was looking

at it like it was an adversary. Wood picked up on it and Jack as well that Vera was fearing the sword. That much was obvious, the rest wasn't as forthcoming.

"We need answers, Vera. Now would be a good time. We need to get back to Randall."

Jack's coaching her to reach wasn't working as Vera wasn't herself at all. Since coming down in the cellar she had been taken. The Vera Jack and Wood knew had left the building and they were now dealing with someone they didn't know. Jack really wished Maggie had come, as for now, he was out of his league. Vera was clutching the locket. Wood watched as she held it as if she were protecting it and he grew concerned. "What's in the locket, Vera? Anything we need to know about?"

Vera looked down at her hand. She slowly opened it and the silver locket came into view. "I gave it to Hope," Vera said softly.

Extending her hand, she offered it to Wood. He examined the locket front and back and then pressed the release lever on the side. It opened with an old photograph on one side, an inscription on the other. Wood scratched at the inscription and read aloud:

"For Mother, Always, Rebecca"

Wood squinted in the shadows at the old photo and let his thumb clean it as much as he could. He looked into the face of the picture, looked up at Jack and said, "I think we have a problem." He then offered the locket to Jack, who examined it like Wood did.

"Look at the picture," Wood instructed as he stood looking Vera up and down.

Jack took the opened locket and studied the picture, lowered his hand and said, "It's Vera." Turning to Vera he said, "You apparently have a history here. Can you tell me why the person in this picture has your face?"

"It's not another person, Jack." Vera confirmed. "It's me. I am Rebecca. I lived two hundred years ago where I walked in her body. I lived in this place with Hope and Daniel Blanch. My half-sister was Pamela, who now lives as Maggie. I know that now. I gave the locket to Hope, my mother. She gave it back to me when she was imprisoned and told me to keep it to remember her by. It was before she turned dark. She was once good. She was once my mother."

Jack and Wood were dumbfounded. Vera had come here because she felt drawn. It was a pull from beyond.

"Was that you calling to yourself to find you?" Wood asked. "You said you heard 'find me.' Who was that, Vera? Was that you telling yourself to find you? Why would you do that? Was it the Sword? When you found you, you also found the sword? That's gotta be it."

"The Sword is not what you think it is," Vera said.

Jack was taken aback by her assessment of recent events.

"Not what we think it is? Vera, or Rebecca or whoever you are, I don't have an opinion about that sword one way or another. I just know for some reason we have been worried about finding it for God knows what. I don't think it's anything. What do you think it is?"

Wood stood aside with his eyes fixed on the sword. It was in itself beautiful. He was a junk man at heart and had the Antique Barn before Maggie bought it. He kept that eye for finding antiquities and that sword was pushing his buttons. It was the dumpster dive find of a lifetime.

Jack's frustration was obvious. Now Vera's actions were compounding an already tense situation.

"Well, Vera?" Jack asked. "What is the Sword of God for?"

"It's a key, Jack. A very important key that has abilities to connect to things previously considered out of reach."

"Keys are for locks," Wood injected. "Do you know what lock this key opens or closes?"

"You wouldn't understand it. You will, but not now," Vera spoke.

"We will know what it's for?" Wood questioned. "How do you know that?"

Vera then announced, "I have to stay here for two more days."

"Stay?" Both Wood and Jack spoke in chorus as they realized what Vera proposed.

"You can't stay here for two days, Vera," Jack confirmed. "No food, water, bathrooms. It's cold down here. It's not happening."

"I'll get a room," she said. "Get a ride back to the airport and leave me the car. I need to be near this place for a while."

Wood and Jack were surprised by Vera's wanting to stay, but it made sense. Her body was there, Rebecca's body.

"Why do you want to stay?" Wood asked, concerned.

"I need to be here when it happens," Vera answered.

"When what happens?" Jack countered.

"When the door is open and there is sight before the door and through the door," Vera calmly stated.

"Well, that clears it up," Wood mocked. "I need more than that, Vera. We're in a shit storm down here and anything you can tell us about doors or lockets or Bevan or anything else sure would be an asset now. We don't have time for riddles."

Vera walked to the wall where Hope was entombed. She put her hand out and let it rest on the cold stone.

"A door will be opened soon. It's been opened before and will be opened again. I can't explain it any better. I need to be here when it is offered. In two days, the anniversary of the fire will be at hand. On that night, every one hundred-ten years, the door will open."

"Every one hundred and ten years?" Jack seemed both frustrated and confused. He began to pace and then saw reasoning.

"You say the door opens once every one hundred-ten years and the female descendants of Bart Campbell, and anyone involved with them, have to deal with it. That scans. It's their invitation to the shadow world and I can't believe I just said that. The revolving clock thing must be to ensure that the women cursed indeed have to face that realization. This whole thing will reenact itself over and over until something stops it. The math says this has already happened once since 1802 and we have to assume that nothing was done to stop it because it is about to happen again. I'm assuming 1802 because that is when the fire was. We need to know how to stop this thing or it will continue on for another century. And why it's a hundred and ten and not just a plain century is darned inconvenient."

"It is every one hundred and ten years because that's how old Bevan's mortal body was when he made his first transition. I can't explain it any more now," Vera said with a hint of frustration in her own voice.

"Bevan lived to be a hundred and ten?" Wood questioned. "Back then that was a long time."

"His evil kept him on this plane," Vera tried to explain. "Bevan grew old and powerful."

"Not powerful enough to beat death." Jack added.

"Mortal death, yes." Vera searched for the right path to let Jack and Wood understand. "Bevan is as much alive in the spirit world as he was here. Maybe more so. That is where his power grew so he could resurrect himself in a cycle over time. He won't go away unless he's forced to."

"And that's where we come in," Wood finished. He turned to Jack and said once more, "That's where we come in."

Jack got what Wood was insinuating. They were the first line of defense against Bevan's clock. It was going to take all of them to give what they could to beat this thing. It may even require sacrifice. They had already lost Cat. Another "lost" person around Maggie, the former Abigail Long, wasn't anything they could afford.

"Vera, where is Cat?" Jack asked. "Do you know? Other than she's where she is supposed be?"

"She is on the other side of the door. You can't see it yet, but you will," Vera calmly stated. "Two hundred years ago a man named Bartholomew Campbell accused my mother, Hope Blanch, of making his crops sour in the fields. She never did anything to his crops or anyone else's. Hope Blanch was peaceful until her heart was darkened by Bart Campbell. She then put the curse on any female descendant of his to receive an invitation to the shadow world. Lovey, Grace, Maggie and I have received our invitation and have acted accordingly. Lovey is a medium. She has psychic abilities, yes, but she only sees what comes to her. Grace is a clairvoyant medium like Lovey. Maggie sees what she wants to but doesn't realize fully what she is yet. Maggie and I were together before. I knew her."

Jack saw an opportunity. "You knew her how, Vera? How did you know Maggie? Was she at Bethel Church during the fire? She says she was involved somehow but doesn't know in what capacity. We need to know for her sake and everyone else's. And what do you mean that she doesn't fully understand what she is yet? She is a descendant of Daniel and Hope Blanch. If you are as well, then you are related in more ways than one."

"Maggie is a descendant of Daniel Blanch. Daniel married Hope and they had Pamela together. Hope was my mother before she met Daniel. Pamela was my half-sister. Maggie is the reincarnation of Pamela Blanch."

Vera was adamant. "The answers are coming, Jack. Go back to Randall. When the time comes, you'll know."

Jack looked at Wood and shrugged. "Looks like she's staying."

Wood looked at Vera standing in front of Hope's tomb and nodded. "Yeah, she's staying. When you get back to Randall, tell Lovey I had to stay here and watch after her niece."

"What? You're staying here, too?" Jack barked.

"I need to be here with Vera, Jack. I can't leave her here in this place knowing what she's facing. Hell, I'm not sure I know what she's facing, but she can't do it by herself. Go back to Randall and let's see how all this works out. If it's a bust, we'll be back in a couple of days. Besides, Lovey would kill me if she thought I left Vera here alone."

"That she would," Jack agreed. "Okay. But I damn well don't like it. What about the Sword, do I take it back to Randall?"

"No," Vera stated. "The Sword is a key and the lock to that key is at hand. It has to stay. That is why it's here in the first place and not in Randall."

"Everything else is in Randall, why would the Sword be here?" Jack asked.

"Because someone or some...thing wants it here. It's all falling into place," Wood assured Jack. "I can see her diligence, Jack. You need to go back to the girls. I believe a 'strength in numbers' moment may be at hand. Burn one for me when you get in."

Jack was stuck. His best friend was staying with Vera in Virginia while he had to go back to Arizona and try and see if he could make sense out of any of this with Maggie, Lovey and Grace. This time it was he who was pulled. He knew he had to go back to Randall to be with Maggie, but for what reason? There was a war coming and he only hoped he and everyone else would be alive to see its aftermath.

Jack pulled Wood's van into the driveway of the big house back in Randall. He sat for a moment collecting his thoughts on what to tell the girls as to why Vera and Wood opted to stay in Virginia. The front door opened. Maggie came out and walked to the side of the van as Jack tried to be cool. "Hey, doll. You looking for a good time?"

Maggie was relieved to see Jack who was especially glad to be out of the basement and back to the land of the living. She wanted details. "Everything go okay in Virginia? Did you find the sword?"

Jack rolled his eyes. "Yeah, we found it."

"Where's Dad and Vera?" Maggie asked now noticing Jack was alone in the van.

Jack hesitantly answered, "Back in Virginia. Vera said she had to stay because something is happening in two days on the anniversary of the fire and she has to be there for it. We have a part in it as well, but I have no clue as to what that is. This is frustrating shit, darlin'. I ask for answers and all I get are more riddles."

"In two days? She said we'd know in two days?" Maggie was beginning to feel as frustrated as Jack.

"Now you know all I do," Jack advised. "Vera became something down in that basement, Maggie. She wasn't herself."

Concerned, Maggie grew even more attentive. "Who was she?"

"You ready for this?" Jack was winding up. "We found more than a sword in Fredericksburg. I knocked through a wall and we found the body of Rebecca Middlebrook Blanch."

"What?" Maggie recoiled. "You found Rebecca?"

"Yeah. Turns out that Vera had been calling out to herself through time. Vera took a locket off of the corpse we found in the wall and there as an inscription that read, *'To Mother, Always, Rebecca.'* There was a picture in the other half. Maggie it was a picture of Vera's face. I'm not shitting you; it was Vera in another time. Another life. She was Rebecca Brook Blanch in a past life. Our Vera was talking and acting like her. She said she knew the Sword was a key and in two days the door would need the key as it does on the anniversary of the fire every one hundred-ten years. I guess to keep the women decedents of Bart Campbell on their toes as to the curse."

Maggie was dumbfounded. It was a lot to take in and Jack hadn't even gotten out of the van yet.

"What do we do now?" she asked. "We have two days to do what?"

"I'm stuck again," Jack admitted. "This shit is beyond frustrating. I guess we wait it out. Vera said we'd know what to do and when and something happens in two days. Maggie, Vera also said that Lovey and Grace are clairvoyant mediums that can see what comes to them, but she said you didn't fully understand what your place in all this was yet and didn't know what you were. I have no clue why she'd say that, but unless you have some superpower you don't know about yet, there is something stalking you. I had to tell you. Good or bad at least now you know."

Maggie wanted to know as much as possible, but it was a long drink of water. She needed time to take it all in. "Did Vera mention Cat? Does she know where Cat is?"

"She did mention Cat, but only when I asked her. She said Cat was on the other side of the door. That's all she'd say and that I would understand soon enough. I guess we need to be somewhere in two days. I have a feeling where."

Jack looked down at Maggie and they both said at once, "Bethel Church."

Jack and Maggie walked into the big house and Lovey and Grace met them in the front room. As Lovey approached Jack he said, "Wood stayed in Virginia with Vera. It's a long story."

Jack recalled the events of the last evening to the girls as best he could. They understood his frustration. "I'm telling you, Vera became someone else. She didn't feel like Vera, you know? Her demeanor was different. Her speech changed somewhat. It was a crazy thing."

"What did she say to do with the sword?" Grace asked.

"She said it was a key. Wood said that a key needed a lock and Vera or Rebecca or whoever said the lock was at hand and we'd know the time to act."

"Act on what?" Grace wanted to know. "The time is at hand for what?"

"And that is the million-dollar question," Jack confessed. "I don't know, but Vera said Maggie would know. Vera said Maggie doesn't understand her part in all this and doesn't know what she is capable of. That's all she'd offer. I'm telling you, standing down in that place with six bodies wasn't where any of us wanted to be. That's four life sentences. Rebecca and Hope aren't tied to us. Maggie, you don't have lifetimes of jail time to appease Bevan or Rebecca or anyone. Whatever needs to happen in two days better be worth it."

"If we get Cat back it will be," Lovey injected. "She is caught between worlds. I feel that."

"Yeah. I feel that as well," Maggie agreed. "But the thing is, I get a feeling she is where she is by choice, not against her will."

"By choice?" Grace questioned. "How can she be there by choice?"

Jack reminded her, "She got into the casket on her own, Grace. She wasn't forced. Now that action has put her somewhere that she either can't escape from or chooses not to."

"Well! Listen to you, Jack Reynolds," Maggie mocked. "When did you become an expert on paranormal dimensions?"

"I picked it up somewhere," Jack answered as he looked at Maggie with a fondness that lit up the room. "In two days we'll see how good we are, people. Vera said the basement at Bethel Church and the bottom of that tool shed in Virginia were connected somehow. That old tool shed is sitting on top of the former home of Hope Blanch. The wicked witch of the… pick a place. We have every reason to believe whatever we know up until now, will be tested. She said we needed to be at Bethel Church in two days. That's where we'll be."

Lovey began to pace. "In two days. She specifically said, 'In two days.'"

"That's what she said," Jack confirmed.

Lovey sighed, "Well then, I think we have at least one of our answers."

"We actually have an answer to something?" Jack mused. "Holy shit, spill it! Answers are welcome, believe me."

Maggie encouraged Lovey to continue. "What is it? You have an answer? To what, exactly?"

Lovey looked at everyone and took a deep breath. "Why this is happening to Vera and to us is that Rebecca, according to Jack, said that every one hundred and ten years somebody has to deal with this curse. A series of events re-occurs to keep Bevan out of this physical world. It's already happened at least once. The anniversary is at hand. So, any spirit, ghost, entity, call it what you will, that has anything to do with Bevan gets awakened, so to speak. Vera is a direct reincarnation of Rebecca. All this is simply timing and the timing for Bevan's return is at hand. Anyone having the blood of Bart Campbell running through them will receive an invite. Vera's arrived right on time which is the real kick starter. All this has been in the works for a hundred and ten years and unless we figure out how to keep Bevan at bay, he will be ushered into our world and nothing but evil will follow for another one hundred and ten years."

Maggie became restless. "You say that Vera is in this because of her being a descendant of Bart Campbell. I'll go there, but Lovey you are also a descendant. Has any of this affected you that you can tell?"

Everyone looked at Lovey.

"No. Not that I'm aware of. That is odd, isn't it? Why would Vera be affected by the date and not me? Grace, you said you've been getting visions. You saw the casket in the basement in your head before you actually came here. If you and I have the same mother, why aren't I affected like you? I had a moment at the museum, where the old gallows were, but nothing like what you and Vera are having." Lovey seemed almost cheated somehow. "Well, I guess I'm lucky until now, at least."

Grace almost laughed out loud. "I'll say you're lucky! Maybe your part in all this hasn't surfaced yet. I hope for your sake it doesn't. This is not where you want to be. Trust me."

"So, what do we do for two days until that happens?" Maggie asked inquisitively.

"I'm tired, babe," Jack confided. "I've been rolling around in this thing for a while. We either need to wait it out, or we need a miracle. I'm at a loss. Again!"

Chapter 16

WOOD IN VIRGINIA

Wood and Vera left the tool shed shortly after Jack. The public began arriving at the cemetery and Wood suggested they leave while they were still undetected. Slowly walking along the path back to the road, they casually read the tombstones.

"If you see any wildflowers on one of those keep walking, okay?" Wood suggested.

"I'll do that," Vera replied as she scoured the area in reflection.

"Wood, I remember being here and I can still hear the sounds from when I was a child. I see the crude buildings, the people. I can remember it like it was me actually living it." Vera stopped by a statue and took a deep breath, closing her eyes. "I can see Hope. She was peaceful, Wood. There was a time when Hope never did anything evil at all until Bart Campbell accused her of killing his corn and Daniel Blanch sent his daughter, my half-sister, Pamela to live with him. You knew that, didn't you? It was in the ledger Maggie found last year. Hope, apparently in her afterlife, in some state of cumulative angst and woe, hated that Daniel sent Pamela to Bart Campbell. Why Daniel sent their daughter to live with the one guy who had Hope executed, I can't say. We will never really know the reason."

"It was Rebecca when you think about it," Wood concluded. "If Pamela went to Bart Campbell, maybe he did that so Rebecca wouldn't be accused of witchcraft. She could have been accused easily being Hope's daughter. Giving Pamela to Campbell was Daniel Blanche's way of ensuring that he would not accuse you or Pamela. I guess he'd rather have one daughter with him than two on the gallows. Why he never mentioned Rebecca more in the ledger, I don't know. Maybe he wanted to keep her a secret. He was a genius who created tools and concepts far ahead of his time. Some of those drawings he did in the old ledger were remarkable. God knows what he was thinking."

Vera nodded to what Wood concluded.

"You are right, Daniel Blanch sent Rebecca away to Randall at that time to hide her. He loved both daughters, but Bart Campbell was in love with Pamela. This was a hard time for Daniel as it was reflected in the ledger. That may be where the name 'Middlebrook' was born. It was to hide her identity as a Blanch from whoever might come looking down the road."

Vera looked at Wood and had questions. "Wood, you have magic inside you. You know that. You are a warlock and I can feel it. Last year you said you were tested, and it seems you passed. You're still healing, aren't you?"

"Come here," he said as he ushered them to a concrete bench. "Sit and act natural." Wood looked around and saw no one coming near that could hear him. "Last year I saw where it could all lead. The purpose of it all. I'm talking about the shit we did when we were serving her. Serving Hope. We were hollow. Living on remote control and everyone just accepted it. If a guy didn't meet Maggie's standards, he got delivered to Hope on a back road and made it to the Wall of Shame."

"Wall of Shame?" Vera asked.

"It's a… never mind. Just something else crazy. I'm not proud of any of it, Vera. I did it. We all did it and then something happened. A small turn of events. I saw Maggie with Jack. I had a distinct feeling that if I took the amulet, all that potential love they could have, that I could see they could have, would just fade into the land of 'what if.' So that's why I didn't take it. It was for Maggie and Jack and I think that's the first time I actually said that." Wood sat back. "People can change, Vera. It's a matter of choice."

Vera sat quiet for a moment and let what Wood said filter in. Change. She looked around her at what was now a cemetery where it was once an open wooded area where she played as a child, in another life. Now it was devoured by tombstones. Vera once more took in a deep breath and closed her eyes.

"Hope changed as well," Vera said with a certainty. "She was caged as her execution neared. She was put in a dungeon awaiting the day to come, growing more and more angry like an animal full of rage clawing to get out. All that darkness had no place to go but inside. She wasn't part of Bevan. She turned into a dark magic unto herself in Fredericksburg."

This time Vera leaned in as if someone could hear.

"When her neck snapped at the end of the gallows rope, she didn't die. All that hate and anger fueled itself and healed her, then she later walked out of the cemetery a cloaked and hidden entity of evil. She lived out her life in seclusion until she sealed herself up in that wall here in Virginia. Daniel thought she was dead. After he died, she stayed here, down there." Vera motioned towards the toolshed. "She had put all her power into the amulet you destroyed last year. All that hate and anger was released. It went out, Wood. Think. What happened to the spirit of Hope Blanch after you smashed the amulet?"

Wood was caught off guard. "You just saw all that? Jesus, Vera. You are coming into your own." Wood adjusted himself to the light coming through the trees. "When I smashed the amulet, I was feeling the loss of the grip at that time. We were all feeling it. It was like someone standing on your chest for as long as you can remember, then they suddenly get off. You don't really notice anything else around you at that particular time. I didn't see or feel her going anywhere but away from us when I smashed it. Are you saying she was too powerful to die?"

"Maybe," Vera admitted. "Wood, I'm sorry. I know you think you killed her, but I have a feeling…"

"Sorry doesn't cover it," Wood interrupted her. "I'm sorry for a lot of it, but what gets you, what grinds your gut is that deep down in all of us, Hope found a way to tap into the primal instincts we all have. As humans we had to survive at one time any way we could. We killed to live. At one stage of our evolution we heralded the kills we made because they meant survival. We did the same, but for Hope. We killed so she could live and then patted ourselves on the back for it." Wood shuffled on the cold concrete bench. "All it proved was that in the end we all got played."

Vera sat assessing the obvious. She was indeed getting stronger by the day as Wood could see. Having a conversation about something she knew totally nothing about a week ago only fueled her questions, which in turn, made her look for answers. She could see how things happened in her past life as long as she was involved. As the anniversary of the fire at Bethel Church grew closer, Vera was becoming something no one could have predicted.

"Tell me, Wood. You have magic. Why aren't you affected like the rest of us. Or are you? Are you feeling any of this?"

Wood had been called out. He had a chance to clear the air with Vera as well as with himself. "Yeah, I've been getting stuff," he admitted.

"When we were at the museum the first day you and Maggie got hit by the gallows by being on that spot. I felt it as well. I knew what happened there just as you did."

Vera understood. "Why didn't you say something?"

"Because none of this is about me, it's about you. We don't need to worry about me getting visions when you are the one targeted here."

Vera shook her head in question. "Jack said we are all targeted by whatever this thing is. How do you keep all this at bay? Why aren't you like Maggie, Lovey, Grace and me, trying to deal with what we are shown?"

"It's the weed," Wood confessed. "I smoke a lot of pot

because it keeps most of it, the visions and such, away. When I was younger, I began to have visions like you and Maggie. I was really scared of them. When I smoked a joint, the voices calmed down. I barely heard them at all. Everyone talks about the medicinal properties of grass. It works for me. I hear Lovey all day long and that's the only voice I want to hear."

"So that's your secret. You don't react to the visions because you found a way to keep them away from you," Vera assessed. "I thought you were just an old stoner."

Wood laughed. "I am! Only it's not something I can walk away from. There would be an adjustment period and the weed doesn't keep everything away. I still feel things, but not as I would if I didn't smoke at all."

"So here in Virginia you didn't bring any pot because you thought you were going right back to Arizona. Now you're here for a couple of days without it. Are you feeling any, how did you say, knocks on the door?"

"Actually, yes," Wood confessed. "It'll get worse over the next forty-eight hours."

"You mean you'll get stronger, don't you? Without the weed you have to, what, evolve?" Vera asked. "We need all the help we can get, and you know that. Sit your pot down for a while and we may have a better shot at this Bevan thing. Are you okay with that? Can you do it?"

"I can do it," Wood confessed. "I've done it before, to see if the shit still hits me. I'll go a day or so now and again, but when I start getting flashes, screw it. I burn one. It's who I am now."

Vera sat back and looked at the little man that fate had given her. When she first met Wood, she had no idea the role he would play in her journey to finding out answers. Here in this memorial garden, she began to chisel away the rough pieces of the man and see for herself who was underneath. Throughout history the greatest knights have turned out to be the most unassuming people.

Vera and Wood found a motel and got adjoining rooms. They had a lot to try and figure out. Both wished their significant others had come, but for now, they were on their own.

Chapter 17

MAGGIE SEES THE FIRE

When someone tells you that you don't fully understand what your purpose is, it can be jarring. Maggie had taken some time to take in what Jack had said about her not knowing what she was. That bothered her. Did she have a superpower that needed to come to fruition before she could use it? Had the time come for her to step into her destined self and become something more? She thought about where she was now and how far she'd come. It was then she decided to take matters into her own hands and see exactly what all the fuss was about.

Jack was sound asleep. Maggie smiled as she watched him purr into his pillow after his long journey to and from Virginia. She thought of how lucky she was that she and Jack had found each other and she was absolutely sure he had a place in her life, but at the moment Maggie knew she didn't have much time to figure some things out. She decided to take a leap.

Maggie couldn't get what Jack had told her out of her head. "Abilities" kept coming and going in her mind.

"Okay, here we go," Maggie whispered to herself.

"What happened that night in 1802 when Bolt chained those four women in the church…. It's 1802. I can see it. I know I can see it. I was there. I know it. It's 1802…. 1802…. 1802…."

Maggie felt like she was flying by putting herself in freefall where she was receptive and exploring. Sounds began to come of an angry crowd and she could feel the heat as she drew closer. Like looking through a smoky mirror she began to see the burning church and hear the screams of the young women.

Maggie could see the whole scene play out as if it were the night of the fire. She could see inside the church as the four women ran from window to window trying to get out. Bevan was inside with them, motioning for them to go down into the basement. Once down there, he went to the wall where the casket had laid, pushed in a corner brick and the wall moved to one side offering a space big enough for the girls to slip through. On the other side of the wall was as she'd suspected all along; Bevan's cellar.

The women were shackled to the walls. She could hear Bolt in the yard yelling that The Sword of God had won out over evil, then Maggie let herself be taken where she could see Bolt standing in front of the engulfed structure. Sheriff Carriage arrived and the scene was playing out until Maggie saw a man standing just outside the reach of the flames on the side of the church. Once more, Bevan.

Carriage began yelling at the preacher. "What did you do? Who's in there? Who's in there you fool?"

Carriage then fell to his knees upon hearing his daughter had been confined to the inferno. He raised his head to see Bevan standing outside the flames pointing a gun at him. Carriage pulled his revolver at the same moment Pastor Bolt crossed their paths with his bible in hand as both fired at the same instant. Carriage's bullet hit the side of the blazing church as Bevan's bullet, meant for the Sheriff, found Pastor Bolt instead. Bolt fell to his knees still clutching the blood-stained bible. Looking up through the flames, Carriage could no longer see Bevan. The townspeople arrived and rallied around the sheriff, with the dead pastor now face down in the sand. Carriage was proclaimed a hero for shooting Bolt. Something he never did.

Carriage then took out a leather envelope from his coat. Maggie could see "Mine No. 8" written on it. Then an explanation came to her. Sheriff Carriage had given his daughter to Bevan in exchange for the deed to Mine No. 8. It was the shaft Vera found herself in when she went through the mausoleum door. It was made clear to Carriage that it was indeed a productive vein. Bolt's torching the church sealed the entrance to that mine and any riches that were to come from it. Carriage must have thought Bevan was in with Bolt and they burned both the church and his daughter, sealing the mine to swindle Carriage. The Sheriff fired at Bevan in desperate anger but missed. In a twist of fate Bevan's bullet found Pastor Bolt, who now lay dead in the churchyard.

Maggie opened her eyes back in her room with Jack. She laid there staring at the ceiling trying to place it all in sequence. Then she said aloud, "The wall. The corner brick. Did that just happen?"

Jack momentarily woke up after hearing Maggie speak. "What's up, babe?" he asked her while turning over.

Still staring at the ceiling, Maggie softly said, "I saw it, Jack. I just saw it all."

"Saw what?" Jack asked.

"Jack, I think I found out what was meant by me not knowing what I was. I let myself go back to the night of the fire. I saw Bevan shoot Bolt. Carriage sold his daughter to Bevan, supposedly to take her back to Germany to live with the wealthy Waechters in exchange for the deed to Mine Number 8. Bevan was never going to take the Sheriff's daughter anywhere but down in the cellar where she would become one of the hundreds tortured. There's a passage into Bevan's cellar we never found. Carriage shot at Bevan outside the church at the same time Bevan shot at the Sheriff. Bolt got in the way and Bevan's bullet hit Bolt. Bevan left and the townspeople rallied around the Sheriff and hailed him a hero for shooting down the crazed preacher. That was the thunderous gunshot the townspeople heard. It was actually two shots fired at the same time."

Jack rolled over. "What? You just saw that?"

"Yeah," Maggie confessed. "Crazy, huh? This really

doesn't help us to know what happens now with the Sword. It does indicate a passage into Bevan's cellar. I think we need to see what's in there."

"You just laid there and conjured all that up?" Jack asked, still trying to soak it all in. "You can see into the past now? With clarity?"

"It was more like watching it from a distance. I can't really describe it. I know what I saw, and it makes sense."

"It makes sense but doesn't add up," Jack concluded. "Those four girls never made it out of the fire, according to history, yet you're saying they did. It's not jelling."

Jack's cross-examination made sense. Now Maggie had to decide whether or not to believe her own vision, or let logic play its part and go with the obvious. But, as Maggie so well knew, with the paranormal there is no 'obvious.'

Maggie was up early the next morning after not sleeping well. When Lovey got up, Maggie gave her a complete run down of what had happened in her vision. Lovey was floored. Maggie had indeed come into her own. She was not only capable of remote viewing, she could do it after something had already happened as long as she was involved, like Vera. Her saying she was "involved" somewhat in the 1802 fire was true. She had just visited it and observed another version of what she was told. Lovey wondered if that was the extent of her involvement or was there more to it? Was she there in another capacity as someone else?

The revelation that Vera was Rebecca Middlebrook in another life was enough to scare most people off into a panic. Maggie wanted more answers. She'd soon feel them coming, but it was going to be a challenge.

When Jack came back to Randall without Vera and Wood, he said that something would happen in two days. Two days was now here. This night was it and she knew she'd be face to face with Bevan before it ended. She told herself she was ready; she just didn't know for what.

Chapter 18

SHOWTIME

Vera and Wood left the motel at nightfall and began their trip to the old tool shed at the Fredericksburg Cemetery. Wood drove along the roadway as Vera sat next to him with her eyes closed and her hands folded neatly in her lap.

"You okay, kiddo?" Wood asked.

"Yeah. I'm good." Vera could sense the anguish in Wood's voice as he did not want to be going where they were going but had little choice.

It had been a while since Wood had smoked any pot which led him to get flashes and visions more frequently now. He kept everything tucked away as not to alert Vera, but since arriving in Fredericksburg, Vera had come into her own as a lady of vision and had moved into seeing her potential as a focused witch. It was something she would come to know as both sword and shield.

"Don't be panicked about tonight, Wood. Everything will unfold like it's supposed to." Vera let her hand reach out and land on top of his. "Thank you for staying here with me in Virginia. I know you didn't want to. Last year you were given a choice, and now you're re-living it. You didn't do anything wrong."

"Then why does it feel like I did?" Wood asked. "Every time I see that tool shed it comes back. I see the amulet, everyone was there and then it was as plain as day, I had to smash it."

"That's because you're one of the good guys. People are given a thousand choices daily. They define us and push us to go in places we wouldn't normally go and do things totally foreign to us. Hope Blanch wanted you for balance. She needed you so she could be reborn in you. If you'd taken over as High Priest, we wouldn't be here today, Jack and Maggie wouldn't still be together, and Lovey would be dead."

Wood was shocked. "What? Wait a minute, what does that mean? Lovey dead? Why? How?" Wood's demeanor had changed to one of alarm at the thought of losing Lovey.

"It would be the final move into your new position. Hope would have asked you to sacrifice her as a gift of loyalty. Her soul for more power. Eventually you would have lost all your humanity, even conceiving of killing Maggie and Grace. See? None of it happened because you simply made a choice at the right time."

Wood was stunned. He couldn't imagine himself ever hurting Lovey or Grace. Maggie was unthinkable. He let his hands sink into the steering wheel and tried to imagine himself taken over like that. He couldn't. That was too big of a jump for Wood as he just shook his head.

"Bevan," Vera began, "…is a Master Spirit. That's a spirit that controls other spirits. He became evil incarnate from the witch trials. He took hundreds of women into his cellar and did what he chose for how long he chose until all that death and pain came to a climax and swallowed him. He wanted power, but dark magic is something that happens when all hope is gone. Bevan created that situation over and over. Now he exists in the echoes of the pain he created."

Wood understood the situation well. "And you think you know how to send this centuries old pain monger back to where he needs to be for another hundred and ten years? Vera, I want to help you and be there for you but damn, I'm pretty freaked out about all this and I'm seeing shit. You know it, I can tell. It's like I'm walking down a road and I can see places and people from long ago. I'm somebody else. I turn it off when I get too deep, but man, I wish Lovey was here."

"You're seeing through the eyes of someone else, Wood. Let it come. We may be able to see something to get us through all this."

Vera removed her hand from Wood's. "You'll see Lovey soon enough." Then she sat back in her seat and got quiet.

Wood glanced over at Vera and let his mind race to the "what if." He was trying to anticipate the events that were to unfold but was lost in so many scenarios he let out a deep sigh and just kept driving, at last pulling up to the curb down the road from the cemetery. It was now dark, and they hoped everyone would be away from the tool shed they needed to get to.

"You ready for this?" Vera asked Wood.

"Not really," Wood admitted, "...but since we're here..."

With that, Vera gave Wood a look and they both exited the rental car.

"Walk slowly," Wood advised. "We're just family walking up to a graveyard. Nothing out of the ordinary."

Vera smiled at Wood's cautiousness. He was indeed her knight at the moment. Wood, if tasked, would give his own life for Vera's. She knew that and took it in as a strength.

They walked through the graveyard in a casual stroll that would lead them to the tool shed. At its entrance, the two stopped and glared at the lock that was now on the tool shed door.

"Houston, we have a problem," Wood observed. "We gotta get that lock unlocked."

Vera looked at the lock hanging there and reached out to it. She let her middle finger barely touch the outside as she ran her finger up and down the shiny steel that held them currently at bay, and then "click." The lock fell open.

"Holy moly! Vera, that's handy. How did you...?" Wood stopped as he saw the blank expression on her face as she removed the lock and let it fall to the ground, then pushed open the door and stepped inside. Wood picked up the lock, put it in his pocket and followed Vera inside, closing the door behind them.

Wood went to the closet, cleared the way, then pulled the release lever to open the trap door leading down to the forgotten home of Daniel, Hope, Pamela and now Rebecca Brook Blanch.

"I hate this place," Wood admitted as he closed the trap door behind them.

After the two hit the ground, Wood lit a little flashlight. "We got to keep the lights down in here. Someone outside may be able to see. We can't take that chance."

Vera looked around the room and up at the ceiling. "Wood feel this. This room is now acting like the room Mrs. Jenkins showed me and the Bethel Church basement. We are between worlds. Your light won't matter now. No one will see."

Vera walked to the brick wall that was disturbed when Rebecca was found and put her hand out to feel the cold hard stone.

"I have to meditate now," she said. "It won't be long."

"Go for it," Wood acknowledged. "Don't mind me. I'm just scared shitless over here."

Vera feigned a smile and got into meditation mode. They both knew something was coming. Neither wanted it to.

Maggie was at the house in Randall when she heard a whisper in her head.

"Maggie," came the first one. Maggie stopped and wondered if what she'd heard was real. Then again, "Maggie, listen to me."

Maggie sat down in her room and closed her eyes. "Vera, I can hear you," she thought.

"Maggie, the time is here. Go to the church. Bring Grace, Jack and Lovey. He's waiting for us."

Wanting to verify exactly who was waiting for them came to mind as she'd just received a thought from someone states away. Trying to grasp what may lay ahead was now rapidly becoming all too real. Maggie Styles gathered herself and walked down the stairs.

Trying not to show too much anxiety, she decided to go over the top.

"Showtime! We need to go to the church now."

"Now?" Jack questioned. "Already there."

"How do you know, Maggie?" Lovey asked.

"Vera is getting ready in Virginia. We need to do our part."

"Our part?" Jack answered. "Does she mean to say we know what that is?"

"Let's get there," Grace injected. "We will know what to do when the time comes."

Jack asked the obvious. "So how do we know to do all this?"

"I can hear Vera now," Maggie sighed.

"Did you hear from Wood?" Lovey asked.

The ride to the church was quick and they had lost their desire for candid entry. Now was destiny's moment and they were right in the middle of it. God help anyone who interfered.

"Let's do this," Maggie said as they got out of the van.

"You sure do know how to show a guy a good time," Jack joked as they made their way to the front of the steps.

As Lovey was about to turn the key to open the door, she heard a rumble of thunder off in the distance. "Is that perfect, or what?" she asked as she nodded towards the thunder.

"Yeah," was all Maggie could say as they entered the church.

"Take this in, will you?" Grace commented as she looked around the church. "This is not just a night; this is something that has been in the works for a hundred-and-ten years." She turned to the others, "Take this in."

They all paused for a moment at what Grace was saying, then Maggie walked to the back and opened the small doorway. "Let's get this done," she snarled as she stepped through the door. Once landing on the dirt floor next to Bolt's casket, they all turned to her.

"What now, Mags?" Grace asked as she tried to focus in the dark.

The one thing each acknowledged was the absence of the casket Cat left in. They all remembered seeing it, but where it went with their counterpart, nobody dared make a guess.

"Sit here," Maggie instructed.

They all took a seat on the dirt floor beside Bolt's casket.

"I need a minute," she confided.

Maggie closed her eyes, took a deep breath and let the world turn around her for a few minutes. Her breathing steadied, then she opened her eyes.

"Soon Vera will let us know what to do. This room here, this basement of this church is connected to the Blanch home in Virginia. They are both rooms between worlds. Through time, Vera will know when to come through."

"Vera will let us know what to do?" Grace bantered. "Good lord, what are we?"

Maggie looked up at Grace and answered, "Witches. That's what we are. You know it, Grace, as does Lovey. We are part of a magic that's older than we can guess. We have an obligation to do what we can to balance out an equation. An evil power has come to fruition in our time and we can't have that, and you know it."

Jack sat looking at the girls. "I'm sorry, but I'm not a witch. Buzz kill! You guys may be, but I'm just an ex-cabin salesman from Georgia."

"When you are with me," Maggie confided, "You share any powers I have. You're part of me now, Jack Reynolds. My power is yours."

Jack heard what Maggie was saying, but how exactly all that worked was a little overwhelming at the moment.

Grace hung her head and took a deep breath. Releasing it she leaned back while still sitting on the dirt floor in front of Bolt's casket and admitted, "Good lord. It's true. I've never said the words because I thought it was Hope back then. The things I did, the things I simply assumed would happen and they did. I'm a witch. A broom flying, spell casting, ugly nosed witch. Well, shit. There goes my day."

Jack looked at Grace and quipped, "Dude, you have a broom?"

The wall they were sitting by began to vibrate as dust fell from the bricks.

Jack stood up. "You seeing that? Something's shaking this place."

"The wall!" Maggie shouted. "Get away from it!"

They all got up and backed away. The church wall was now humming as it vibrated.

"What's happening?" Grace shouted.

The bricks began to emit a white light that was bright, but not hard to look at. They backed up a step as the swirling began to form a funnel as the wall took on a transparency that allowed them to see Vera and Wood on the other side.

"Wood!" Lovey called out. "I can see you. My goodness!"

Wood and Vera were fighting off their own bombardment of light. Looking up through the swirls, Vera steadied herself.

"Something's happening!" Grace yelled out.

The wall was consumed by the swirling light and faded into nowhere as the two rooms, both between worlds, collided.

The five now stood on the same dirt floor that stretched across both rooms and into Bevan's cellar. The pulpit was there like it was at the beginning in Vera's vision. Then a voice: "Through time, we are together again. We will always be together, until there is no time."

The voice echoed through the cavern as footsteps could be heard coming behind them. Jack reached down and picked up a shovel as a hooded figure came around the corner. Maggie put out her arms as to shield the others from who she knew was now with them. The hooded figure walked in and made its way up to Maggie.

"Pamela," the figure said in a deep voice. Then with a pull of the hood Maggie was looking into a familiar face.

Lovey, Grace and Jack all said at once, "Cat?"

Jack stepped forward and asked the obvious; "Cat, what is going on?"

Maggie warned him. "That's not Cat, Jack. Not the Cat we knew, anyway."

Grace asked, "Maggie, what's going on? Is that Cat or not?"

"It's Bevan," Maggie confirmed.

Bevan, using Cat's body, stepped towards them. "I'm taking her like I took the others. Hundreds of others. They begged and screamed to get back to their miserable lives. I gave them purpose."

Maggie stood her ground as she confronted her adversary. "Bevan Nicholas Waechter, I presume."

"Hello Pamela." Maggie heard Cat's voice, but knew it was Bevan.

"I've come back for you. You'll serve me, like your pitiful father was supposed to serve Hope Blanch until he gave into weakness and forfeited her power."

"My father is not weak. Damn you!" Maggie yelled.

"Too late," Cat snarled. "Already there."

Maggie was on the border of rage when she heard Vera's voice in her head.

"Maggie. Maggie don't fight him. It's Bevan. He's taken Cat's body. She's still in there. It's the hour Maggie. The one hundred and tenth anniversary of the fire. We have to act now."

"Pamela. Pamela Blanch," Maggie said to him. "I once lived as Pamela Blanch?"

"Yes, you did," Bevan stated with authority. "We all have been around. Except you!"

Bevan's eyes were glowing a hot red as he pointed at Jack. "You aren't part of this."

Jack stepped up to Bevan with little expression. "If Maggie is involved, then I'm involved."

Bevan walked over to Grace. "You. I've watched you. I've seen you fight things that were out of your control, still you lingered on, trying to find answers other than the ones I gave you. You served Hope well. You brought her souls and did her deeds. Why do you fight me now?"

Grace felt frightened at first, then she unloaded. "I don't fight you. I don't even acknowledge you. You exist deep in the psyche of us all and pull strings we never knew we had. You try and manipulate us through fear. Fear and curiosity."

"Curiosity?" Bevan recoiled. "Curiosity. I suppose there is a fascination with the weak. You people are taken in so easily. You believe what you are shown. I had hundreds of women who appeared mortally dead but were not. People believed the act. I hung the women, yes, but they were never really in any harm, until they woke up here. In this place is where it all began. In a way I was born here."

"Yeah, and in a way you'll die here as well," Jack said defiantly.

"You're not part this you pitiful man!" Bevan responded, still in Cat's body.

"You want us to fear you?" Jack laughed out loud. "Like the good Pastor Bolt here feared you? He never feared you, he defied you and died while doing it. There is a difference. I don't think you squeezed as much fear out of him as you think you did. He was a man of faith. It's hard to break that."

"He was a fool!" Bevan shouted through Cat. "A man of faith who had no idea of his ancestry. Bolt was convinced his clairvoyance came to him through his faith in his God. As he grew in power, he took it to come from some Heavenly deity. Jeremiah Bolt came from a long line of warlocks. He never had a teacher, just a belief in a God that he was convinced would help him clear the evil that his own ancestors shared for centuries."

"What?" Jack got up to walk over to Bolt's casket. "We read what he wrote in his bible. Cat, you're still in there. It was you who mentioned the wildflowers. Remember how you said a man who sat reading in a field of wildflowers couldn't be all that bad? You see? Bolt had a choice. He knew he had abilities but made the choice to turn them into acts of good, not evil. You had the same choice. As for who or whatever is inside you, look at you now, living out what meager existence you can masquerading as a little girl. Pretty sad."

"Sad?" Bevan echoed.

Maggie could feel the anger that was taking the room as Cat stepped forward and confronted Jack. "Sad? You call me sad? You have nothing! You're a weak little nothing with only a witch with great potential at your side. You cower behind her and use her flesh for your own enjoyment. There are far better pleasures you could use her for, but you have not the will nor the courage to accept what you would find out about your own self."

Vera and Wood were watching all this unfold. The rooms had joined, and Wood slowly took steps toward Lovey. Standing beside her, he reached out and took her hand. Vera was frozen. Staring down what was left of Cat; her lover, her friend, her everything.

"This is about me, isn't it?" Vera said as she approached Cat. "This is why we are together? So you can do what? Be reborn?"

"That's not Cat," Lovey reminded Vera. "It's Bevan."

Wood released Lovey's hand and slowly walked over to Bolt's casket. He was looking down into the aged face of the dead pastor.

Bevan asked Wood, "Why do you look at that fool?"

Wood stood quietly by Bolt. Maggie watched him, waiting. Something was up and she knew it. Wood glanced at Jack and then to Maggie. As he did the ground began to tremble.

"It's here," Bevan said defiantly. "The time is now. One hundred and ten years is now over. I'm alive!"

As the ground shook it began to split. In earthquake fashion the ground laid itself open as the six people in the now conjoined rooms stood in awe. Flames began to shoot out of the crevasse but released no heat. Maggie could see into the opening and heralded, "It's the church fire! I can see it. It's 1802."

The six watched as the flames parted. They could see the four women inside the now flaming church going from window to window trying to escape as they screamed in desperation. The door to the cellar was locked shut. Then, a man. Bevan! They could see him come from the shadows, unlock the door and take the women down the stairs into the basement to his personal chamber where torches and time awaited. The fire raged hotter

Wood yelled out, "The girls! They went down into the cellar with Bevan! Maggie, that can't be. The paper said it took days to find what was left of the bodies. There has to be bodies...."

It was then Wood looked over at the black plastic bags that lay against the far wall that Maggie feared would someday be found from the Abigail Long trials.

"Jack!" Wood yelled out. "The bodies! Help me!"

Jack looked at the bodies in the back and into the crevasse. He got what Wood was saying and he ran to help. One by one Wood and Jack threw the black plastic bags into the opening and watched as they descended through time to land on the floor of the now blazing church.

Vera stood defiantly and said, "Through the Sword, windows are opened, and deaths are erased."

Wood turned to the wall where Rebecca's body was hidden and then to Hope Blanch's resting place in the far wall.

"No!" Vera shouted. "They have to stay here."

With the walls now heaving, Bevan walked to the edge of the flames with hands high in the air. "Life!"

Jack looked at Grace. "Lock and key. It said in your book your grandmother gave you that under the Sword, windows are opened, and deaths are erased. It's a lock and key, remember?"

Vera was walking toward Maggie. She had the sword in her hand behind her, hiding it from Bevan.

Wood turned to Jack and whispered, "She has the Sword."

He then put his hand in his pocket and felt the lock he put in there when he and Vera entered. She touched it and it fell open. He felt it in his hand and realized, "Keys need an exact fit to work. The mold. That's the key! That Sword is looking for the mold that made it."

Frantically looking around the room Wood called out, "If that's the key, we need the lock. The mold has to be the lock."

Maggie went within herself. If she had a power other than what she knew, now was the time to recognize it. She looked down at Bolt laying in his casket with his gaze looking down towards his feet. Suddenly it hit her. She walked over to Bolt and reached under his head to see what was making him look down and felt a box. She pulled it out and slowly began to open it as a light shown from inside. A mold to a small sword with the same lettering that was both on the casket and on the keypad at Bevan's mausoleum revealed itself.

"That's it!" Wood yelled. "Jack, that's why someone buried Bolt down here. It was to hide the mold, not him!"

Maggie heard Vera in her head as Vera stood stoic as the scene unfolded around her. "Maggie, stand ready. Hold open the mold case."

Bevan saw what was happening and stood in front of the opening. A loud gunshot could be heard coming from the flames.

"That's Bolt getting shot!" Jack yelled.

As the words left Jack's mouth, the sound of pain could be heard coming from the casket. They all turned to see movement. A hand reached up from inside and then a man, youthful and very much alive, raised up and stood before them.

Maggie's eyes widened and everyone stepped back. "Jeremiah Bolt?"

The Pastor got out of the casket and began to approach Bevan in front of the crevasse.

"Holy shit!" Wood heralded. "He's alive!"

"You!" Bevan shouted at Bolt. "You are long dead. You do not belong here. Back to the ground..."

As the words were leaving Bevan's mouth, something interrupted him. Grace yelled out in pain and had to steady herself against a timber.

"Grace?" Wood yelled out. He went to her and held her up.

"I'm okay," she said to Wood.

Bevan stood in Cat's body trying to speak when a light blue glow began to take the room. Confronting the now resurrected Jeremiah Bolt, Bevan seemed to be in pain. He dropped to his knees as the glow became more intense.

Lovey called out, "Maggie? What's happening?"

Maggie looked at Vera who seemed to be fighting something off as well.

Bevan cried out, "No! You witch, you are part of me now! You are in my soul! You are in my…"

They watched as Bevan in Cat's body fell to his knees in agony and began to convulse. The blue glow darkened as Bevan turned to the corridor. A figure approached them from around the corner. It was an old woman with her face looking down at the ground as she walked in, every eye was on her.

Bevan became enraged and pointed at the figure. "You are mine! You are part of me!"

The woman stood at the cellars' entrance. Her voice came thundering into the room as everyone cringed at the volume. "You will release her!"

Bevan countered with, "You are of me now, woman! You gave yourself to me. I am your life now, witch!"

The woman turned to Vera. As their eyes met, her lips could be read saying a silent, "Rebecca."

"Mother," Vera instinctively heard herself say.

"Mother?" Wood echoed. He studied the woman and their situation. At last he said coldly, "Hope Blanch."

Everyone stood in shock.

"Hope Blanch?"

Maggie assessed the situation and had no clue what was unfolding. Here, by some means, Hope Blanch had appeared in the flesh. The witch that had controlled them for most of their lives was now here in the fight alongside them.

Bevan appeared to be regaining his composure. "We made a deal, you lying witch. Now that deal is going to hell with all of you."

Bolt began a slow walk to the crevasse. The flames roared from the 1802 fire and shot out around Bevan as he stood in front of the flames. Hope fixed her eyes on Vera's and walked to her. Hope reached up and removed the locket from around Vera's neck and almost seemed to smile. Vera looked back into the eyes of the two-century old spirit in front of her and whispered the words from the locket, "For mother, always, Rebecca."

A mother's love goes beyond time. It's a bond that is set in stone at its creation and survives countless bombardments of life's trials throughout. Here in a musty cellar between worlds, a mother two centuries old reached out and touched her creation.

Hope turned and moved towards Bolt. She stood beside him in front of Bevan who was using Cat as a vehicle for his tortured soul.

Bolt turned to Maggie and reached out his hand.

"Give him the mold, Maggie," came into her head. It was Vera coming closer. "Give it to him."

Bevan shouted at Bolt. "You and that lying witch do not belong in this time, this place! It's mine. I need more life, more souls!"

Maggie held out the mold and Bolt took it. He swiftly moved towards the flames and turned to Vera. Bolt opened the box and held it in front of his chest. He turned to Bevan, feigned a smile, reached out and took Hope's arm and began to fall backwards through the opening into the flames as Bevan yelled, "Go back to the ground you fools!" As he fell, Vera revealed the Sword and raised it over her head.

Jack yelled, "Now, Vera! Now!"

Vera threw the sword at the mold the now falling Pastor held up. As the Sword left her hand, Bolt dropped the mold into the flames, letting the Sword fly precisely into his heart. An explosion of light came from the wound as it engulfed both Pastor Bolt and Hope as they fell back into the flaming abyss. Hope pointed at Grace as she fell and commanded, "Serve me once more!" With his hand on the Sword in his chest, Bolt could be heard saying, "The Sword of God has won...."

The crevice began to close as Bolt reached out and grabbed Bevan in Cat's body, pulling her with them into the void. She let out a chilling scream as they all descended. The ground closed. In a moment, it was over.

The wall returned and the scenery around them reverted back to present day. Maggie, Jack, Wood, Lovey, Vera and Grace stood breathless looking around the hazy room.

Vera stood quiet as the shock of the event passed. She tried to come back to the reality of where she was both in time and place. Oddly, she could feel her sensitivity begin to cool. The visions and whispers that had driven her the past week were now absent. Her mind was clearing. Vera Chase was on her way back.

"She's gone," Vera whispered. "He took her. Bolt took Cat with him."

Lovey took her first breath after the event. She heard Vera's voice and understood. Trying to focus and being glad they were all still alive she tried to calm Vera and herself as well.

"No, Bolt took Hope and Bevan with him. I guess Cat was collateral damage. She chose this, remember?"

Vera was still trying to recoup from what had happened.

"Because she got into the casket on her own, she chose this. She chose it for me. Cat got into the casket trying to find me and now she's gone. I know the object of the game was to stop Bevan, but my girlfriend just fell into a flaming crevasse."

Vera took a deep sigh and looked at Maggie. "If I'm really a witch I can now tell you firsthand that witches feel things. The heart of a witch has great power to love. They also feel the loss of that love with great depth." Staring into the dim light of the musty room Vera admitted, "I never knew that until now."

Jack went to Maggie and wrapped his arms around her. "You okay?"

Maggie smiled back and nodded.

Wood was looking at the empty space where the four bodies were. They were gone. He felt a sense of relief come with a thousand questions. He'd learn to live with most. "Holy moly, it was her. It was Hope Blanch. I stood on the same ground with her and yet I never felt the need to kneel.

There was a time when I would have done anything for her. She was my queen."

Wood stopped and remembered Vera telling him Maggie, Lovey, Grace and Jack would be out of his life if he'd not refused Hope's amulet. He would have sacrificed them in return for more power and status as a warlock and lost more than those closest to him, but what bit of humanity he himself still harbored would be extinguished for something far more sinister; power and recognition. That direction was as foreign to him now as he could imagine, and he was free. He told himself then and there he'd closed the door on her. Hope Blanch was now in his past.

Wood kicked the dirt floor in front of him. "I thought we'd seen it all when I smashed the amulet last year. Man, we were just getting started. I don't know how to feel. Part of me wants to say we beat the bad guy and the other part wants to go get Cat. How can that happen? We need to get her back somehow. There's no way we can just walk away from this with her… wherever the hell she is."

Grace gathered herself. She had stayed silent since the shock of Hope pointing at her, commanding her, "Serve me once more!" It rattled her big time. Almost frozen with fear, she at last put something to words.

"Holy Lord, what did we just see? It was her. It was actually Hope Blanch. She pointed at me." Looking at Wood she asked, "What did that mean, Wood? Serve me once more?" She's dead in that crack with Bolt. How can I serve her? I was once like you. I called her queen. I'd have done anything for her. And Jeremiah Bolt? He was long dead and came back to life when the guns fired. I once called her queen and would have…", Grace stopped herself and turned to Maggie. "…Done anything for her. She told me to serve her once more. What the hell does that mean? As for Bevan this marks the one-hundred-and-ten-year anniversary. It was the time of Bolt's death. That started the clock. At that moment he came back, rose up out of that casket and sacrificed himself and Hope? Is that what he did? Maggie? What was that?

Where did they go? They are now in 1802 Randall, aren't they?"

"Bolt was the lock," Maggie confirmed. "We knew the Sword needed a lock and that lock was here, somewhere. It turns out Bolt himself was what the Sword wanted. If Jack hadn't thought to dig him up, Bevan would still be in this world."

Maggie turned to Jack. "Everyone here knows what they are capable of except you. You came here with no magic, no history or any idea where all this would lead. On your own, using only your intuition, you managed to find Bolt, shed light on a two-hundred-year-old mystery and while doing it, unveiled the lock to the key that would eventually send Bevan back to the land of the dead. Thank you, Jack Reynolds. You saved us all."

"Me?" Jack sounded. "I think Vera here gets credit for throwing that sword." Turning to Vera he asked, "How did you throw it so precisely?"

Vera was coming back to her normal personality. She was still trying to clear her head. "I threw it, Hope guided it."

Lovey was shaken. She knew her regressions were helpful to people, but this was off the map. All her clairvoyance and meditations had not prepared her for what she'd just seen as now they all would be forever changed. She took a breath and turned to Grace.

"Grace, you know that our bodies are only vessels in this lifetime. When we are done with them, or they with us, we move on to another plane and time. Bolt and Hope have done that. Maybe they're ghosts or something, I don't know, but it does show us that the man who collected wildflowers wasn't all that bad. He dedicated his spirit to keeping Bevan out of the real world. At his death he could have moved on but chose to stay here to do battle with Bevan every one-hundred-and-ten years. He does have eternal life, only now it's with a mission."

"What about the tool shed in Virginia?" Grace asked. "Are Hope and Rebecca exposed?"

"It doesn't matter now," Jack clarified. "Even if someone finds those bodies they won't be connected to Maggie. They are two hundred years old. Hope and Rebecca were long dead before Maggie was even born." Turning to Maggie he smiled. "Congratulations Abigail Long. No victims, no crimes."

It was a relief to say the least. Maggie was virtually out of the hot seat when it came to the missing students. They were now lost in time. Victims of a two-hundred-year-old curse that a crazed pastor took a step too far. Maggie was feeling a wave of release.

"Dad, you saved me. Throwing those bodies in the crevasse was genius. They are now part of history. I can't believe it. Those were the four bodies history recorded the townspeople exhumed from the church fire, burned beyond recognition. We always knew somehow we would have to deal with those four bodies. In 1802 nobody would have recognized a male body from a female body if it were burned to a crisp, which is, I guess, what they were. Indeed, under the Sword, windows are opened, and deaths are erased. At least the bodies are, anyway. The deaths will haunt me and a lot of other people for a long time to come. Count on it."

"What now?" Wood asked. "We going to stand here all night?"

Looking around the room Wood spoke for them all when he said, "Good riddance you musty ass basement."

As the six were exiting the church, Maggie noticed the sound of their footsteps had changed somewhat. The echoing sound of a hollow basement was gone and as they walked, it felt solid.

Maggie spoke up. "No boom. Listen, it sounds solid now."

Jack went back to the door to the basement and found only a smooth empty panel. He pushed and prodded, but the door was gone. He shook his head as he walked back to the others. "Door's gone. I guess that pretty much seals up the basement at Bethel Church."

"It was all for Bevan," Vera sighed.

Lovey was with them. "Good riddance indeed, but this could keep going around in circles forever."

Wood looked up at Grace with a look she'd seldom seen. "Thank you, Grace. If you had not brought your book, we'd never have figured all this out. We owe you for that. Don't forget it. Thank you."

With that Wood reached out and took the back of Grace's hand and kissed it as Jack had done back at the Grizz.

Grace heard herself say, "I love you, too, you freaky little nut case."

Vera didn't go to the van with the others. It was the middle of the night and she was heading straight for the back of the cemetery to Rebecca's grave. The others said nothing. They realized where she was going and they all followed. As it came into view under a moonlit night sky Vera sped up her gait. There on Rebecca's tombstone were the wildflowers Mrs. Jenkins had given her. They were back.

Maggie saw the flowers. "Hey, look at that. A thank you from beyond?"

Vera took the flowers and held them. "Just a hello from Mrs. Jenkins. She is resting now."

Lovey turned to Maggie and Grace. "She's got skills."

Grace looked at Vera. "Yeah, and we've got some catching up to do. What do you say you come up to the mountains for a while before school starts? It's beautiful up there."

"Agreed," Jack admitted. "It's home."

The following daybreak found the six exhausted people in the living room of the big house in Randall having fallen into their own spaces. Wood rolled a joint, lit it and announced, "I'd like to propose a toast."

"A toast to what?" Jack asked as he waited for Wood's come back.

"I'd like to propose a toast to us," Wood said defiantly.

As he took his first hit off the joint, Vera looked at him and smiled. Wood took another hit and then passed it to Jack.

He remembered letting Vera in on his "medicinal" use for the weed. It did keep the visions down and at that moment Vera was glad Wood found a way to cope with himself, something everyone needs.

Maggie reflected, "We all played a role in this. Lovey's insights with helping Vera regress to find answers was and is crucial. Dad's determination to stay in Fredericksburg with Vera was heroic, Grace bringing her book that led us to the Sword, Jack seeing more than a dirt floor in the basement, Vera and Cat, well need I say more."

Everyone got quiet at the mention of Cat who had fallen with Jeremiah into the past. It would be another hurdle explaining it to whom ever asked about her.

"And you!" Lovey barked at Maggie. "If you hadn't fluffed up the Mayor, we'd never be here."

And then the laughter began. Another moment of release. The wave went around the room until fatigue claimed the day. It was time to crash.

Jack sat back in his chair and reminded Wood, "Hey, you do realize there is a rental car somewhere near the Fredericksburg Cemetery with my name on it, unless you thought to return it."

Wood replied, "Her fault," as he pointed to Vera. "She wanted to stay."

Jack confessed, "I've got to get some sleep."

"I hear that," Wood seconded. "Why don't we re-group in a few hours and..." Wood stopped mid-sentence. Then, "Cat!"

"Cat?" Everyone answered.

Everyone turned around to see Cat coming down the big staircase.

"Holy shit! She's back!" Wood sounded.

Getting up, they all walked towards her. Cat was yawning and stretching in a just woken up state. Seeing Vera and the others looking at her, she asked, "Vee? How'd you get out of the mausoleum?"

"Cat?" Jack asked. "Are you, you?"

Cat was confused. "What? How did we get back here? We were at the church and… that's all I remember."

"You got in the casket," Maggie reminded her. "When we left you stayed and got in. What happened after that? Do you remember?"

"I got in? In the casket? Why the hell did I do that?" Cat asked still dazed. "It must have been that damn pot. Wood's crazy great weed blew me away and I don't remember much. You say I got into the casket?"

"Yes, you did," Maggie stated. "And you don't remember anything?"

"She wouldn't." Lovey reasoned. "If Bevan came into her then it was always his play."

Cat looked at Lovey. "Have you found anything in the Bible we can use yet? That's the last thing I remember, Lovey going through Bolt's bible. Did you find anything to help us send him back to 1802?"

They all realized Cat didn't know anything about what they'd all been through. To her, Bevan was still an adversary to be dealt with.

"We did it, Cat," Jack said. "We sent Bevan back to where he needs to be."

"You did?" Cat asked. "How? Was it in the book? Was it really The Sword of God that did it?"

"I'll fill you in," Lovey assured her. "We need to let the dust settle on this first."

Cat walked over to Vera and asked again, "Vee? You okay? How'd you get out of that stupid mausoleum? Come here." With that Cat wrapped her arms around Vera and laid her head on her chest. "You scared the shit out of me, you know that? Don't do that again." Cat looked up at Vera and again asked, "How'd you get out?"

"Never mind that," Jack began. "How did you get here? We watched you fall into a …"

Maggie raised up her hand. "There are things we are going to have to just accept. After seeing her fall with Bolt, anything is possible. We can only assume that after Bevan was returned to 1802 where he belonged, Cat didn't belong there and was returned here."

Vera nodded. "I ended up sitting on Rebecca's grave the same way."

"What?" Cat barked. "I was in 1802? When the hell was I in 1802? And Jack, where did I fall?"

Everyone was fascinated by Cat's loss of time. She didn't remember anything from the point she got into the casket.

Vera looked over at Lovey and shrugged.

"Later," Lovey mouthed.

"Is Bevan back where he should be?" Cat asked.

Jack confirmed it. "Yeah, for another one hundred and ten years, Bevan is under wraps."

"I'll fill you in later," Vera promised her. "You're not going to believe it, but I'll try."

They all stood looking at Cat. For all intents and purposes, she was dead to them; gone where she could never be found yet here she was wide-eyed asking questions about an event she was a part of. It was both a relief and a mystery.

The following day Grace had gotten up early and was ready to head back to Colorado. As she sat in the driveway of the big house everyone had gathered to see her off.

"Stay a while, Mom," Vera coaxed. "Why are you heading back so soon?"

"I have pot roast to make," she mused. "The mountain needs me, as does Pete, Sam and the Grizz. I have a place in this world and I'm getting back to it." Grace looked at Maggie, pulled her close and asked, "Is it done, Maggie? Is this the last of Bevan and Hope Blanch and all the shit that comes with them? I need all this behind me, as do we all."

"I can't say that, Grace. We thought we were done with it after Dad smashed Hope's amulet, but that wasn't the case. For now, go make pot roast."

Wood put his hand on the back of Grace's. "See you on the mountain, you old battle axe."

"Be careful, Wood," Grace said with a confidence. "See you up high."

Grace motioned for Lovey to come to the truck. As she approached, Grace held out the book she'd brought her grandmother gave her.

"Here. Keep this damn thing because I don't want to see it anymore. I was told I'd need it and know when and that time has passed. I'll leave it in your hands in case you want to see something in it. It's weird isn't it? I find out I'm a witch and here I am giving up my crystal ball."

Jack injected, "See? If you had your broom you could fly back."

With that, Grace waved a goodbye and headed off to Maggie Mountain. Wood stood there with a mournful expression as Grace's truck disappeared. Wood didn't like it. There was more to it and he felt it. It was in Grace's nature to want to go home, but so soon? Things weren't jelling.

As Grace made the left-hand turn towards home, she felt something come over her. It was subtle at first and then she caught herself in what was like a daydream. She shook her head and blinked. When she did, she looked over at a mileage sign. She'd just raveled twenty-eight miles and didn't remember any of it. She took a deep breath. "I've got to get some coffee."

Grace had turned a corner and was beginning to own her magic instead of fighting against it. She thought of Jeremiah Bolt raising up out of that casket and Hope Blanch, her former queen. Grace could see Bolt walking toward the crevasse, reaching out for the mold and then exploding into light as the Sword of God split his heart, ending a cycle to be played over and over every one-hundred-and-ten years. As Bolt and Hope fell, Grace could still hear Hope point to her and say, "Serve me once more," then the shrill scream Cat made as she was dragged from this world into the past.

"Bolt had magic, but made the choice to do good with it," she thought to herself. Grace had a long drive in front of her, in more ways than one.

Chapter 19

VERA GETS IT STRAIGHT

Lovey asked Vera, "Are you ready for your answers?"
Hesitantly, Vera nodded. It was time.

Jack wanted to know, "Answers? What answers? I thought we wrapped this up."

"Really," Cat agreed. "What more answers do you need?"

Maggie and Lovey had filled Cat in on current events. She was dumbfounded. Bolt and Hope Blanch coming back alive, then falling through a crevasse with flames shooting out of it? Then Bolt gets hit in the heart with The Sword of God that really did exist, then he grabs her and pulls her back with them to 1802? It was an earful.

Maggie and Lovey got a vibe that something was up with Vera. She seemed determined to find answers, but reluctant to tap back into what they'd all already gone through.

Lovey asked her, "What is it, Vera? Are you wanting to let all this lay?"

"No," she answered. "I cannot get on with my life with a big blank at the end of an equal sign. I have to find out why."

Jack was reluctant as well. "What do you need to know that is so important you can't leave it where it fell?"

Vera confessed, "I have to know what started this whole thing. When I was doing the ghost tour, Rebecca's voice came in my head and said, 'Have you sought the answer?' We did find Rebecca and we did stop Bevan, for now at least, but the answer is still out there: Why did Jeremiah Bolt chain those women in that church? We've seen the aftermaths of it, but the real motivation, the reasoning that made a man who collected wildflowers in bibles, or at least one bible, chain four young women up in Bethel Church in 1802 and set the place on fire, I have to find out."

"So how does this work?" Jack asked, hesitantly.

Maggie stepped up and said, "I need you here on this, Jack. Remember my powers are your powers?"

Jack had to laugh. "Yeah, is that like hot spotting off a cell phone? When I'm close to you I get a signal?"

Maggie was serious. "You need to understand it more, Jack. This is important."

Cat rolled her eyes. "Unbelievable. Out of the frying pan and back into the fire."

Maggie began to pace. "Dad, can you see your way to help us help Vera? We need you, and you know what I mean."

"You know what I mean?" Jack questioned. "You mean like warlock power magic shit?"

Lovey tried to calm the situation. "Look, I know it sounds crazy after what we've been through, but together we have a lot of vision. We can help Vera see and give ourselves a closer look as well. We need to do this. We both have the curse as does Grace. The blood of Bartholomew Campbell runs through our veins. I may be next in line for something we can't foresee, I'm not talking crazy here, Jack, you know. We need to see it."

Everyone sat quiet, then Jack asked the obvious; "When do we start?"

Maggie looked at everyone looking at her. "We do this now."

Wood declared, "I gotta burn one. I can't get in the spirit world without some degree of headication."

"Church!" Jack answered. "I'm in."

Lovey was pissed. "Are you guys listening to yourselves? This is serious."

"So are we!" Wood confirmed. "With the shit we just saw? I gotta get ready."

Cat was again reluctant. "That's my cue to go take a bath. You guys enjoy your dead friends. I'm not feeling any more reunions anytime soon."

Ten minutes later, Lovey, Wood, Maggie, Jack, and Vera were all sitting cross legged in the living room. Contrary to Lovey's wishes, everyone had gotten mildly stoned, even her. Now doors were unlocking as the six people gathered all their luck.

Jack sat next to Maggie, holding her hand. She told everyone they were going back to see through the eyes of Rebecca Brook Blanch.

"We will see what she saw, we will, to some degree, feel what she felt. She was a prisoner who was supposedly tortured under Bevan's hand. Are you all ready for this?"

Everyone looked around the circle at the others. A resounding "No!" followed. Maggie began to take deep breaths.

"It's 1802. We are seeing through Rebecca Brook Blanch's eyes. It's 1802, the night of the church fire in Randall, Arizona."

Nothing happened. Minutes passed, still nothing.

"I don't know what's wrong." she said sounding frustrated.

"I need you all on this. Together we can do this, I know we can. Look, we all have to be there in the past. Say it with me. It's 1802, the night of the Bethel Church fire. It's 1802 the night of the Bethel Church fire."

"Why are we doing this again?" Jack asked. "It's not working, babe."

Maggie tried to explain that remote visions happen when someone believes they can see something from a distance. You have to let go. Don't doubt it. It's like turning a knob on your radio and knowing it will come on. Be that sure. Now let's try this again. Please!"

"Why are you so into this?" Jack wanted to know. "Damn girl, maybe we all need a breather here. I know you want to help, but here we are trying to go back to open doors we seemed to have somehow closed. Does anyone else feel burned out? Is it just me?"

"I hear you, buddy," Wood sympathized. "Look, we are all hesitant. That's why the train won't go."

Everyone glanced at Maggie trying to be in control, but momentarily fragile from her own experiences.

"Okay, busted," she confessed. "I admit to being on guard, but if we don't let Vera see this, she'll never quit trying. We are not as strong as we were before the anniversary of the fire. We were all seeing beyond what we were used to."

"Amen to that!" Wood agreed.

Vera broke. "I feel terrible. I'm sorry to cause all this. It's because of me we are all here in the first place. I was fine, then Rebecca knocked on my door and everything went sideways. I can't ask any of you to go and do anything you don't want to because I know what we do and what we see seems all too real. That's our combined visions and that can come with carrying the memories of what we see as well. It's a risk. But we are witches and it's our right to see. So please, let's try once more. Maggie, I'm driving."

Maggie didn't say anything. Everyone sat repeating what Vera fed them. Over and over until the missing ingredient showed itself; belief. They had to believe it.

Vera's voice led the others down a road seldom traveled, then like falling into a dream, the sounds of a crowd could be heard. Trying to focus, Vera narrowed her "search" to the town square, then the gallows.

Vera and the others began to see the crowd of people that gathered in the town to watch the witches be hung. Rebecca was atop the gallows when a voice came. "Now Rebecca, be a good girl and die for the crowd." Then another voice; "May the Lord have mercy on your soul and save you from the grasp of Satan himself. I am sorry Rebecca."

Maggie stirred. It was Bolt! Jeremiah Bolt was on the gallows with Bevan. It made sense that a minister would be present at a public execution, but still they hadn't counted on it.

Bevan could be heard as he put his hand on the lever that would drop Rebecca to her supposed death. "Rebecca Brook Blanch, you are found guilty of witchcraft and sentenced to die this day,"

The vision was becoming blurred. Rebecca looked down at the woman with the Holy Water that stood by the gallows. Every woman was forced to drink some before they ascended the steps to the executioner. The water was drugged with a sedative that knocked the women out as their time came. The women had been starved for three days to purify them, so the drug worked fast. Rebecca was in the throes of the effects as she passed out. Bevan pulled the lever.

The next vision was of Rebecca waking up. She could feel someone taking a harness of some sort off her back. Still trying to focus, she felt Bevan. "Rebecca. You died well tonight. Now, you're mine."

Maggie and the rest could feel the cold steel shackles as they were forced on Rebecca's wrists. Weeks passed in fast forward as the vision saw Rebecca and two others shackled against the wall of Bevan's cellar. One morning as the women awaited their usual torment, Bevan approached them and said, "You're a part of me now. You serve me. You live for me. I am all you know, all you think, all you want. You are now mine until I deem you useless. After that, we'll find some more satisfying ways of using our time together."

The vision saw the women unshackled and cleaned up. Robes were given to them as they were told never to show their faces in public. Hoods were drawn so the cloaking was complete. As they stood taking in their new roles, four more women were brought in and shackled.

"Service these things. Feed them, water them, keep them alive. They are for me when I decide."

Why he had opted to keep Rebecca and the other two women, Maggie and the others couldn't see. What seemed like an eternity for them was actually mere seconds to Vera. As the others watched with her, she could only anticipate what was to come.

The vision saw Rebecca and the other two women coming and going through the church. They carried covered buckets and jugs with food and water for the shackled women below. The townspeople whispered and pointed at the hooded women and tried to see their faces when opportunity came but were denied any reveal leading to their identity. These women were supposed to be dead from the hangman's noose. Obviously, they weren't.

Bolt was seen arguing with Bevan and pacing while his anguish and resentment mounted. Bevan was using his church as a front to his cellar where he eventually killed the women he stole from the gallows.

At last Bolt could contain it no longer and had to know who the women were. He stopped the three after they entered the church that hid the entrance to Bevan's cellar and the entrance to Mine Number 8. He grabbed Rebecca's arm and pulled back her hood.

"You!" he shouted.

Studying her face, he said, "Rebecca. I watched you hang. I saw you die with the rest of them…."

He then pulled the hoods off the other two women.

"I watched all of you hang! Witches! The Devil is at work here. The Devil and Bevan Waechter. You're a coven of Satan worshippers. That's why you live! That's why you come and go. You serve him! There's no hope for any of you now. Witches!"

The girls said nothing to Bolt. They replaced their hoods and silently continued down into the cellar with their food and water.

Days passed. Sheriff Jonathan Carriage was seen coming and going talking to Bevan. At last he showed up at the church with his daughter, Sara. Bolt watched as Carriage, Bevan and Sara went into the church, then returned to the street a short time later. Bevan gave Carriage a paper which he signed and placed in an envelope.

"The deed to Mine Number 8," came into everyone's head.

Maggie and the rest could see Bolt in deep prayer with his

hands clasped as he struggled with a solution to the evil that he was sure he'd been tasked by God to exterminate. He walked to the blacksmith barn, found a chain, picked it up and closed his eyes. When he opened them, they could tell Bolt was now on a mission.

Still sitting in a circle on the floor, Vera continued to carry the group through the events that lead to Bolt chaining the women and starting the fire.

Bolt went to the church and waited until the town was dark. All was quiet as the three women came to the church steps and stopped. Bolt could see Bevan walking towards them with Sara Carriage, the Sheriff's daughter. Bevan met the other three and instructed Sara to go with them. Bevan left as the four women entered the church.

As the doors closed, they could see Bolt holding the chain up as if he were sacrificing it, then he motioned it towards the door. The chain flew across the yard and wrapped itself around the door handles. Bolt then threw a lamp which exploded in flames. The dry wooden structure was consumed in minutes.

"The Sword of God has won out tonight!" Bolt began crying out. Then, like clockwork, Sheriff Carriage arrived, shielding himself from the flames.

"Goddammit preacher, what did you do?" It was then the screams of the women could be heard from inside. Carriage grabbed Bolt's coat and yelled to his face, "Who's in there you fool? Who's in there? Tell me or I'll shoot you right here and now!"

Bolt let his gaze burn into the Sheriff's eyes.

"They are all in there. Your daughter and the coven of witches that walks this town. Devil's work. No more!!"

"What?" Carriage yelled. He looked up at the blazing structure and screamed "Nooo!"

A man could be seen outside the church. Bevan! Carriage was sure Bevan was in with Bolt and had robbed him of his daughter and gold mine. He drew his gun while Bevan drew his at the same time. Both fired, producing a thunder that shook the town. Carriage's bullet hit the side of the church as Bolt stepped in front of Bevan heralding The Sword of God, taking the bullet meant for Carriage. Bolt fell forward into the churchyard.

Seconds later the townspeople arrived and gathered around Carriage for shooting the obviously crazed Pastor Bolt. Something he never did.

Maggie felt herself coming back. She slowly opened her eyes and looked around at the others.

"Holy moly," Wood asked, "Did everyone just see what I did?"

"Think so," Jack chimed in, trying to focus. "There you have it. The reasoning behind the fire. Bolt was sure the women were a coven of witches. It looks like Bolt was really a witch himself. That was what that was, when he did the thing with the chain and torch?"

"Yeah," Maggie answered. "That's what that was."

Maggie had gotten a replay of what she'd seen earlier when she first tried her projected viewing. This regression confirmed her recollection of what she'd seen. Silently, she felt a sense of relief that she now could indeed mine the past for answers.

Lovey was stirring trying to put it all to memory. "My goodness! It's all true. Bolt thought the three were evil, serving Bevan. They were more his hand maidens except for Rebecca. She was his pet. Sara Carriage was at the wrong place at the wrong time. She was the fourth. But if Bevan took the women down in the cellar, what happened to them after that? It was the bodies Jack and Wood dropped through the crevasse that were found days later."

"More so still," Vera began, "We owe it to ourselves to find out who the other two women were. We know Rebecca and Sara Carriage, but who were the other two?"

"Vera, darlin', to be frank, who cares? Let this be," Jack coaxed. "You keep opening doors. Just learn to keep a few closed."

"He's right," Wood verified. "Right as rain. Let this stop now, Vera Chase."

"I'm only talking about research." Vera was hiding her true feelings. She wanted to wrap it all up. No unfinished business. It had become an obsession with her, and everyone knew it. Yes, she was now owning her identity as a witch and had come to the moment in her life when everything went sideways. Now she had a purpose and that was to use what powers she could to identify those two remaining women who died in the church with Sara Carriage. She had to know their names. Rebecca didn't die there that night, she ended up in a wall in the old Blanch house in Virginia.

"The list. The one in Bolt's jacket," Maggie reminded them.

"It has more names on it. We can reference that and see what comes up."

"Let's start there, tomorrow," Jack advised. "Give it time, Vera. Take today and give us all a breather."

Chapter 20

WHO ARE WE NOW?

Since the anniversary of the fire had passed, Maggie, Lovey, Wood and Vera were feeling more like their old selves. When the date was at hand, their powers multiplied. Their sensitivity was more apparent, but with Bevan gone, most of that extra kick was fading.

Vera had now owned her situation. She was a witch. Her demeanor changed somewhat, but at the core she was still herself. Maggie was watching her because she knew Vera wanted answers. At the moment Vera held that single spark that remained alive from a fire that was hopefully extinguished. That single spark could come back to haunt them all and turn into an inferno. Maggie, Lovey and Wood knew that. It's a witch thing. Jack suspected it and he let his intuition guide him.

Cat was distant. She was told she did things she didn't remember at all and for someone as inquisitive as she was, that was a lot to take in. She loved Vera, that was apparent, but Vera had been through something extraordinary. The Vera that was going to have a mock funeral for her masculine self was outta there. Cat had always seen themselves as equals, but now there was more to Vera than she could ever know, and that was becoming a problem.

The afternoon was quiet. Jack and Maggie had retreated to their room for a "nap." Lovey and Wood were up on the top deck. Vera and Cat were in their room with Vera looking at the list of names from Carriage's envelope. Vera had read the names over and over.

"Vee, Jack was right. You need to give this a rest. I know you're obsessed, but damn, when are you ever coming back from all this?"

Vera seemed startled at Cat's voice. She was somewhere between memory and fantasy as she tried to see who the other two women were she was bound to in Bevan's cellar.

"Vee?" Cat seemed frustrated.

Vera seemed hazy at best. "I'm trying to see it, Cat. I have glimpses, but nothing I can put a hand on."

Her receptive powers were fading and she was trying to cope with the loss. It was understandable. Vera's heightened magic came to her because of the anniversary of the fire and everyone associated with it was "awakened." Vera's first experiences as a witch were in an accelerated state. She understandably missed it.

Cat laid down next to her on the bed, resting her face on Vera's chest. Vera didn't react at all, she kept staring at the list of names.

"What are we now, Vera?"

"What?" Vera responded, interrupted.

"You and me. What are we now? Last week were we planning a funeral for your masculine self to go for a walk on the wild side and now, look at us. We have been through something crazy and are laying in the aftermath with you trying to go further. I'm asking you, Vera Chase, what are we now? Witch and Cat? Am I your sidekick or something? Do you even still want me here? Vee, I need some help. I don't know what or how to feel."

Vera was surprised. She was so into the past she forgot she'd planned a future with Cat. Here was this person who'd literally gone to hell and back for her and she wasn't feeling anything like she used to. She saw the dilemma. Laying down the list she turned her attention to Cat.

"I don't understand much of this yet. I'm sorry for making you feel this way but look at what's happened. I feel like I've been reborn. I was once afraid of the, what, 'shadow world?' I guess Bart Campbell's curse did more to me than I was aware."

Vera wrapped her arms around Cat. "You're still my girl. Hey, you know that? Look at me."

Cat looked up from her hug.

"We are still us," Vera assured her.

Cat was cautious. "How can we be us, if one of us has been reborn? I may still be Cat to you, but Vee, you have to admit that you are not the Vera you were. Not to me, or any of the others that helped you see this thing through. I'm not a witch, Vera. It freaks me out to even use that sentence because that leaves the obvious; you are. I'm trying to see how we can do this. One day you said you wanted to transition into a man, then you transition into some kind of a witch. What am I to think?"

Vera recoiled at what Cat was proposing. She was facing losing her. Deep down she knew that, but it didn't sit the way she'd expected. There was only one thing to do. When going gets tough, the tough have make-up sex.

Vera let her face drop down to Cat still laying on her chest. She whispered, "Hey."

Cat looked up and into her eyes. Vera remembered her standing there in the throes of being invaded by Bevan. She looked up and re-focused, then leaned down and kissed her forehead. Cat understood the gesture. She raised up to Vera and kissed her as deeply as she dared to go. Vera felt Cat's attempt at closeness. She slightly opened her eyes in the kiss and saw into her face. Vera got a flash of Cat standing in Bevan's cellar once more, engulfed with his spirit as he, living in Cat, pointed and stared right at Vera. It was frightening.

"What is it, Vee?" Cat asked as Vera turned away from her.

Vera got up off the bed and walked across the room to the chair she'd slept in days earlier, sat down, silent, and looked out the window.

"I was going to have a funeral to bring out the man living inside me. It turns out you were the one with the man inside you. It's a little jarring. I need a minute to file it in my head."

Cat didn't say anything. She rolled over, got up and went into the bathroom, turning on the shower. Vera sat in her chair, motionless as the memory of Cat standing before them, taken by evil, taunted her from the past. Would she ever be able to get those images out of her head? Only time could tell, but at that moment, Cat and Vera were on the outs.

Vera looked at their bed and the paper on it. The list. She got up, walked to the side of the bed, took the list and stood still listening to the water running. There was a time when Vera would have gladly added to the steam in the shower by joining her, but that wasn't happening. Cat had a point. What were they now?

The list only offered nine names. She read them over and over hoping one would jump out at her. The only person who could help was Maggie. Vera sensed that and wanted to speak with her about she and Cat's "problem." Seeing Maggie and Jack's door closed made her go for plan B; Lovey.

Wood and Lovey were on the top deck. She walked up the stairs and into the sunlight.

"Well, Vera Chase on deck!" Wood announced.

"There's my sweet niece," Lovey purred. "You getting yourself back to the land of the living?"

"I am, I guess. Cat's not. I can't seem to look at her now without seeing her in the basement with Bevan's spirit inside her. The terror, the evil. She was there with him and we all saw it. I keep going back to the moment when she fell. When Bevan reached out and grabbed her arm, pulling her down into the crevasse. Aunt Audrey, I felt good about it. It was a relief. It was Bevan on one hand, but on the other, I was in a way glad to see Cat die. I can't get past that. She's everything to me and yet, there we were, I see her fall and I feel the emotion. I wasn't unhappy about it and now I don't know how to feel."

Wood told her, "Don't beat yourself up. You saw your

significant other compromised. It wasn't her. It was her body, but we know now Cat was an innocent in all this. It was her wanting to get to you that did this to the both of you."

"Wood's right," Lovey injected. "Cat was willing to do whatever she could to get to you, even if it meant her own troubles."

Vera wanted to remember. "But didn't we say that Bevan invaded her before she went through? When the casket arrived, Cat said she had to see it. Remember? I think the arrival of the casket started something. It was close to the anniversary of the fire and Cat wanted to see the casket."

"That was her and it wasn't, Vera," Lovey reminded her. "Cat was used. The casket was meant for her because Bevan needed a body to take human form and be reborn. Cat was convenient. She was standing next to you when you were at Shelia's funeral and you said you wanted to be reborn as a man. Remember? She was there through it all, with you, never faltering or leaving you. That part was Cat. That's the part you've got to see. If you can't find your way back to her, and re-see her as she is, your girlfriend, then you'll never be able to continue as you are. As a couple. Vera, you don't need a clairvoyant aunt to tell you that."

Lovey had spelled it out perfectly. There was no regression to do or any sword to find. The solution to Vera and Cat's situation was laying in Vera's hands. She needed to take control. But in matters of the heart, a firm stance won't help anything. You have to want it and Vera simply had to convince herself Cat was someone she still indeed wanted in her life. Having to ask herself that was hard. It was a self-examination she hadn't seen coming.

Wood got up and walked around to Vera. The sun was bright and warm as he stood in front of her. "You're a good kid, Miss Vera. You do realize you are dealing with shit that you can only deal with when you love someone. This duality you're testing yourself with is understandable. If Lovey had turned into a monster, I'd be wary of her, too. That would screw anyone up. Give this time. It's not going to be a quick fix. You say you are hell bent on finding out who the other two women were in the fire? You have two women here who you need to find first: You and Cat."

"Wood's right, darlin'," Lovey agreed. "Before you go looking for more answers, make sure you have all you need here. Tell Cat you love her. That'll go a long way now. You do love her, right Vera?"

Vera looked at Lovey and Wood and couldn't answer. She turned to slowly walk to the stairs. Reaching them she turned to Wood as he took a hit off his joint. "I might need some of that," she said, referring to Wood's admission that he smoked to keep the visions at bay.

Still holding his breath Wood said, "I always knew you had potential."

Maggie and Jack got up later in the afternoon. As Maggie walked into the kitchen, she could see Bolt's bible laying on the counter.

"Oh, shit! Bolt's bible. We still have to return it. I forgot about it," she said as she slowly picked it up. "No visions this time," she said to herself.

She carried it into the living room where everyone else was sitting and being glad to still be alive. Cat had come out and she and Vera were being civilized sitting together talking to Lovey about their situation. It was obviously Lovey using her professional skills.

Maggie said she had to get the Bible back to the museum and asked, "Anyone want to run into town?"

"I'll go," Vera spoke up and said. She turned to Cat and gave her a light kiss. "We are going to get through this."

Jack asked Lovey, "Hey, what happened to the newspaper Vera found in the ghost room at the courthouse?"

Lovey scratched her head as her long dread locks swayed. "I looked for it last night. I guess it got taken back, like I said. Some things are not meant to be here. It went home."

"Amen," Jack added.

The drive to town was short. Maggie and Vera talked about Cat and how healing takes time. Vera said Lovey had offered a degree of hypnosis to help her not see Cat as a monster.

"I'll think about it, but I'm not the kind to be hypnotized," Vera admitted as they turned into the museum parking lot.

Maggie agreed. "Some people aren't. Let it rest for a while. All this will fade into a 'remember when?' One day you'll see."

Maggie and Vera sat quiet for a minute when they pulled into the parking lot. It was a reverent moment of them remembering the hundreds that died on that spot. It was the gallows. They remembered seeing the people chant, hungry for the witches' demise.

Maggie turned to Vera and asked, "No visions. You?"

"I'm good," Vera confirmed.

"Let's give Bolt his bible back," Maggie said exiting the car.

As they walked into the museum the same kid was at the front counter. He saw Maggie and lit up like a Christmas tree.

"Hey, doll," she cooed as she walked up to the kid. He did his traditional hard swallow and gave Maggie his full attention. She was in a tee shirt now. No buttons to undo. The halter was now a fond memory.

"We wanted to return Jeremiah Bolt's bible before you called the cops on us." Maggie flipped her hair around to keep the kid's attention.

"Do you need to call the mayor to call the insurance company to open the case?"

"Nah," the kid replied. "They are closed now anyway and the mayor leaves at three o'clock every day. I'll put it in the back with the rest of the Bolt stuff. The mayor will deal with it when he does, I guess."

"The rest of the Bolt stuff?" Vera turned and asked. "What stuff?"

The kid was nonchalant. "There is a box in the back with BOLT written on it that the bible came over here in a long time ago when this place was first built. This display thing was at the old courthouse until they built this place. They boxed everything up and labeled it, then brought it over here. The lady who put together the displays said the papers that were in the Bible didn't fit into her vision of the display, so she left the contents in the box. It's nothing, really. Just pages of writing."

"Why didn't you mention that before when we said we needed it?" Maggie asked.

"Because you never asked about anything else, just the bible," the kid said. Once more looking Maggie up and down, he confessed, "I really wasn't thinking about boxes in the back room when you were here before."

Maggie almost blushed, then leaned in really close to the kid.

"Do you think you and me could go in the back room and see it? I'd be really appreciative."

The kid was already halfway to the storeroom by the time Maggie finished. "It's in here."

Maggie motioned for Vera to follow them. Once in the room the kid pointed up. "There. Top shelf. See there? The one with BOLT on it."

He then inched his way up to the box and handed it down to Vera. She set it on a table and removed the lid. In the bottom of the box were pages of parchment. She reached down and Maggie stopped her.

"Wait. Don't touch it, remember? If it's Bolt's, you never know."

Vera recoiled. "But we have to see this."

Vera was adamant on seeing the parchments firsthand. Maggie began to notice something changing. She watched as a blue light began to take away the dullness of the storeroom. Maggie saw the kid taking notice as well as she went into spin control. "We need to see this over the weekend. I'm sure the mayor won't mind."

The kid broke the news. "I'm sorry. I can't let anything leave this place without authorization from the mayor. It's my ass if I get caught."

It was Maggie time. She turned up the flames a notch and got in the kids face and said, "Please…"

"Look," the kid began, "It's really not my call."

Vera butted in. "Nobody even knows this is here except us. We are at the end of our ropes here. If these are actually Jeremiah Bolt's notes, they are worth more to us right now than you can guess. We won't say anything to anybody. I'll owe you a favor! Yeah, you'll be in college soon and I teach there so…"

Vera stopped herself as she heard the voice of a pleading woman. She was in a free fall of uncertainty and grabbed a ledge. She saw herself as a witch now and that comes with a degree of assuredness she suddenly felt. Looking at the kid she let her gaze lasso his, then felt something. The world was slowing down and suddenly there was no fear of anything. She gently blew in the kid's direction as he became lost and slightly dazed.

Vera was cold. "Thank you for letting us borrow the Bolt artifacts. We will return them soon, so you don't need to mention this to anyone. Go back to work."

The kid nodded and returned to the front of the store.

Maggie watched her. "Do you realize what you just did, Vera Chase?"

Vera was riveted in the moment with her potential was showing itself. She was excited and yet still maintained her coolness. Willing someone into submission, on her own, here, in this place, Vera tasted her own magic and was immediately intoxicated.

Maggie whispered, "We need to get out of here."

Taking the box, she and Vera walked to the counter where the kid was standing. Vera leaned in and kissed his cheek. The kid's eyes blinked.

Vera whispered, "Thank you."

Startled, the kid replied, "Ah, did you just get here?"

Maggie called out to the kid, "You were magnificent!"

The kid stood wondering if he'd missed anything life changing.

They pulled into the driveway of the house with Vera

holding the box. As they walked in, Jack saw it. "For me? Is it my birthday?"

Vera mockingly replied, "No, but it may be mine."

With that she sat the box down, opened it and revealed pages of old parchment.

Jack looked at the parchment and then at Maggie. "What?"

Maggie shook her head. "It's Jeremiah Bolt's notes. They had them stored in the back room at the museum. The display designer apparently thought they didn't fit the motif, so they stuck them in a box and forgot them. There they sat, quietly waiting."

Looking at Vera, Maggie motioned towards the kitchen. "Get the gloves, we need to see this."

Lovey was stunned. "Oh, my Lord! His actual notes? How on earth did you just happen to be somewhere this was?"

Maggie had to wonder that herself. Fate had once more played a role. "It was the kid at the museum."

Wood was waiting. "Oh shit. Here comes a story."

Maggie had to laugh. "No, really. He said he'd put the Bible back with the other stuff. We asked, 'What other stuff?' And here we are."

Jack looked at Maggie and Vera with their treasure. "There's more to that."

Vera got the gloves and put them on while staring at the parchment. Several pages of notes were rolled up and tied together. She laid the first page out on the table. It was beautiful. Faded ink from the quill of a desperate man searching for the answers he had all along. His magic was his own.

"What's that one?" Jack asked. "Looks like a grocery list."

Vera scanned the parchment and read the numbers followed by names of women. Thirteen women were counted and named. The following pages were the same. It appeared the entries were made at different times.

"These are names of women," Vera assessed. "I guess they are women from the executions. Maggie?"

Maggie looked over the parchment reading the names one by one.

"Could be. There are no dates. This would be really handy if we had dates to go by."

Vera moved the pages around to see if there was anything else. Seeing a different format on one of the pages she picked it up then read aloud to the others.

> *"I have seen their faces. The cloaked ones who walk this town. They died and rose up to be here and serve that Waechter family. Witches! They come to my church and enter at will. Bevan Waechter owns the land Bethel Church sits on. I can not stop them from coming."*
> *I now know the names of those who were taken. I'm am pained by it.*
> *"Rebecca Brook Blanch..."*

Vera froze. Rebecca's name. Her name.
"Go on," Wood coaxed.
Vera took a breath.

> *Rebecca Brook Blanch was hung on the gallows for her witchery. She is one of them. After she was dead, she rose up by way of the Devil inside her. Now she walks cloaked and silent. Satan has her. She is in front of the others as they come and leave the church.*
> *Rebecca was not meant to be in God's eyes. It was not her fault there was love between her real mother and father. Now she's damned, because of love. I can watch her service to the Waechters no more. I'd rather send her to hell than see her liken herself to a warlock's handmaiden. I am sorry."*

Vera dropped the paper down to her side. "He did it for

Rebecca. That's why he burned the church. But why her? He said it wasn't her fault her parents were in love. That means Rebecca was a love child. We never knew her father. Bolt must have known something about where she really came from. He said he was sorry.

Lovey was fascinated. "Only he will ever know, Vera. Maybe someone he held close came to him like in a confession or something and told him how they loved someone and a child happened. He must have known something. Whoever it was, it served as enough motivation for him to burn the church with them inside."

Cat understood. "The man who collected wildflowers finally snapped. With all that was going on around him I can't say I'm surprised."

Wood had to agree. "Ain't that the truth. There was a heck of a lot happening to him. Poor guy. He could have just moved, but he made a choice to live there and do battle with the bad guys. He was really the hero, not Sheriff Carriage."

Lovey looked down at the parchment paper in Vera's hand.

"Is there more?"

Vera held it up and read,

> *Mary Ellen Jones lived with the farmer Joneses by the state road. Her brother stole a cow from her other brother and she put a curse on him and made him get the sickness. Sometimes I hear her humming. I can not hear what she sings, but the sounds are sweet and her own. It's Satan and his tricks. I don't listen. God gave me my own magic using his word. I don't need any other.*

"His own magic," Jack realized. "Bolt did have magic but didn't really understand it. I guess when you're a backwoods preacher and you pray for something and then it happens because you're a warlock and don't know it, things can get confusing. This leans towards that."

"Looks like it," Wood said.

Vera kept reading.

> *Erma Beckett kissed the boys after church when
> she was little. The Devil had her early. Satan
> made her body tempting to the men and she used
> her magic to persuade them to do her will. I've
> seen her and her evil walk. It's damned. She died
> with the others on the gallows the witch she is,
> now she lives for him. No more will I tolerate the
> evil that walks this town.*

Cat sneered, "She had an evil walk. No pictures I gather."

"None," Jack sympathized.

Lovey was hanging on every word. "Shhhh! Let her finish."

"Sorry," Jack offered as he held his hands up and backed away.

"What else is there?"

Vera continued reading.

> *God needs the chance to redeem these souls and
> I have to do it in his name. The Sword of God will
> win out over the evil that rests here this night.*

> *Pastor Jeremiah Bolt*
> *September 3rd, 1802*

Vera held the letter down to her side once more. Something was stirring as she felt a knock on her door. Something was wanting her attention.

Wood peered into the box. "Anything else there in the Jeremiah Bolt time capsule? Anyone have any other revelations about all this? Vera, looks like you got your wish. You now know the names of the women who served Bevan. Feel better?"

Vera studied the pages before her. She tried to see the faces of the women on her own. She had the names, but through time, she could not recall them. It seemed that now she was trying to come to a conclusion.

There were still questions she wondered if she'd ever know the answers to. She wasn't one for unfinished business.

"Maggie," Vera began, "I've been thinking about the Sword and how it was already made with Rebecca and Hope in Virginia. It must mean that the two rooms were joined before. Those two rooms are like the basement at the church and the storeroom I found the newspaper in. When that happened, Rebecca was there like we were when the wall on her side disappeared. When her wall reappeared, somehow, she was on the Virginia side of it, holding the Sword. She must have kept it hidden in the wall and at her death, did the same thing Hope did. She walled herself up and died."

Wood spoke up and said, "Holy moly, that sounds like a plan. Let's go with that."

Jack nodded his head in agreement.

Vera turned to Lovey. "I'm going to have to come to terms with how I got out of that mausoleum. I have the blood of Bartholomew Campbell running through my veins just as you do. This isn't going anywhere and you know it. I have to know."

Standing before the pages of parchment a man filled long ago, Vera Chase was trying to come to terms with the past. Was this enough? Was it time to let it all go? Deep down she knew the answer.

Wood was about to close the lid when he saw one of the rolled up parchments. He reached in, with no gloves, and took out the roll and removed the string around it. "One for the road," he said as he unrolled it.

Lovey leaned over to see. "What is that? Looks like..." And she stopped. "Oh my. Does that say, 'Last Will?' Could that be Bolt's last Will and Testament?"

Vera reacted and immediately looked to see it for herself. Everything she was at the moment pointed to what Wood held.

Wood read it aloud;

My name is Jeremiah Bolt. This is my last statement to the living.

God has been good to me and gave me all I need to fight the evil in this world. My possessions are meager. What I have I give to the unfortunate. I have no family that will be alive after this night. It hurts my heart to see how Satan has twisted the mind of the innocent. Once young and beautiful, now I have to see her walk in the throes of his wishes.

I stood on the gallows as the evil in this town claimed life after life. I prayed for their souls and got only heartbreak. I watched as she who is of my flesh descended and had her mortal life cut short because her parents were never married in the eyes of God. Now she walks this town cloaked and silent. It is my punishment for the sin I committed. I loved her mother before Satan took her under his wing and made her spoil another man's crops. Now she is dead and the only thing that remains of her to me has fallen to soiled hands.

I pray for God to forgive my offspring. I will fight for her soul.

My service to the Lord is why I was put here. My service to the Lord is what will send me home.

Jeremiah Bolt

Everyone stood silent. Wood lowered the parchment and looked around the room. Then he turned to Vera. "I think you have some soul searching to do. All this points to Rebecca and Hope Blanch. I think Bolt had an affair with Hope before she went bad. Remember, you said Hope was peaceful until she was charged with spoiling Bart Campbell's crops? She once knew real love and bedded Bolt. They produced a child. Rebecca Brook Blanch, and here we are."

Jack began to pace. "Oh, my. Jeremiah and Hope hooked up and she had Rebecca. Pamela was Hope and Daniel's kid. Maybe that's why Daniel never mentioned Rebecca in the ledger. He knew she wasn't his and didn't acknowledge her."

Vera was shaken. "I knew there was something I was missing. I felt it. Night after night when I gave the ghost tours and told of how crazed Pastor Bolt killed those women, I had no idea I was incriminating my own distant relative."

Cat was mesmerized. "Vera, you're actually a descendant of Pastor Jeremiah Bolt. Are you okay with that?"

Maggie stood trying to take it all in. The one villain she'd known in her life was at one time most human. Hope Blanch fell in love with a man of God and bore his child. Because someone thought she spoiled his crops, she was taken and caged, keeping her from those she really did love.

"Knowing there was a chance that Pamela and Rebecca would be charged as witches themselves, just for being Hope's children, she angered to a point that turned her heart cold as stone. The hatred she had for those responsible still lingers. That hate is why we are still with this. Hope's child, Rebecca, grew into someone who called out to Vera through time when the anniversary of the fire was at hand. Now we are standing in the wake of it all. If knowledge is indeed power, we just upped our game."

Vera looked at Maggie with desperation. "Maggie, I have to know. I have to know now how I got out of the mausoleum. There is more to it. It's like I've been asked a question I know I have the answer to, but it's hidden. It won't come for some reason."

Maggie took a leap. "Rebecca was the daughter of Hope and Jeremiah, that much we know. I can see why this is happening now. Vera, you are the reincarnation of a woman whose parents, both of them, were witches. That means you have a powerful lineage because the offspring of two witches has a purity. It is combined magic that takes many forms and this magic will not die. It has stayed alive through time and now has settled in your back yard. There's more to this. We have to do another regression or Vera, you're going to go nuts."

Jack couldn't believe it. "Oh, God. Here we go again. Damn, Vera! This shit is going to eat you alive. When are you going to let this lay?"

Wood agreed. "Jack's right. You are at a crossroad, Vera Chase. You can walk away knowing what you do, or you can jump back into the fire and see if you can find answers. Somehow, Bevan saw to let you out of that mausoleum. Alive at that. I say you better quit while you're ahead."

Maggie was hearing both sides. One was the safe play, the other risked something not of this physical world. Maggie felt sorry for Vera. She understood needing to know how all this came to be. She felt like Vera was supposed to be given that choice and it worried her at the moment. Maggie wanted to run. Why was this happening to Vera? It would take a miracle to get this straight, but one way or another she knew they both had to find out or Vera could never rest. It would always be there. The missing piece.

Maggie jumped in. "I'll do what I can for you, Vera. I'm at a loss as to the reasoning. Something is pushing me to go back with you. I guess we better go."

"Ahhh, shit!" Wood let out. "There goes my day, again!"

Chapter 21

CAN THE BROOM JOKES

Back on Maggie Mountain, Grace had been trying to adjust. Her vision of Bolt rising up and encountering Hope Blanch wouldn't leave. She muddled through her day to day tasks but mostly found herself on the back steps smoking a cigarette and trying to focus with a feeling something wasn't right. Hoping everyone was safe and sound, she opted to call Jack instead of Vera. Grace needed answers and felt he would be the best avenue for that. Jack was with Wood up on the top deck when she called.

Jack's phone rang. He looked down and saw GRACE and looked over at Wood. "Hey, it's your arch enemy."

He held up the phone and showed Wood who it was.

"Give it to me," he said with his outstretched hand.

"Wood talking on a phone? Holy shit! This is an occasion."

Wood took the phone. "Hey," he said as he answered.

"Wood?"

"Yeah, it's me. You okay up there?"

Grace could hear the cautious attitude. "I guess. It's...hard."

Wood knew it. Something wasn't right with Grace and he felt it when she left for the mountain. His intuition had served him well in the past, now he pointed it towards Grace and didn't like the outcome.

"Grace, I got a feeling you're not saying something. We

are trying to put this all to bed down here. Didn't you get that when you left? You getting anything we need to know about?"

Wood could feel her on the other end. She was scared. He got that in spades and wanted to help her. Over the years he and Grace shared a playful banter that carried them through their lives together. Deep down, she meant a lot more. Grace was his friend. Hands down. He knew that and saw her as a strength. If she needed any of his, then he was all about giving it to her. A true friend is a powerful thing to have.

"Grace, Vera is needing answers and thinks there is more to know about her relatives. Are you hearing me? She wants to regress back and find out some more about them."

Grace was reading between the lines as to what Wood posed. She had been getting flashes of Cat standing in front of the flames and Bolt rising up and exploding into light. Then, a shadow. There is something dark in the vision. There was a cold presence she felt, but none of the others did as if someone or something was looking over her shoulder.

"She's going back? Oh, Lord! Wood, you can't let her do that! Tell her it's done. Why on earth is she going back? Is it Maggie? Is she behind all this?"

"No," Wood reassured her. "Vera needs answers, Grace. We found out some things since you left. Maggie and Vera returned Bolt's bible and found a box with his original letters in it. One page was a list of the names of the hidden two women she was searching for. Another was Bolt's last Will."

Grace was shocked. "His Will? Lord! What did it say?"

Wood paused and felt Grace's concern grow. He decided to try something. "Grace," Wood calmly said, "You know what we found, don't you?"

Grace got quiet on the other end of the phone. Bolt's Will. She closed her eyes and breathed in. Slowly, she saw it. The manuscript a man wrote two hundred years ago as his dying testament to the world, but she was seeing it through Vera's eyes.

"He loved her," Grace whispered. "She loved him. They had a child. Rebecca! No!"

Wood realized Grace had just gotten the memo. Vera, her daughter, was reincarnated from Rebecca Brook Blanch who was suddenly the product of a two centuries old love affair between a witch and a warlock that produced a child. A witch's reincarnation is more cosmic than physical, but how Grace had seen it was uncharacteristic. Wood knew Grace was a witch, but a witch who uses the sight? One who can see remotely? No. That wasn't her. Not that he was aware of, anyway.

"Jesus, Wood! You have got to stop her! If she goes back down that road, she will be resurrecting him. Maggie knows that. Why is she doing this? Tell her to let it go. We can't risk Vera any more than we have to. You know what? Screw it! I'll tell her myself. I'm flying back today. I can't stand by and let this happen."

Wood had to try. "Grace, Maggie won't be resurrecting anyone. Bevan is gone. We locked him out of this world with the Sword of God and Jeremiah Bolt. He's not coming back for one hundred and ten years. Why do you say she will be resurrecting him? All Vera wants to know is what the events were that led her to get out of the mausoleum. Both Vera and Maggie can see things as they happened as long as they were involved. That's what this is. Nobody will be bringing anyone back from anywhere."

Grace was set. "I'm coming back today. I'll fly in."

'Today?" Wood asked. "You sure?"

"I have to see her, Wood. I can't not be there. She's my child! She was someone else's in another life, but here in this one that's my kid and if anyone from ghost land wants to have a chat with her, she's not doing it without me there."

Wood couldn't say anything to change her mind. He was feeling something from Grace. Something else. It wasn't the mommy/daughter thing pushing her. There was more to it. Grace was convinced the regression would throw gasoline on what sparks remained from dealing with Bevan and Hope. He knew that and softly said, "We'll be here."

Grace hung up and Wood turned to Jack. "Here's your

phone. A hundred different organizations probably heard what we said. You know that, right?"

Jack took note of Wood skating his phone line paranoia to talk to Grace. He must have thought it important. "Maybe she should have sent a pigeon. She cool?"

"She's flying in tonight. Can the broom jokes." Wood got up and walked to the top of the stairs. He turned and asked with no expression,

"You ever hear of people lifting cars off loved ones with a burst of adrenaline? They get excited and focused. Somehow they get super strong and can do things they wouldn't normally."

Jack was taken aback by the question. "Yeah, sure. I've heard about it. Why?"

Wood leaned up against the door and tried to explain. "Jack, when a witch or warlock gets excited, really angry or even super sad, their powers can mimic an adrenaline burst. It usually means there is a danger to someone close. I told Grace about finding Bolt's Will and understandably she got excited. She asked me what it said. I took a chance and told her she already knew what it said, and she stopped, focused and nailed it. She told me what I was going to tell her. She saw it, Jack. Grace has always been a witch whether she chose to wear it or not. Now, all that gentleness is taking a holiday. She's getting crazy stronger all of a sudden and I think it has everything to do with Vera trying to tie up loose ends with how she got out of the mausoleum.

Grace is on her way back here. She will be here later tonight; I just hope she is the only one coming. There is something off with her, Jack. I know her. I can tell. She's thinking that if we do the regression with Vera that we will be bringing Bevan back into this world. He's gone, Jack. We saw it. There is something more here."

Jack took in what Wood told him. If he'd not heard it from Wood, he'd have passed it off as bad sci-fi. "What do you mean, 'The only one coming?'"

Wood looked at his friend and decided to take a chance. "I

have a bad feeling about something, Jack. Last year when I smashed the amulet, Hope's dark magic, her essence, her power, went out into the world. It was really strong and I believe it went…" Wood stopped and looked out across the desert landscape. Jack was looking at Wood's expression and finished his thought for him.

"You think Hope's power, magic, call it what will, went into Grace, don't you?"

Wood was caught out in the open with his feelings showing.

"Yeah. I get that. Vera told me when we were in Virginia that Hope didn't die."

Jack tried to put the pieces together. "How would Vera know that? She wasn't there."

"Jack, Vera is a reincarnation of Hope Blanch's daughter, Rebecca. We know that. Vera is apparently really sensitive to anything surrounding Hope. When we were in Virginia, Vera asked me where Hope's spirit went when I smashed her stone. I didn't have an answer, until now. Grace was there, as was Sue, Sam and the rest of us. She would have been a target seeing how Grace served Hope for all those years, as did we all."

Jack was amazed. "You think Grace has been invaded by Hope Blanch. If so, why is she just now finding that out?"

Wood shuffled. "It must be the connection she has with Vera. Mother shit. Grace saw the Will through Vera's eyes. Think about it, Jack. Vera and Grace have a connection, so it only makes sense that Hope and Rebecca have the same thing. Mommy, daughter. If Vera is going to regress back in to see the what's and why's of how she got out, then Hope, Rebecca's mother, would feel that. You see? We have two generations of mommy/daughter shit going on here."

Jack's head was spinning. "So how is this going to play out? Are we looking at something like what happened with Bolt in the church?"

"I have not a clue, Jack. I know Grace and Vera are headed

for something. I can only try and be there for them when it happens. I better tell Lovey and Maggie. I'll be downstairs."

Jack watched his best friend disappear into the stairwell. He turned to look out over the desert and wondered how on earth he ended up in Randall, Arizona with a flock of witches, one of which he was absolutely in love with. He remembered finding the old ledger at Maggie Styles' Antique Barn and where it took them all, then he remembered his boss and friend Seth Holiday and the image of him with a bullet hole in his forehead for simply being a possible recipient of the ledger.

Jack really missed Paris Frances, his friend and someone who's sharp eye saved them last year and helped them find the tool shed with Hope hidden underneath it. Jack hoped she was well and still with Steven Winters, AKA "The Snowman." He had considered including them in this when he was thinking of hacking Elliott Security to get the Bolt's bible, but passed for fear of she and Steven being drawn into the craziness he and the others had landed in.

For a brief second he actually missed traveling around, trying to sell prefabricated cabins to anyone who'd buy one, including Maggie, who actually said she would buy one. Circumstances changed when Seth was shot to keep the ledger in play. At the end of it all was Maggie. He really was a part of her now. He felt that and let everything else fall to the desert that sprawled out in front of him. His life had indeed gone sideways.

Wood told Maggie and Lovey that Grace was coming back. He explained their conversation and said he didn't like it at all. He explained his Hope theory and the girls didn't blink. They got it.

Maggie had her hands tied when it came to Wood and Grace. There was a lot there, only she just wasn't sure how much of what.

Wood looked around the house. "Where is Vera?"

"She's upstairs with Cat," Maggie said as she motioned to the top of the stairs.

Wood went up and knocked on her door. After a pause, Vera opened the door wrapped in a sheet.

"You got a minute?" Wood asked.

Vera saw his sincerity. She looked back at Cat whose eyes were coaxing her back to bed. After a deep sigh she gave in to Wood. "Yeah, I have a minute."

Cat could be heard from the bed complaining. "Hey! I don't suppose this could wait another ten minutes or so, could it?"

Vera glanced back at Cat, smiled, then turned back to Wood.

"Let me get dressed. I'll be a minute."

Wood led Vera out into the driveway next to his van. He opened the double side doors and sat down as Vera stood in front of him watching him gather his thoughts. She didn't like what was happening. There was something wrong.

Wood looked up at Vera and for an instant remembered seeing her face in Rebecca's locket. It was her, plain as day. "Hope's daughter," he silently thought.

Wood needed answers he hoped Vera could furnish and he hoped they were the answers he wanted to hear.

"When we were in the basement in Virginia, you asked me where Hope's energy went. Remember? Why did you ask me that?"

Vera remembered the conversation. She understood some things, not all and got concerned. "Why are you asking me that?"

"Explain it to me again," Wood asked Vera. "The part about Hope's energy going somewhere."

"Oh," Vera said surprised. "When an entity as dark as Hope Blanch gathers all their energy and puts it into an inanimate object, like an amulet, it is unstable. A living host can be made to bend a little and accommodate a presence. Sometimes that host is not aware there is anything going on. The entity simply resides inside them until the time for it to show itself. It happens when there is unfinished business. Hope seems to have had some of that. Why are you asking me this?"

Wood shuffled and kept his gaze down to the sandy driveway.

"Kid, how do you know that? You've only been aware of your powers a relatively short while and you seem to have a knowledge that goes far deeper than your time with the craft should allow. It takes experience to know this shit and you simply spout it off like you've known it all along. Vera, you're not adding up."

Vera was made aware of how she was coming across. How did she know all that? It was there in front of her and she simply responded to the question. "I have no idea how I know that. Don't you? You have been around all this longer than I have."

"Vera, Grace is flying back tonight. She wants to be here when you do your regression to clear up how you got out of the mausoleum. She says it is important and insisted. Grace has it in her head we are going to resurrect Bevan. He's out of the picture. He went back to 1802 but Grace is adamant that if you regress, he will come back." Wood decided to take another chance. "Your mother will be here soon enough, but there is another matter we need to talk about."

Vera felt awkward. This was uncharacteristic of Wood. It wasn't like him to go deep.

Wood asked, "I need to know if there is any way the spirit of Hope went into Grace when I smashed the amulet. You asked me where it went. Grace was there. She would have been susceptible. There is something about your mother that's wrong. I'm not sure why, but I believe she has a passenger she doesn't know she has, yet."

Vera was stunned. "You think Mom has the spirit of Hope in her? Why? Why do you say that?"

"When we were down in Bevan's cellar, Hope showed herself. Grace went into a convulsion of sorts before that. I believe your mother was used as a vehicle for Hope to survive in this world until she was needed again. When the anniversary of the fire came to be, she woke up. Do you remember what Hope said to your mother before she fell into the crevasse with Bolt? She looked at Grace and said, 'Serve me once again!' I think when Hope said that, she put her essence back into Grace. Only now, that spirit isn't just hiding, it's making waves. Grace is seeing shit she can't deal with. I know her better than I know myself, and I'm telling you, I believe Hope is with her still."

Vera was shocked. "I don't know what to say, Wood. I felt something from Mom when I hugged her goodbye, but I blew it off. You really think you see Hope inside her? How do you know?"

"Your mother and I have been cat calling each other for longer than I can remember. It gave us something to do. While we were at it one day, she laughed at something I said. That was it, just a casual off the cuff remark, but something about it struck her funny. She laughed and couldn't stop. It happens. There's nothing weird about it, it's simply something that let me see past the bullshit. I saw past the guard she kept up. Under all that, I saw an equal. Someone no smarter than me, no stronger than me. Grace was not any threat to me at all. That laugh was hypnotic."

Vera understood. "I know she's fond of you, too. Anyone can see that."

Wood stood up and walked to the side of the van. "When a witch really lets go and opens a window to let the fresh air in, it's a magical thing unto itself. I saw her colors, Vera. I saw the blues and the chorus of sounds that went with them. She never admitted to me before the other night that she knew she had the craft. She'd really never said it, but I knew. We have a way and you will come to see it. It's a gift of nature. It's who we are. It's like animal instincts, we simply know. I've had her back ever since that laugh, and I will firmly say, she's had mine. It's because of that I need to know if there is a chance she's been invaded. If she has been, it's my fight as well."

Vera saw the honesty coming from Wood's voice. She was glad he was there for her. Wood had been her knight while they were in Virginia and now here, he was about to go into battle again for someone else. Vera's view of him was changing. The little guy with a heart of gold was turning out to be more. He was giving of himself. That's big magic anywhere.

Grace drove to the airport after telling Pete something needed her attention in Randall. He had his own keys to the bar, so all was well. Grace arrived at the airport early. She had a short hop flight to Phoenix from Denver and had parked in the parking lot trying to steady herself. Terrified of flying in the first place, Grace was not having a good day. She leaned back in her seat, closed her eyes and tried to ease her breathing. As she did, she felt herself falling asleep and couldn't stop. But it wasn't sleep that took her.

Grace could suddenly see herself in a wooden room filled with angry, yelling people pointing and throwing things. A pain on her arm made her cry out as someone's rock, thrown in anger, found its mark. She focused and could see a man pointing at her. It was Bart Campbell.

A loud bang happened by her head. She turned to see a judge hammering his gavel shouting, "Guilty as charged! Hope Blanch you are sentenced to hang by your neck until you are dead on this earth!"

Grace felt out of control and couldn't stop it. She felt herself thrown into the dungeon where the hordes of women had been and still were kept to their deaths, whether on the gallows or by the flame. Either way, Grace was re-living Hope's last days.

All that time wanting to get out, being hounded by the guards, not being allowed sleep, the rage began an unstoppable climb. She was burning inside. Her witchery broke free and she boiled from the hatred. At last there was an explosion inside her. A manifestation of all her anger, all her hate, all her love sucked from her heart leaving the pure entity of a lost, broken soul. Hope Blanch was re-living her birth from light to dark, inside Grace.

"Water!" Grace could feel her parched lips soaked with liquid. She felt the swallow that tried to cool her. She wanted more but was pulled away and felt the pain in her feet as splinters cut her step by step as she climbed to the gallows.

Hope was led, then placed in position. A black bag was put over her head so only darkness prevailed as the crowd became more inflamed when the rope found her neck. Hope's rage intensified into something dark and unholy. She immediately wanted to be fed. She wanted souls to keep her dark spirt aware. The lever was pulled. Hope felt herself fall and then heard the snap of her own neck. She hung there as her body twitched and swayed in the Virginia sunlight, but life would not leave her. Her soul was never tempted to fly. Staying quiet in the pile of death the gallows had produced that day, Hope slowly moved her neck. She heard the bones crack as they moved back into place. She laid still and silent until darkness fell and the crowd went home. She then rose up off the pile of corpses unnoticed and showed her face to the world for the last time. Pulling a veil over her, she slowly walked out the courtyard and into her life of searching for souls to nourish her own now pale existence.

Grace slowly came back to herself. A two-hundred-year-old witch had found a way to stay alive living inside Grace. Hearing the roar of a jet engine passing overhead, she readjusted herself and tried to place what she'd just been shown. Grace served Hope for years. She now understood what Hope meant as she fell into the crevasse in Virginia. "Serve me once more!" roared through her head.

Hating airports, she got out of the car and looked into the terminal. Regardless of who or what was living inside her, she felt Vera needed her and she was hell bent on getting there. With a huff she took out her suitcase and began to pull it down the walkway. She looked around at where she was and thought of what she'd been shown. It was official. She was scared to death.

After sweating through the flight, Grace got a rental car and headed for Randall. She had more time to think. The closer she got to Randall, the worse she felt as she was experiencing a duality. Hope was apparently aware of her situation. She was coming back to life.

Steadying herself, Grace kept driving. The sun was setting and brought out an array of colors that flooded the desert as she drove along the flat road. She noted the beauty, only to be swayed by the obvious fact that beauty only lasts so long. Grace blinked and found herself miles down the road, once more not remembering how she got there. Thankfully, Randall was coming into view.

Chapter 22

HOPE'S SHOWDOWN

Wood was still sitting in his van waiting for Grace to arrive and was worried she needed him. At last he saw the lights from her car sweep across the front of the house as she pulled in. When she got out, Wood was standing by his van waiting for her. "Back again. You make good time?"

Grace was bending and stretching from her being in the car.

"Pretty good. I hate airplanes. They scare the shit out of me. It's not natural to be up in a flying tube like that. Where's Vera? She getting ready?"

Wood didn't have to wait to bring up the regression. Grace was focused on it. He wondered about her need to come back and be with Vera. There was something else and he knew it. Wood once more opened the double doors of his van and sat down. Looking into the eyes of his friend, he unloaded.

"You're not telling me something, Grace. I know you better than I know myself, so I'm telling you I think there is something you need to clear before we start this regression. You hearing me? Spill it. What's up you aren't saying?"

Grace was a bundle of fragility. She was shot. Visions had been coming she could not explain, feelings of horrible possibilities flooded her and now here she was back awaiting further trials no one even knew about. Standing in front of Wood she could feel it all coming to a head.

"I saw her, Wood. I saw Hope. I saw her at her trial when

she was found guilty of souring Campbell's corn and I saw her in the dungeon with countless others proclaiming their innocence. It was then I felt her hatred for the people that tormented her and the other women.

Hope was terrified her daughters would be accused of witchery just for being her offspring. She got dark, Wood. She got so, so dark. I felt it. I now know what it's like to be hung for something you didn't do, to feel your neck break at the end of a rope and then not die. I felt her thrown onto a pile of death until she mustered up enough of her dark magic to rise up and deny the world the pleasure of her true demise. She's here, Wood. She's here with me. I know it and Vera is the key to giving both of us our sanity back. I had to be here."

Wood was both glad to be shown his instincts were indeed on target and at the same time he was sorry to know what Grace had been through. It wasn't fair, but what in this crazy scenario was?

"I'm sorry, Grace. I don't know what to say except that you got me. I don't know what I can do to fix this, but whatever it is, I'm here as are the rest of us. You're not alone in this. Know that."

Grace walked to Wood and put her head on his shoulder.

"Why is this happening, Wood? We let all this go a year ago and it's back worse than it was."

"That's because we never really put it behind us. Grace, Vera is sure, as am I, that Hope went into you when I smashed the amulet. Hope used you as a vehicle to survive in this world until the anniversary of the fire. She obviously knew that was coming. She wanted this and needed you to help make that happen.

When Hope fell into the crevasse with Bolt, she pointed at you and commanded, "Serve me once again." I think at that point she went into you to stay on this plane for Vera. She wasn't done because Vera wasn't done. Vera is Rebecca incarnate. Hope is trying to protect Rebecca still, only it's not Rebecca, it's Vera."

Grace had just been given a review of what deep down she

already knew. She was a host for an evil she once worshiped. At one time she would have felt honored, now it was a mother's duty to protect her young, and Grace as all about it. She asked Wood, "Does she know? Does Vera know all of what you just proposed?"

"I'm sure she does. She's advanced to a state I can't explain. Grace, she knows things she shouldn't know. Vera has only recently been introduced to the craft and she knows things it would take an average witch a lifetime to understand. I'm lost as to why that is, but your daughter is special, Grace. Vera Chase is something I've never seen. Accelerated, smart, aware. I'm telling you, she's quite a specimen."

Grace almost had to smile at the compliment. Her daughter was indeed special. "Is she in the house?" Grace asked looking up at the big Victorian.

"Let's go see," Wood said as he squeezed Grace's hand.

As they walked into the house everyone turned to see Grace and the state she was in. She looked awful and Maggie got up and wrapped her arms around her. As Maggie hugged her, Hope came through. Maggie felt her as she had also been a slave to Hope and, luckily for her, the four bodies she put under the tool shed she brought for Hope were now lost in history.

Grace stepped back. "I had to come, Maggie. Vera is going to need me, isn't she? I can't let her go through that without me."

Maggie, Lovey and Wood were studying Grace when she suddenly changed tempo. "I have to be there! I have to be there for Rebecca! She needs me, I know it."

Lovey countered. "Rebecca? You are here for Vera, Grace. Your daughter. Grace? You are here to help her. Right?"

Wood had seen enough and turned to walked back outside. Jack had been up on the top deck when Grace arrived and was coming down to see Wood walking out. He walked to Grace, reached out and put his arm around her, saying, "Hey doll. Couldn't stay away from the flat lands?" Then he walked away glancing at Maggie. Something was up with Wood and they both knew it. Once outside, Jack saw Wood sitting in his van, walked up, opened the door and got in.

"What's up out here, buddy? You got another rolled one in here someplace?" Jack was walking softly. After the talk they had earlier, he wasn't sure where Wood's head was. Now he was acting funny over Grace's arrival.

"She's there, Jack. I can see it. I can feel it. Hope Blanch went into Grace. I understand it all now. Vera told me Hope's energy didn't die when we were in Virginia, now I see it alive in Grace. Hope Blanch is in her, Jack, saying she's here for Rebecca. That's Hope's kid. I'm telling you, she's there. Hope told Grace to serve her once more when she fell. I think Hope went back into her for something."

Jack was sympathetic. "Man, I don't know what to say. We have Vera wanting to go back and see things and Grace says she's got to be there. You say Hope is with her. What does all this mean and how the hell does Vera know so much about it?"

Wood tried to put it all in perspective. "What it means is that we can't be sure who wants what. Grace is Vera's mother. Hope Blanch was Rebecca's mother. Vera is the reincarnation of Rebecca. So that means Grace is here to help Vera. Hope, for some reason has decided to show herself and be there for Rebecca. See? How Rebecca factors into this now, I haven't a clue. All we need to know is who is waiting for who on the other side. Hope Blanch is alive, Jack. Buried in that crazy ass woman in there who's only claim to fame is her pot roast. She didn't ask for this. None of us did, yet here we are."

It was a crazy scenario, but Jack had learned to go with crazy. Wood had seldom been wrong about anything to do with paranormal exploits. He was a real warlock and could see around corners Jack couldn't. If he was worried, then Jack was worried.

Inside, Grace was talking to Maggie and Lovey when Vera and Cat came down.

"Mom. You made it. You came back here for me? You want to be part of my regression? Why?"

Grace hugged her daughter. The closeness made them both feel the duality inside Grace. Pulling back, Vera could see it as Wood had. The connection. She felt Hope needing to come forth.

"I had to be here," Grace admitted. I couldn't risk you bringing him back."

"We aren't bringing anyone back," Vera explained. "Maggie and I can see things in the past as long as we were involved. It's a viewing, that's all. It's not a conjuring. We aren't resurrecting anyone; besides, I have no idea how to that."

Grace stood in the room unsettled. Everyone felt it. "It's all my fault," Grace confided. "It's because of the shit I did that you are here. I can't not try and make amends for all the years I served Hope and not my own daughter. I kept you at bay from the rituals, the deaths associated with it and what it took to live that life. Now if there is a chance we can clear up some things, I have to know that you are at peace. I need to see you healing, Vera. Don't try and take that away from me."

Grace paused a moment, swayed and said, "I love you Rebecca. You need to know that."

"Rebecca?" Maggie questioned. "Grace, this isn't Rebecca, it's Vera."

Lovey stepped in front of Grace and looked into her eyes to find the longings of another lost mother. Hope was coming through Grace loud and clear. Lovey saw it as well as Maggie. "My goodness!" Lovey said as she studied Grace. "It seems there is more wanting to happen here than a viewing."

Cat seemed restless and uneasy. Seeing them all about to go back down a scary road was not where she wanted to be. "I'm going to sit this one out. I'm not ready to go back into that place, even if it is only a memory. I'll be upstairs. Happy landings." With that she turned and headed up the stairs. Everyone watched her walking away and they all understood. She'd been through a lot. Nobody blamed her at all.

It was ten o'clock. Everyone gathered in the living room. The lights were dimmed once more as they sat in a circle and held hands. Grace and Maggie sat next to Vera and felt her wet palms as the tension of the moment was showing itself.

Maggie took the wheel. "Tonight, we find answers."

Vera felt a knot in her stomach. After a deep breath she adjusted as Maggie tried to coax her further. "Re-live it, Vera. From the moment you walked in and the mausoleum door closed. What did you see?"

Here it was. Vera had to believe the missing pieces were on their way. She had to believe it. This time the vision they all shared came quickly. Letting it come, she could feel an energy coming from her hands holding Grace and Maggie's. Vera and the others could see they were on the other side of the mausoleum door where she first stood in the darkness. The torch lit. They could see the five marble containers, the last one with the name, 'Bevan Nicholas Waechter,' then Mrs. Jenkins' door. Everyone could see through Vera's eyes as she walked through it and down the deep stairwell. At the bottom was the long pathway.

As Vera's vision took them slowly down the corridor, the mining artifacts came into view as did the large number "8" that hung over the shaft. At last, they could see the chamber with the rounded brick ceiling where Bevan came to be. They saw no tables with bound women or any sign of Rebecca or Bevan. As Maggie led them deeper into Vera's memory the sounds of an angry crowd began to be heard. Then the voice, "My sweet Rebecca, be a good girl and die for the crowd." The sound of the lever being pulled jarred them as they suddenly felt themselves falling. This was all Vera remembered. They had come to the fork in the road where answers needed to surface.

Vera let the vision of the gallows cool. She was seeing herself inside the cellar on the floor. As she got up, she could hear footsteps. Her eyes scanned behind her to find a familiar face once more. Cat!

Everyone watched as Bevan, using Cat's image, slowly came into the room. Vera heard the thought, "Do you know what you are?"

Vera paused as the vision of Cat falling into the crevasse with Jeremiah Bolt and Hope Blanch flooded her. "Yes, I know. I am the reincarnation of Rebecca Brook Blanch. I lived two centuries ago as her. I… served you as her."

"You will always serve me. Every life you live, for centuries to come, you will continue to serve me. We are two. Forever together… until there is no forever!"

The room began a dark transformation. A cold mist began to form in the air causing Vera to shiver in the freezing chamber. A blue glow took the room in a familiar moment; It was her.

"You will not have her!" Thundered through the cavern.

Vera and Bevan turned to see an old woman walking toward them.

As the mist cleared, a woman dressed in seventeenth century garb addressed them. "You will not have her!" once more roared through the chamber.

Vera and the rest felt her. It was Hope Blanch. Wood was right. The spirit of Hope went into Grace when Wood smashed her amulet last year. It re-established itself in her when Hope fell into the crevasse with Bolt and still harbored deep inside her.

Bevan laughed out loud. "You have no say here, witch! Look where you are."

Hope came closer. She could see behind Cat's eyes into Bevan's dark soul. She stared into the now red glowing eyes in defiance. "You will release her!"

Bevan laughed again. "Release her? It was you who gave her to me. It was your curse. The curse you put on the lady descendants of Bartholomew Campbell."

"Any woman having the blood of Bartholomew Campbell running through their veins is hence forth cursed to receive an invitation to the shadow world."

"But you never saw your own child, Rebecca, being reborn from Campbell's bloodline, did you? All that rage, all that pain you had cursing the innocent. Now look. She and Vera have both been handed to me on a silver platter."

In the room where everyone sat locked in Vera's vision, Grace began to convulse. Vera could feel her hands begin to shake.

Hope asked Bevan, "What do you want?"

"Want?" he said with distinction. "I want for nothing! I starve for nothing! I have what I want. My sweet Rebecca has served me well. She will continue to as long as I desire, unless…"

There was a pause. Bevan was pondering a move. Hope stood watching as everyone looked on in a dream state. "You know the price for Rebecca, witch! You give yourself to me freely. I watch you die and I take all you are."

Hope countered. "You want more power to hate. To hurt, to kill. It won't last. Nothing you do will sustain you for much longer. The anniversary of the fire is at hand. You will not be in this world when it passes."

Bevan roared, "I am the world you pitiful woman! I am and will be all there is!"

"In your world, you are all you are," Hope solidified. "But in the world of the living, you are nothing more than a direction. A choice. Nothing you do can carry you further. You will not survive the anniversary of the fire."

Bevan almost laughed. "You sad woman. My one hundred and ten years are up. I will be set free and souls will be mine!"

"You won't survive it. I'll see to it you will not survive it! Release Rebecca. Let her go. If it's me you want in return to end the curse, so be it. She is my child. Her children will not be chained by you."

"You give it freely? Your witchery? This is not the same as putting all you are into an amulet, Hope Blanch. You put all of who and what you are into me. I will be all you are."

Hope paused and studied Bevan's stance. "Release Rebecca first. Put her back into the world she knows. It stops here. I started the curse; you need to release her to end it."

Bevan looked at Vera standing in the room. "She will be released."

"Now. Release her now!" Hope commanded.

Bevan pointed his eyes at Vera standing in awe. There on the ground in front of them a mist swirled. Visions of Rebecca in 1802 begin to flash. Her entire life ran past them, then Vera's life. From child to womanhood, bits and frames of her life shot by, until the scene showed Vera doing her ghost tour, finding the casket, and at last it showed her swirling in the mist as it expanded above Rebecca's grave. In a free fall through the hole in time Bevan had created, Vera fell from the world of shadows into the world of the living and landed exhausted on Rebecca's grave. There it was at last; the answer to how Vera got out of the Waechter mausoleum.

Bevan stood in front of Hope. "The child is herself free, now you have a debt to pay. Kneel. Kneel down and know who is taking your witchery."

Hope, in the cavern, walked to Bevan, knelt down and immediately went into excruciating pain. They watched as she writhed in agony. Suddenly in the circle back in Randall, Grace's hand left Vera's and she fell forward seemingly mimicking Hope's agony.

Everyone wanted to help her when they heard Maggie. "No! She's leaving!"

No one could move. Grace was lying in front of everyone while the vision continued. Everyone watched as Hope Blanch slowly turned back into the Hope of old. She rose up from the floor of the cavern, whole and youthful and turned to face Bevan, who was in the throes of absorbing Hope's last ounce of dark sustenance.

The evil one. The entity that brought them all to their knees now stood in front of them free of the hate, the pain, the evil that plagued her for two hundred years. She looked up at the ceiling of the cavern and held her arms outstretched. Everyone could see her going back into her time. The time before the trials, the time when she was in love.

Maggie and the rest could see her walking across a field of wildflowers holding hands with Jeremiah Bolt. It was their time. A time of wild innocence and unfortunate deceit, as Daniel Blanch, Hope's husband, knew nothing of the affair.

Slowly the vision began to fade. They could see Bevan draining the last of Hope's dark heart until she was pure of evil once more. Hope Blanch vanished from their sight as Bevan roared with his newfound dose of Hope's witchery. It was over. Everyone began to come back.

Jack broke the silence with, "Vera, I hope you are happy now. Like it or not, you have your answers.'

Grace opened her eyes. "She's gone. I guess she wanted to stay here, in me, until Vera had all her answers. It all makes sense now."

Everyone looked at her. The visions she'd been fighting off for days all became silent at once. Grace was left with herself and the memories of what was.

"You okay?" Maggie asked Grace.

"Yeah, I guess." Then she shifted to Vera. "Hey, Vera."

Vera had been through the ringer. She had answers but didn't have the pieces in line yet. "You good?"

"Yeah," she said looking around the room. "It's calm now. Storm's over."

Wood was coming back and beginning to focus as well. "Anyone want a shot at what we just saw? I need a minute."

It was Lovey who put it together. She stood up and collected herself. "Jeremiah marked passages in his bible with wildflowers. Remember? The last verse was Mark 3:26; *And if Satan opposes himself and is divided, he cannot stand: his end has come.*

"This verse, I believe, is where Hope was headed. She let Bevan absorb her magic, her witchery. She went into him and according to Bevan became part of him. When we were in the cellar on the anniversary of the fire, Hope became conflicted and left Bevan for Rebecca and Vera's sake. This plays like the verse: 'If Satan opposes himself and is divided, he cannot stand. His end has come.' Like we said, Bevan is not Satan, but the rule apparently still works here. Evil is evil, regardless of the label."

Lovey smiled and stretched regaining her presence a little more. She looked at Vera and reflected, "I told you there was something in that bible we were missing. I felt that. The problem was, we simply didn't have all the pieces yet. It seems Jeremiah Bolt left us all we needed, including the mold to the Sword."

Jack was wondering, "Lovey? How do you think Bolt knew about the Sword in the first place? He just started yelling that the Sword had won out over evil. That works for us, but for him? Where did he and Sword come together?"

"I can't say," Lovey replied. "It's a good question. We can go back and…"

"No!" Everyone said in chorus.

Wood spoke first. "I'm out! If anyone wants to see more shit from back in 1802, they are on their own. This little warlock is on the bench."

Maggie had to agree. They had a sense of closure they could live with. Anything else would have to wait.

Chapter 23

"WE'LL BE BACK!"

For the next two days Grace and Vera got to experience what having a real mother/daughter relationship was like. It had been long enough. Grace wanted to be a part of Vera and Cat's future and once again invited them up to the mountain. The invitation was accepted with pleasure. It was time to head home. Grace was going to drive back with Wood, Lovey, Maggie and Jack in Wood's van. She'd had enough of air travel. In the driveway once more, Grace said her goodbye.

"I'll be available should you need anything at all," Grace advised Vera.

"You need to see if she's got lunch money," Jack mocked.

As they headed out of town, they saw the Randall Museum and wished it a fond farewell. Two hundred years ago this site set things in play no one could have imagined. Now it only existed in visions that had been indefinitely put on hold.

As they stopped at the light by the museum, Lovey made note of the kid unlocking the door to start the day.

"There's your admirer, Maggie. On the job once more. If he hadn't mentioned Bolt's box, we'd never found out what we needed. We sort of owe him; you know?"

Jack turned around and looked at the kid, then at Maggie. "You wanna give him one for the road?"

"What?" Maggie questioned. Then she saw Jack's grin. He motioned towards the kid then looked down at Maggie's chest.

Maggie scoffed. "Jack Reynolds! What do you think I am?"

"You're a horny old history professor, remember? Go on, flash the kid. He'll be behind the counter all morning."

Wood turned around and said, "I'm not seeing this."

Maggie rolled down her window and called out, "Hey, doll!"

The kid looked up to see Maggie in the van at the light. Maggie positioned herself in the window, lifted her shirt and exposed herself to the kid.

"Thanks for the help!" Maggie yelled. "We'll be back!"

The light changed and Wood drove off with the kid still standing with his key in the lock.

Readjusting her shirt, Maggie fell back into her seat.

"I can't believe I just did that."

Jack busted out laughing. "That kid is going to be setting off alarms again in that bathroom."

Wood had to join in. "He'll be in there all morning!"

Lovey couldn't help it. "I wonder if the mayor saw that. My goodness! He'd be in there with the kid!"

Grace shook her head, "My lord, Maggie."

Laughter. It's nature's ways of telling us no matter how bad life seems we can always laugh about it later. It was the cure-all they needed as Randall, Arizona was now finding its way into their rear-view mirror.

Jack reached out, took Maggie's hand into his and asked, "You never really told me what all was involved in me having your powers when we are together. Is that something I'll actually need?"

Maggie sighed, "You never know, Jack. Let's get home. Right now, I'd say we're needing a break."

"Amen!" Wood heralded. "Put it in the can."

The following week found Maggie, Jack, Lovey, Wood and Grace back on Maggie Mountain. Scenery can go a long way in healing. Jack stood on the back deck of their house looking out over the valley recalling the visions and trying to find a place for them in his life. The memories weren't going anywhere so it was best to try and decipher the events while they were fresh. It would take time, but the clouds were parting and there was sunlight head.

As Jack stood on his deck, he heard the sliding glass door open and footsteps coming behind him. Jack's gaze was with the gently blowing trees in the valley as a small bear ran across the field down below. He remembered seeing one the night Sam shot out his tire and took him into a world he couldn't imagine. His life had not gone the way he'd planned, but whose did? Rolling with the punches was Jack's way.

Not turning around he said, "Hey, it's a beautiful day out here. Come stay a while."

No response. Jack waited and still heard no response. Turning around he was confronted with Maggie wearing nothing but a smile.

"Holy sh….!"

Maggie put her hand over his mouth. She loved him. He loved her. There on Maggie Mountain life was really trying to get back to normal.

ACKNOWLEDGMENTS

I'd like to thank Ryan Almario for taking the time to do the covers of my books. Both The Dark Ledger and The Ghost of Bethel Church covers were photographed and Photoshopped by him freely because he wanted to help me in my writing endeavors. That's a friend.

I want to thank my wife Karla and my daughter Amelia who have never questioned why I chose to write songs or books. It makes things easier when you have the support of those around you. They also make me laugh at least twice a day. Each day with them is a blessing.

ABOUT THE AUTHOR

Wil Hodge is both an author and a recording artist. His CDs and music can be found on most of the popular streaming formats including Itunes, Spotify and YouTube.

He is an avid motorcyclist as well, who finds both solitude and inspiration on the winding roads of the North Georgia mountains.

Wil lives in Marietta Georgia with his wife Karla and daughter, Amelia.

He can be contacted at wil@wilhodge.com

www.ingramcontent.com/pod-product-compliance
Lightning Source LLC
Chambersburg PA
CBHW031945110726
47902CB00001B/307